Daughter of the Queen

By
Becca Patterson

Daughter
Of the
Queen

First Print Edition:February 2016

Acknowledgements

Special thanks to Ekaterina Beaumont, Devin Harnois, and Milli Gilbert for their advice and support through this process. I must thank my husband as well for putting up with me and my rants against computers. I couldn't have done this without the inspiration of all my students who prove that young minds aren't spoiled by rules or tradition.

Emalynn

Emalynn guided the little shuttle to land precisely on the mark they'd given her. She savored this victory. King Levon started it with his trick of announcing her official lineage on *Hot Topic* before talking to them about it. Then, despite *Hot Topic's* following segment on her navigations midterm simulation, he insisted on sending a boarding team to put a "real" pilot on the shuttle. The Other pilot didn't like that idea and repelled the boarding party until they gave in. This was shaping up to be the most epic parent-child battle in the history of the universe.

Tristan kept out of it as much as he could. Emalynn didn't blame him. He'd grown up fearing his father's anger. He might even be right that she'd been rude. She just couldn't believe etiquette for royals was really that different from the way everyone else behaved. It's not like she called him names to his face or even where he could hear her. In her opinion, he'd been rude, so they were even.

"Nice landing." Tristan released his safety harness but remained in his seat.

"Thanks." Emalynn finished the landing and release sequence on the control panel. The engine noise, so constant she'd forgotten it was there, dropped out. The silence of a landing always surprised her, despite the number of times she managed to pull off decent touchdowns "Are we in trouble?" She pointed to the line of guards coming toward the shuttle.

Tristan looked, counted, then gave one snort of a laugh. "No, we're being honored."

Emalynn looked again. There were more than three dozen guards out there.

"I'm not feeling all that honored."

"Me either. I miss..." Tristan sighed.

She guessed he was thinking of his personal guard this time. Techani Kenchi had been his mentor and protector when everything else he relied on disappeared in a puff of smoke and debris. For Emalynn, he was just a name

Baba had spoken of with reverence. Then he disappeared in that puff of smoke and debris to draw attention away from them. He was just one of the changes to the universe that would have long-lasting consequences.

Emalynn unhooked her harness and pushed herself up against the full gravity of Prime. After months living in less than full gravity, she struggled with her weight. Another reason to delay leaving the shuttle.

"Are you ready?"

Tristan looked up at her from the copilot's chair. "Are you going to make a scene about the guards?"

He knew her too well. "By scene, you mean will I yell at them to leave me alone?"

"Don't do that." He pushed himself to standing and steadied himself with the back of the chair.

Emalynn sighed. "What should I do?"

"Talk only to the one who talks to you and ignore the rest."

How was a smuggler-raised brat supposed to ignore that many women in uniform? If she thought of them as the goons of a kingpin, she just might make it through this without offending too many people.

"I'll try."

He smiled. "Oh, and you're going to have to go first."

"What? Why?" She turned on him so fast he fell back into the chair. "They're your people." She thrust her arm at the door. "You've done this your whole life."

"And you're firstborn." He stood again, nose to nose with her. "That makes you the heir, which means you're the important one."

How ridiculous. How did birth order, especially of twins, have anything to do with this? This was Tristan's home, and she was visiting for the first time. He should be leading her into the house. If she argued, he'd just tell her about the rules. No, etiquette was supposed to be about making the people around you comfortable, not about who was born first. The first daughter of a great pilot could end up better suited to being a chef. If her parents couldn't understand that simple principle, it would become part of their war.

Tristan put his hands on Emalynn's shoulders and turned her around. "You're going to have to get used to this."

"I don't want to get used to this."

"Then when you've managed to prove yourself well enough that people in the palace respect you, you can change it. Either way, today you are the heir and you're going to act like it." He propelled her toward the back of the shuttle.

She let him push for two steps, then took back her pride and walked the rest of the way on her own. She could feel him smiling behind her when she hit the release with a little more force than necessary.

The shuttle doors opened slowly, forcing her to stand there and wait like some overpowered pompous lady who expected things to happen just because she wanted them to. On a smuggling ship, once that button was pushed, they would have been scrambling to get the cargo ready to shove down the ramp. Speed in unloading was the first rule she'd understood about what Baba did. The second was run from anyone in any kind of uniform. All of Baba's rules had helped them survive.

Baba also taught her to act like everything was normal even when it wasn't, so by the time the ramp was in place, Emalynn had put on her character and strode down the ramp to meet the triangle of guards as though it were the most natural thing in the world.

"Princess Emalynn. Prince Tristan." The guard in front bowed, bending her knee almost to the grown before rising again. Her hair showed a few hints of gray, but the rest of her suggested she was barely old enough to have graduated.

Emalynn nodded but said nothing. Tristan knew what to say; he should be doing this. No one looked to him with more than a cursory first nod.

"Welcome home. I hope your travels were..." What could the guard say, with honesty, about the travels that had been broadcast across most of the net? Even the financial channels had carried parts of it. "Exciting."

"They were," Emalynn said when the silence grew uncomfortable.

The guard nodded, clearly relieved she'd picked a good word. "We have chambers ready for you to refresh in before your official welcome ceremony."

Emalynn nodded again. She wanted to ask about the ceremony. The tension oozing off Tristan warned her not to. The part about refreshing sounded good. Especially if there was a proper shower available. Better yet, a bath.

The guards turned in formation. She imagined them in a dance studio, learning all the proper turns. A cough, presumably from breathing planet air after too long in recycled environments, covered her laugh. She followed them across the landing pad into the building nearby. This building looked more like a high-end mall or luxury spa than a shuttle port. Inside, the marble floor, glass ceiling, potted plants, and water features brought the wilds indoors and attempted to tame them. That was just the lobby. The statues beside anything door-like turned out to be more guards.

Most of the honor guard left them at the main door. Emalynn could breathe a little easier after that. Too many uniforms continued to lead and follow them. Then the statues started bowing at her when she passed. That would have to stop. Lower into the complex, other types of uniforms appeared and they bowed, too. One boy in a black and white outfit that showed more than a decent amount of leg bowed so deep he dropped the load of towels he carried. He became even more flustered when Emalynn stopped to help him pick them up.

"We should continue, Your Highness," the lead guard told her quietly. "You are expected in the spa."

Another guard came to the poor boy's rescue while Emalynn was distracted. They had the towels gathered and were gone when she turned back.

"Then they shouldn't turn themselves over trying to bow to me." Emalynn fell in with the guards again.

"You won't get them to stop," Tristan said.

She thought of several things to say. None of them would have passed muster with Baba, so she swallowed them.

Everything about this building, from the polished stone floors to the sculpted ceilings, had an elegance that whispered how rare and expensive it was. Luxuries that really were all about the comfort and beauty of existence. Everything pretended to be something it wasn't with such skill that, unless she looked up, Emalynn could believe they were walking through a forest under a night sky even though they were three floors below the surface while the local star was high in the sky.

This level, while more compact than the ones above, was still too tall for her to touch the ceiling if she stood on the guard's shoulders. Just because of that, she wanted to touch those stars. Maybe move one out of its proper place so anyone coming after would know it was all an illusion.

She did reach out and pluck a leaf off one of the tame trees as they approached an oasis. The leaf, like all the rest, acted like a living thing. The one thing they hadn't yet perfected in their search for perfect beauty was the art of the flaw. This leaf, like all the others, was perfect, absolutely perfect. That was a state nature abhorred but artists strove for.

"Emalynn." Tristan gasped.

"It's fake." She handed the leaf to Tristan. "It's all fake. Beautifully rendered but fake."

"You didn't really think we could grow trees this far underground," the lead guard commented.

"Then why make a forest where one can't grow trees or see the stars?" Emalynn shot back.

"Because it is beautiful." The guard paused beside an arch made of clinging vines with red and yellow flowers nestled among the leaves.

"There are more appropriate kinds of beauty."

A woman in a tight-fitting uniform that mocked the real armor of the guards around them emerged from the arch. Where the guards were protected but allowed to move freely, she was confined by stiff lines and embellishments that played more for fashion than function. A man in a similar outfit stood behind her. His uniform emphasized his maleness over everything else. Emalynn didn't have to imagine what he would look like without the uniform.

"Your Majesties." The woman bowed to Emalynn.

The man directed his bow to Tristan.

"Your welcome ceremony is scheduled for seven this evening." The woman stepped back, leading them into a room that pretended to be a grove.

The pretense broke down on the far side of the fountain where there were two frosted glass doors with the floral pattern brushed in. Now that was appropriately beautiful. The heavy scent of flowers put Emalynn on edge. It should have been calming, and in a natural setting, it would be, but here among the fakes, she couldn't shake the feeling someone was trying to lull her into stupidity.

"There will be a short public ceremony in the grand hall, followed by a private dinner with their Royal Majesties. Are you in need of refreshments now?" The woman smiled as though truly pleased to be serving them.

Emalynn looked to Tristan. He shrugged.

"A snack would be great." Emalynn shrugged.

There was a moment of confusion.

"What would you like for a snack?" she asked.

Emalynn shrugged again. "Anything really, except a nutrition bar."

Tristan snickered, but the two standing before them looked horrified.

"Cheese and crackers," Tristan supplied. "Any kind of cheese will be fine."

The smiles were back.

"That will be just a moment." The woman shifted in a way that cut between Emalynn and Tristan. "Princess, if you will come with me…"

She guided Emalynn toward the door on the left, while Tristan followed the man to the right. Emalynn resisted the urge to fight them off just to stay with Tristan. She could do this. She'd survived the smuggling routes where an insult could get you killed. A spa shouldn't be that hard to handle.

Tristan

The welcome center reminded Tristan of all the things he'd missed of palace life while enjoying his freedom. It also reminded him of all the things he'd been happy to give up. Out there, as Trevor, he'd experienced what privacy really meant. How he wished he could send the guards away for one last moment completely alone. The lobby of the spa was double the size of the shuttle they'd shared for the past three weeks. Their little hut on Farthing Moon that held their bed, a cradle for Darren, and a small hearth would fit within the boundaries of the glade without needing to move even one branch.

The male attendant brought him to a dressing room that offered no feeling of privacy. He couldn't reach all the way across the room in any direction, and there were no flowering plants covering the walls to provide an illusion of being hidden. A curved couch upholstered in red dominated half the room, facing a set of clothing racks. He didn't have to look to know they were all designed specifically for his body and skin tone. Those clothes, chosen for him by people who were supposed to know about fashion, reminded him he still hadn't had the joy of choosing for himself from the mass-produced options available at the local mall.

"Sire, is something wrong?" The man hovered.

Tristan brushed the tear away from his eye. "Nothing." It was time to be the prince again. He had to put his selfish desires away and be the boy they expected him to be.

"What's your name?" Tristan asked despite the expectations.

The man hesitated. Should he follow the order to do as the prince commanded or the one to keep himself anonymous? In the palace, Tristan hadn't found out the names of his staff because he wasn't supposed to care. Now it felt important to know who they were as people. This man would be the first to feel the difference.

The man dropped to one knee. "Chris," he said with his head down, waiting for punishment.

"Thank you, Chris." Tristan waved for him to stand. Then with a smile, he continued. "I'd like to start with a bath. Nothing special, and I'll wash myself." Tristan ignored Chris's shock. "What I want you to do is pick several outfits from all of this for me to choose from."

"Sire?"

"I trust your judgment about these things more than mine."

Chris blushed beautifully and bobbed one more time before leading Tristan into the bath. Chris directed him to all the options for showers and jets as well as the temperature settings. He pointed out all the soap dispensers and fragrance options as well to cover the time it took to fill the bath.

Tristan sank into the hot water. On Farthing Moon, they'd had a half barrel filled with not-cold water to bathe in until they were strong enough to stand for a shower. Here, he could stretch out to his full length still covered in water. If he could bring this bathtub with him, it would be an easy decision to flee back to that primitive colony. A luxurious bath did not make up for the pressures of living a public life. It would be more enjoyable after a long day convincing sheep, goats, and cows to behave.

Emalynn's voice reached him through the wall that separated their rooms. He couldn't hear the responses of her attendants, but he could guess. She wanted privacy, and they'd been told to teach her how a princess is supposed to behave. They were all going to have to learn compromise or Emalynn would do to the monarchy what Uncle Phillip had tried.

When something thudded against the wall hard enough to create ripples in his bath, he sent Chris to tell the attendants to do things Emalynn's way for now.

Emalynn, he thought, *will make an incredible heir if she can find her way through the etiquette and expectations.* He, on the other hand, would be left with an undefined role. The Other pilot's clear desire for an ambassador gave him something to wish for. Maybe he could turn his training that way and take up the post later. In the meantime, he had a lot of making up to do. He'd thought his tutors meant him to pass the citizenship test like every other citizen of the galaxy. They'd shown him practice tests, which he'd passed with ease. What he didn't know, what most of the galaxy didn't know, was the monarchs didn't take the same test.

He'd seen the study guides and practice tests for the standard citizenship exam while he was pretending to be a standard teenager. He'd also seen the dangers of failing that test when he stopped pretending and started running for his life. His tutors taught him the things he needed to know to be a king and nothing else. Citizens were expected to know about the sciences and mechanics as well as laws and government structures. Even on those topics, the questions confused him because they were from the perspective of the governed, and he'd only learned the perspective of the government. One more reason to resent his isolation in the palace.

He had to sneak away from most of his minders just to get a peek at a shopping mall. If that had worked, Techani... Techani had promised him a day in high school. Tristan would never get that chance now. He splashed the bath water in frustration. His children would. No matter what he became now that he wasn't the heir, he would make sure his children experienced the life other children did. They would know about life from living it, not sneaking vids when their tutors weren't looking.

Tristan sighed to himself. Here he was lying in a bath of a luxury spa, planning to live the rest of his life off script. Not as far off script as the last three months, but not following the plans made by the various offices of the palace. More than that, he planned for his children to be worse than he was about following tradition. He'd changed. A little taste of freedom left him wanting more.

He'd been lucky that he'd escaped the first time in a way that allowed everyone to think he'd died. That wouldn't work again. He'd just have to find some other way to win back his freedom. He couldn't risk being late for the welcome ceremony, though. That would guarantee less freedom than before.

Back in the main room, Chris had pulled one rack forward with several outfits displayed. Each a different style and dominant color. All were also built of several pieces. Chris stood beside the rack, quivering.

Tristan ignored the poor man's fear and looked at the outfits he'd selected. None of them grabbed his attention right away.

"Which one do you recommend?" Tristan avoided looking at Chris in a vain attempt to help him calm down.

"Um... the blue will match His Majesty's suit, or the red will match the queen's."

Tristan looked at both and set them aside. He didn't want to match either. Someone would take that to mean he preferred one over the other.

He just didn't like the green one, but the shirt was a lovely lavender shade that shimmered different hues as it moved through the light. He pushed it aside with his memories of Murphy, who would have loved that shirt. He would have worn it in honor of their dead friend, except it would hurt Emalynn too much. Instead, he chose the rose-colored shirt from the red set with the black pants that were supposed to go with the blue suit and the black vest from under the green jacket. He topped it all with a silvery-white long coat with intricate designs textured in. He finished the look with basic black socks and shoes that matched the coat.

Chris brought a box of accessories for him to look through.

"Do you know what Emalynn is wearing?"

Chris shook his head.

Tristan laughed. "I would guess not. I'll go help her decide."

Chris's eyes went big.

"Actually, I wouldn't go in there just now." Another man walked into the room. He was young and confident and dressed in a designer suit that fit him perfectly. Someone tried to make this colony boy look like a noble.

"Hi." He thrust out his hand, "I'm Davy, your new best friend, according to your publicist."

Davy? The name rang a bell.

"You're M—" Tristan almost choked. "The one who used code fifty-three?"

Davy nodded. He swept into the room, showing how uncomfortable he was in the formal, flare-legged outfit. "Thanks for the warning on that one." He bared his teeth rather than grinned.

"Sorry." Tristan had told Murphy it would get his friend arrested until his status could be verified, rather than shot or just turned away.

Davy flopped into one of the lounge chairs, hooking one of his knees over the arm. "It was better than some cells I've been in, at least as far as the food goes. They wouldn't even let me send an *I'm all right* to my mother, and I missed everything you guys got into."

"Oh, sorry. I didn't know about that part."

"That wasn't the worst of it, but I forgive you." This time, Davy's smile looked genuine. "Besides, I get to dress up like a peacock. Just wait 'til Murphy sees this." He kicked one leg and the flare swirled around.

Tristan choked again. Davy didn't notice and went right on.

"Then they told me I'd won some sort of image contest and I'm your best friend." Davy tossed his head back. "So I suppose I should get to know you or something before we have to go on stage for their Majesties—by which I mean the cameras."

Tristan laughed. He could almost hear Murphy saying things like that.

"Right." Tristan perched on the front of a chair opposite Davy. "So... I'm the prince." He cocked his head to mock the posture he was supposed to use. "I'm sixteen. I have a twin sister, and I like anything my parents hate. My favorite activity is running away."

Davy laughed. "Murphy never said anything about a sense of humor."

"That might have something to do with..."

The silence grew heavy around them. Tristan wanted to keep up the conversation. He should have been able to think of something innocuous to change the subject. His mind went blank.

"Right." Davy's expression faded to neutral. "So how did we meet?"

Tristan heard the raw pain in Davy's voice. He bowed to Davy's ability to keep up the front and let the distraction pull him out of his own paralysis.

"At the mall, of course," Tristan said. "Now that the net knows that's where I was when the transport blew."

"So we aren't going to pretend I've been here all along?" He swung his feet around to sit properly on the couch. "That's what the publicist told me."

Tristan dropped back into his chair. He didn't care about proper posture anymore, not when he was "hanging out" with his "best friend," coming up with a story about how they became friends. "No." He shook his head. "I'm not going to revise that part of my life for her."

"Right." He grinned with an air of enthusiasm. "Then how did we become friends so fast?"

Davy had something against the publicist? They just might be friends.

"Well, you helped get me out of the mall without security noticing it was me."

"Did I get to travel with you?"

"For a couple weeks, until Techani sent you back to tell my parents not to hold an official funeral until all the victims had been positively identified."

"Why would he send me?"

"Because we didn't know who we could trust." Tristan shrugged.

"But I proved myself in two weeks?"

"Make it three."

They were leaning in and grinning like fools. The story would hold up if anyone went looking for proof. All except the part about Davy being on that particular colony that particular day. Those records could be altered if necessary.

"I don't suppose I was with you when you met Emalynn?" He smirked.

Tristan shook his head. "What do you know about her?"

Davy put his head back to laugh. "Murphy said so much about her that I can't believe half of it. He was in love, like for real love, with her. Half the time, she was a typical girl, assuming life worked the way she wanted it to. The other half, she was an ancient ninja warrior with the soul of a dragon, ready to bite your head off. And somewhere in there, she could be the sweetest girl you ever knew."

"The crazy thing is that's pretty accurate." Tristan had seen the warrior side of her more than either of the others. Maybe it would have been different if he'd met her when she was still a typical high school girl. She could be sweet when she was serving as ship's host and when they were living on Farthing Moon.

"And she's going to be queen?"

Tristan laughed at the look of horror on Davy's face.

Karen

Karen checked the mirror one more time to be sure the bruise wouldn't show under the makeup. This wasn't the first time she'd had an Emalynn-shaped bruise. This was the first bruise that came from breaking up a fight. All the others had been from overextending during cheer practice. There was that one that happened during a competition, but Emalynn insisted that one didn't count because Carly misstepped and forced her to trip. The whole team had become skilled at hiding bruises beneath makeup because they weren't content to take it easy.

"Do you remember that one competition when Lou had such a bad shiner that we changed our makeup to match?"

Emalynn shrugged herself deeper into the chair. It was more movement than she'd showed since Karen chased the attendants away to go tend their injuries. Karen didn't have much sympathy for them. Stupid women who continue to fight for things like helping a grown woman bathe deserved a few bruises. Maybe they would learn. She'd chased them out to help Ly calm down. She couldn't afford to have Ly's temper tantrum disrupt the welcome ceremony.

It wasn't fair. After all they'd been through, Ly—and Prince Tristan—deserved a chance to relax before being put on display. Ly especially, since she wasn't coming home; she was living in some alternate universe where nothing was what it seemed.

"You have to get dressed." Karen gave up on trying to cheer up her friend and went with the tough love that usually worked on team members who'd been dumped.

"I don't want to." She again kicked the now rumpled designer suit the attendant had chosen.

"So you're going to meet the king and queen of the galaxy in your bra and panties? With every major news and gossip site broadcasting you on the entire net?" Karen walked over to the racks of suits. No one should have this many formal wear outfits in their closet. "So what colors do you want?"

"What are the king and queen wearing?" Emalynn got up to hurtle the red suit across the room.

"Um, I think the king will be in blue and the queen in red." She was supposed to get Emalynn to wear red, but Karen didn't think that was such a good idea now.

"Ugh."

"So who do you want to honor?"

Emalynn looked out to somewhere across the universe and moved her mouth. No sound came out.

If Karen needed any more proof that Murphy had died, this was it. She didn't need some special death report or body pics to know the reason he wasn't with them when they landed. How had they ended up in such a tangled web? They were just poor kids from an outer ring colony.

"So something purple with subtle flare it is." Karen poked her way through all the outfits but found nothing that fit Ly's mood or personality. Wow, these stylists didn't have a clue who they were designing for. This would be easier at the nearest mall, but she would make it work here. Most of these suits were in multiple pieces, so she threw concerns over the designer's feelings over the event horizon and pulled together an outfit Murphy would swoon over.

Emalynn burst into tears when she saw it.

"Should I try again?"

"No!" Emalynn grabbed the clothes from Karen's hands. She accepted her help when the tears got in the way.

Karen adjusted the mix-and-match suit to hide, as much as she could, that each piece was made by a different designer. Ly looked regal for the few seconds she was able to stop the tears and view herself in the mirror. Then she collapsed into Karen's arms and sobbed.

"It's almost time," Karen whispered when the sobs subsided. "It's time to put on a show."

"I don't want to." Ly pulled away from Karen's embrace anyway.

"It won't be long." Karen shifted to block the mirror. "I promise."

Emalynn's lips twisted upward a bit. "How can you make that promise?"

Karen gave her patented evil grin. "If they take too long, I'll start one of our cheer routines right in the middle of everything."

"You're crazy. You know that." Emalynn sat up. Her smile, though still small and sad, looked more real.

"That's what I'm here for." Karen grabbed her friend's hand and dragged her to a stand. "Hey, this isn't any worse than finals, right. And you're usually the one cheering for all the rest of us."

"I just…" Emalynn fluttered her hands in a rare display of wordlessness. "I don't want to do this right now."

Understandable, really. "That's how I feel when the math test pops up on my tablet."

Emalynn laughed in spite of herself. They'd spent many late-night hours arguing whether math was hard or complicated. Emalynn insisted on complicated because every math problem could be broken down into smaller parts. Karen argued for hard because she didn't want to take the test.

"Look." Karen pulled Emalynn toward the door. "All you have to do is walk down the middle of that big room they always show on the news feeds, bob your head while the rest of us bow, say a few words about how nice it is to be home, and it'll all be over. You can go off to dinner with your parents for the first time and have a normal teenager fight with them for not being there for you all this time. And for the first time in history, you'll actually be telling the truth."

Emalynn laughed. "It's not like it's their fault."

"You're supposed to save that line for after the tears and wailing." Karen looped her arm in Emalynn's and propelled her through the door. "Don't you watch the vids? These things have a formula to them. I didn't spend all this time learning the ways of vid making to have you screw it up."

"That's your thing." Emalynn sounded more like herself.

"Then listen to what I'm telling you."

They made it out to the "oasis" just as Tristan and Davy emerged from their side room with arms draped over each other's shoulders.

There was no mistaking Tristan. Even if she hadn't seen his face plastered all over the net since they were ten, he looked so much like Emalynn she could have mistaken them for one another. Then there was their fashion sense. Tristan's outfit had all the hallmarks of being three different designer suits, too. They'd even managed to come up with matching colors.

On seeing her brother, Emalynn finally broke into a real smile that lit her eyes. Karen let out the breath she'd been holding. The publicist had warned her if anything went wrong with the welcome ceremony, it would be her responsibility. Karen didn't think the woman was really a publicist so much as a director.

"Tristan." Emalynn waved at Tristan's outfit.

"Emalynn." He matched her so perfectly it was fun. "Oh, let me introduce you to my 'best' friend. Davy, this is Emalynn."

Davy held out his hand for Emalynn to grasp.

"Oh, how did you two meet?" Karen jumped in before Emalynn could start crying again.

The boys giggled as they spun an amazing tale of how Davy had helped rescue Tristan after the explosion. They finished each other's sentences just like best friends or good improv partners.

Emalynn refused to look at Davy through the whole thing. Tristan kept Davy's eyes off Emalynn, too. This was far worse than they'd been prepared for. "Just keep those two on script," they'd been told. No need to mention the threats today. Those had been clear enough from the start.

"It's a lie." The growl in Ly's voice gave Karen the chills.

"Put it away." Karen used the "mother voice" Coach had taught them when they became team captains. "Put it away for now. We have the biggest performance of your life to get through."

Emalynn turned away. At least she wasn't going to attack Davy.

Davy shot her a worried look. They both had much to worry about, but worry didn't help.

"Ly." Karen softened her tone. "It's hard. I get that. It's not fair, and they should have their royal asses handed to them on a platter. None of that matters right now. If you don't get up there and play your part today, you'll just finish what that hole-eaten Lord Leblanc started."

Emalynn stiffened, then relaxed into her ready stance. Anyone who'd never seen Emalynn fight would think she'd calmed down. Karen knew better, but at least in this state, they could get her through the ceremony.

"Fine." Her voice had the same deceptive tone as her body. "Let's go."

Tristan stepped over to walk with Emalynn. His eyes flashed with the same fire as hers, so Karen let him take her arm and faded back to walk with Davy. He clenched her arm as they left the spa to meet the guards that would keep them from getting "lost."

Karen feared that moment, too, but Emalynn appeared to ignore them. She glanced at Davy, hoping he would assure her that they were doing the right thing, but he was looking for the same thing from her.

Emalynn

Emalynn set a fast pace as they walked down the central aisle of the grand hall. She wanted to walk with Tristan, but the publicist wouldn't hear of it. No, she had to escort Davy, of all people, through the throngs of people dressed in fashionable suits to the steps of the dais where King Levon and Queen Treylyn sat in fancy chairs. No doubt some of the buzz around the room came from commentators yabbering on about who was wearing what. Emalynn understood now why even the serious news sites spent so much time worrying about fashion during these events. The events were as boring as watching grass grow, and the fashion wars added the drama needed to keep people interested.

In her quick walk, Emalynn picked out three distinct designers who had managed to clothe almost everyone in the room, including the camerawomen. Those same three designers were represented in Emalynn's and Tristan's mismatched outfits. In other words, no one won the war tonight, but they would have thousands of hours of commentary on the meaning behind the royal twins' fashion choices. All three designers would get a publicity boost any artist would kill for.

Emalynn felt like killing because of it.

On top of all that, the failed manipulations of her attendants in the spa became obvious as soon as she saw what the queen was wearing. They wanted her to choose the red to match her mother and make a cute image that could be the center of a publicity campaign. Tristan had probably weaseled his way out of a blue outfit to match the king. No wonder the publicist was so cranky with them. Well, she, along with everyone else, would just have to learn to deal with it. Emalynn had no intention of becoming a puppet.

Davy kept up with her pace easily with his long legs. He even managed to make it look effortless. His breathing gave him away, but only she could hear that. Tristan and Karen followed along behind and let themselves be outpaced. Something about that amused Tristan enough that she could feel it through that bond connecting them.

Everything in this ceremony should have been scripted out, with rehearsals and the possibility of retakes if necessary. Any friend of a first-level vid student knew that. In some way, they expected her to fail. If she failed, she would do it honestly. She'd do what she could to keep their script. So she stepped up to the mark with Davy by her side and bowed her head. Davy dropped to one knee beside her.

The long pause while they waited for Tristan to catch up and take up his position beside her with Karen on the far side left most of the gathered wondering whether they should bow as Davy did or wait for Karen. The crowd scene would need to be reshot for this vid because they missed their cue. No wonder Tristan felt so happy.

"Princess Emalynn and Prince Tristan," a woman in a constricting black and white uniform bellowed.

Everyone stood, and Emalynn looked up into the faces of her parents for the first time. She'd seen their faces every day just as she'd seen Tristan's. No one could avoid the royal family in the colonies. Now they were her parents and they were looking at her.

"Our child, separated from us for so many years, welcome home." The king's voice boomed over the whole crowd and out into the colonies. That stupid microphone attached to his collar took his intimate words and threw them over her head to everyone except her.

They'd clipped one of those to her collar as well, so she couldn't ask Karen to feed her a line that would be formal and accepting—whatever that meant. How could she accept their welcome anyway? All this ceremony before she could meet them. It felt backward or inside out.

"I thank you for holding my place in your heart open all these years." She kept her eyes on the king while she spoke.

His lips twitched up a bit at the corners and his eyes showed a bit more sparkle under her gaze. All around her, people were tensing or shifting uncomfortably. No one had the authority to look so hard at the monarch, as though a gaze were a weapon. Emalynn had just become his daughter, and a child should be allowed to look at her parent. Let him tell her otherwise in front of the cameras.

The queen shifted forward a bit to draw her attention. "There has been a sorrow hanging over our house." She began. Her speech, even more than the king's, was directed at the cameras.

Emalynn tried to catch her mother's eyes and hold them the way she'd held the king's, but the queen didn't notice. She spoke about the hardships of having only her son to carry on the family legacy, as though Tristan weren't standing right there. She talked about the fear they faced when they thought they'd lost him, too. Finally, long after Karen should have started her cheer routine, she welcomed both twins back to the household.

"I wish"—the queen looked down at her without seeing—"we could have done something to change this situation before now."

Emalynn didn't. She wouldn't have traded her life with Baba for life in the palace. If she had a choice, she wouldn't have learned of her heritage until after Tristan had been crowned. They cared more about appearances than their relationship.

"It would have been best had I been raised here, but my experiences won't be wasted." She hardened her stare at the queen. "My unique perspective will be an asset as I take back my place in the family."

The queen froze her expression with a smile on her face. Her eyes, caught in Emalynn's stare, revealed fear. Fear that Emalynn would disrupt the balance of power she'd worked so hard to create. It couldn't be a strong balance if a challenge by a sixteen-cycle girl could topple it so easily.

"My son." The king pulled focus to Tristan. "We are more than pleased you were able to escape the fate others chose for you and return to us. All the better you managed to double our joy by finding your sister among the stars and bring her back to us."

Emalynn allowed the continuation of the ceremony to break the battle of wills between her and the queen of the galaxy. Treylyn was known in the darkness as a woman with a hunger for power. Everyone knew she'd been born to a corporate family and caught the attention of the crown prince. She'd risen to the title of queen, but not the power it should have come with. Among the smugglers and thieves who'd helped raise her, Treylyn represented the worst of the government's oppression. They blamed her for any enforcement effort that got in the way of a big payout.

Levon somehow managed to avoid the stigma of being the head of the government. It could have been that he was handsome, though Baba said he wasn't that much to look at. She swooned for his speeches about the need to improve the education options for colonists and advocacy for research into the citizenship marker so it could be safely given to older people who missed their normal graduation window. Emalynn liked him because he wasn't afraid to smile.

"It's time," Tristan whispered.

"Together or not at all." Emalynn agreed.

He nodded and they walked in perfect step the last three steps to the dais and up the four stairs. Still no hugs or teary greetings here where the cameras were trained to catch everything. Instead, they clasped hands and smiled at each other. Treylyn began another speech about the history that led to this moment, until Levon put a hand on her shoulder.

"I'm sure you would all love to know more," he said, "but we've waited seventeen years to have dinner as a family. And I'm hungry."

The crowd laughed. Emalynn couldn't help but smile. Finally, something resembling a real family greeting.

Music played. Reporters turned to their cameras. Karen smiled up at her with a thumbs-up hidden from the rest of the room. She'd survived, and so had everyone else.

Except it wasn't over yet. Tristan gripped her hand tight enough keep her attention. It also alerted her to the tension that had risen between her parents, despite their broad grins and waves to the crowd. Tristan led Emalynn through the motions of waving to all parts of the crowd before following the king and queen out the door at the back of the dais.

Emalynn let out her breath with relief once the door closed behind them, but Tristan's grip only tightened. This back hall had the same subtle elegance of the welcome center, except there were no guards pretending to be statues. They were safe from the prying of reporters and their net-linked cameras, though not from the security cameras. Those were tucked in corners every few feet. This part of the palace must be very secure if they let the entire family wander about without security. So why had Tristan's tension increased?

Queen Treylyn answered by ripping her arm away from her husband with enough force to pull him off balance.

"Really, Lev?"

"Really." He stared her down.

"I worked on that speech for hours."

"After I told you not to?" He stepped closer to her. "I said to keep it short. Keep it simple. They aren't up for this kind of thing yet." His hand thrust toward them so fast Emalynn found her self in a defensive stance without thinking.

"This was the best chance we had to spin this whole fiasco to our advantage." Treylyn spared a glance at the teenagers, then turned back to her husband to continue the fight.

Emalynn closed her eyes so she could block out the words they were throwing at each other. Tristan took a tighter grip on her hand, and she returned it. They made a good pair here. He knew the rules and the ways. She knew how to keep her head above water in a hostile environment. Sometimes that meant slamming your foot down and fighting it out, but sometimes it meant sneaking away through the underbrush while the wolves fought over who would get to eat you. This was of the latter form.

She tugged Tristan to follow her as she moved slowly behind the queen's back. She couldn't slip behind both of them, and she counted the queen as the more dangerous of the two. She used them to spin her politics.

What else would she use them for?

Tristan stopped her before they were behind the queen and pulled her to the wall. A hidden door pulled back and slid aside just wide enough for someone to slip through. Tristan flashed a sly grin at her before disappearing into the darkness beyond. Emalynn followed him without hesitation into a dimmer, less elegant hall that ran parallel to the main one.

"Where are we?"

"Servants' passages." Tristan snorted. "They're monitored, but it will take time before anyone notices we aren't where we're supposed to be. By then, we'll be back on script in the family dining room."

"How many of these halls are there?" Emalynn marked all the security cameras. She found no blind spots. "And how long does it take them to notice?"

Tristan shrugged. "It depends on whether we've been missed or not. They run all over the palace to keep the servants out of the way and let them get around without interference."

"How long until we're missed?"

A broad smile passed his lips. "Depends on how long they fight. The better joke would be to start dinner without them."

Emalynn nodded. She could have fun with this.

Karen

When the last of the camera crews were escorted from the throne room, Karen let out the breath she'd been holding since she woke up this morning. She'd found a place out of the way on a built-in bench about halfway between the dais and the grand doors. Davy lounged beside her with his head on her lap. He knew her relationship with Dom but insisted on these kinds of intimate displays as often as they could. He called it a safety net. She found it comforting in an odd way.

"They did it." Davy shifted to look up at her. "They made it through the ceremony without any major gaffs."

Karen looked down at him. "Yeah, they did." She couldn't muster any more enthusiasm than that.

"So what are you going to do?" He went back to gazing across the room where the servants were still cleaning up.

She watched them, too. Their carefully choreographed movements looked so natural. Or maybe it was that their natural movements looked choreographed. Either way, they made for a good distraction from the dread neither of them wanted to talk about.

"Go home, graduate, get on with my life." She fell back against the wall. "You?"

"Same." He spoke with less enthusiasm than she felt about math tests.

They'd only met a week ago when she arrived for her "all expenses paid trip to Prime" that King Levon had promised when he announced Emalynn was his daughter. She thought it some kind of joke that she'd won the contest she'd made up to cover the crazy images of Tristan that appeared all over the net. Then the royal guards arrived in the middle of school and pulled her and Dom out of class. It didn't work the way she expected. Now Davy, who'd never met Tristan before, was the only one she could talk to.

"You don't sound convinced," Karen mused when the silence grew too long.

"I'm not." Davy pulled his legs in and wrapped his arms around his knees. "Maybe I'm paranoid, but it's just too easy. And where are our handlers?"

He had a point. They'd been handled just about every moment they'd been in the palace. When they weren't learning how to manipulate their friends to make a good show of the welcoming ceremony, they were watched or locked away in their rooms (for their own safety). They'd never been left sitting like this before.

"Maybe we don't need them anymore?"

Davy snorted. "Have you seen where we are?"

He was right. The guards wouldn't let them wander around the palace unescorted. If they found a way past the guards, neither of them knew how to get to the guest rooms, and they didn't have the access codes to their own rooms. If this represented the royal life, Karen didn't want any part of it.

"This is so not what I expected." She'd said that too many times this week.

Davy snorted again, as he did every time she mentioned her expectations. He had a low opinion of the government and the palace in particular. He had reasons he wouldn't tell her. She kept her secrets, too.

"You don't think they're going to let us go home, do you?" She pushed his shoulder gently.

"No, I don't. We know too much that doesn't support the current story."

He'd said things like this at least once a day since they met. She couldn't deny the logic or the drama of it.

"I'll be missed. Everyone knows where I am."

"And they'll be fed a story to explain your continued absence." He turned to look her directly in the eyes. "You believe what they teach in governance, don't you? That the monarchy cares about all its citizens."

She nodded. Her arms crossed themselves over her stomach. He'd gone down this hole before.

"It's not a lie, exactly." Davy held her eyes with his. "It's just that not everyone gets to be a citizen. You know someone like that. Someone who just quit coming to school before graduation. Someone whose parents lost a job. An orphan."

Charlie.

Emalynn never let them forget Charlie. When so many kids lost a mother in the Corring Mine collapse, he lost his father, too. No one else came forward to claim him as a nephew or volunteered to adopt him. He lived with a hired couple. Until Ly came, he suffered the taunts of the other victims who blamed him for the disaster. No one knew Ly the day she fought off a whole crowd of his tormentors; no one forgot her after.

Karen still remembered what Ly said when the rest of the kids ran off. "Don't let them bother you. There are people who care. Don't wait too long to run away." Then she went on as though nothing had happened.

"You don't see them, the ungraduated who aren't citizens. They are hidden away by the corporation who made them."

"Aren't the corporations required to educate the orphans?" It sounded stupid before she said it. Now it sounded naïve, too.

Davy turned away. "That's what the law says."

"But not what happens."

The law said people shouldn't have been in the Corring Mine with the gas levels where they were. The law said family members weren't supposed to work the same shifts in mines.

"Do you really think they don't know about it?" He pointed a toe at the dais. "Maybe not all the specifics, but they have to know it happens."

Karen wished she could deny it. A year ago, she would have been able to. Then Ly's Baba was murdered and all the details came out.

"How do you know about it?"

Davy looked up at her. His eyelids were already turning red from some sad memory he didn't want to cry about.

"There you are." A pair of women in the palace uniforms stood before them. "Dinner will be served in your rooms tonight. Let's go."

Karen felt like kicking her in the shins, but she smiled instead. "Sounds nice."

The silent guard pulled Davy to his feet and twisted his arm behind his back. Davy closed his eyes against the pain, so Karen kept her mouth shut, too. She stood and walked with them meekly all the way back to their rooms. They said nothing the whole way. The handlers gave an aura of anger, but Karen didn't want to know what they'd done wrong. They'd find out in the morning when Deliah came to get them.

Karen looked at the tray on the little table. She didn't bother to lift the cover to decide she didn't want to eat. Instead, she went to clean the makeup off her face and check the bruise Ly gave her. It was a good one. Not quite round, just under her eye. It could make her look quite rugged. She posed in the mirror. Maybe she could use it as proof she was being abused. That wouldn't work because she wasn't the one being abused.

Best not think of her own situation.

Emalynn was in trouble. The fight with the attendant and little issues of defiance in the ceremony told her that much. Karen could guess Ly had some anger toward her parents. Who wouldn't? Then the fact that Murphy hadn't returned with them said something else. Add it all up, and she found even more gaps in the story.

Karen flopped on her bed and stared at the ceiling. She hoped the idiots who watched her constantly were having fun. Let them speculate all they wanted about what she was thinking. They didn't know Ly the way she did. It wouldn't be long before Ly figured out Karen wasn't acting on her own. She only had to have faith that Dom would be able to wait for them. In the meantime, it was her job to read the hints her friend gave her about the secrets Ly kept from the rest of the universe.

Tristan

Tristan sat in his place at the family dining table and watched Emalynn pace through the space opposite him. He marveled at her control of her body, even in something as simple as walking back and forth. All that control showed just how raw her nerves were. He felt the same, being back in this room, waiting for his parents to finish an argument before they could eat as a family. He wondered how many revisions the menu had gone through already, waiting for the king and queen to appear.

He'd never thought of that before. Now that he knew how delicate foods could be, he understood the cooks had to constantly shift the plan when the royals didn't show up to the table on time. How many of his favorite meals had been the third or fourth choice for the evening? Tonight they had to be on the fifth or sixth option. He'd never known his parents to fight this long when dinner was waiting.

"What are we waiting for?" Emalynn stopped across from him.

"Mother and Father to realize they're supposed to be here."

"Are they still fighting over that speech?" She pushed off against the chair and resumed her pacing.

Tristan held back from joining her, though the temptation rippled through him. He understood her frustration. She didn't know the rules here, so this felt more like a cage than a dining room.

"Try sitting down." He waved to the chair opposite him. "Martisan used to tell me things wouldn't happen until you sat down."

"That's nonsense." She slowed her pace a bit.

"It seemed to work at the time."

She moved toward the chair across from him on the other long side of the table. "How old were you?"

He laughed. "Five."

She growled but pulled out the chair and sat. She stayed just at the edge of it, ready to jump up if needed.

"Didn't you ever have family dinners growing up?" Tristan asked.

"Of course, all the time." She gave him one of those are you being stupid or clever looks that she was so good at. "Whenever Baba could scrape together a real meal. Sometimes we even had a real table. Once we found a table in the storage bay we were using as a base and had a whole dinner with the crew." She let a small smile escape for a moment.

"Did they make you this nervous?" Tristan adjusted his silverware again.

"Why would they?"

"Why does this one?"

She glared at him.

The door shifted open before she could respond. Mother preceded Father into the room, which could only mean Father won the fight and Mother would be looking for perfection, which she wasn't going to get.

"Tristan." Mother set her eyes on him. "We expect better of you. And Emalynn,"—her gaze shifted to Emalynn—"don't scare us like that. Do you-"

"Then don't fight like that." Emalynn shot back, holding Mother's gaze.

This time it was Father who broke it off with a nudge to his wife. "Leave it be, Trey."

Mother fixed Father with that same look, but he ignored it.

Tristan fought the urge to stand up while Father made his way to his seat at the head of the table. Propriety said he should, but practicality told him to keep Emalynn in her seat. That meant keeping his seat as well.

The servers came with bread and salad as soon as everyone had taken their seats. Emalynn sat deeper in her chair and thanked the server. Tristan did the same, despite the glare from Mother. Mother ignored her server, but Father followed his children and thanked his. Battle lines were set now. Nothing would happen while the servers still lingered, so they just smiled at each other and ignored the food in front of them.

"We should discuss the expectations." Mother grabbed and shook her napkin and placed in in her lap.

Tristan kicked Emalynn under the table to keep her from snarking back right away.

"What kind of expectations do you want, dear?" Father's skill with words could be something to witness when he displayed them. Tonight looked like a perfect opportunity.

Mother laid out a practiced list of behaviors she expected from the princess and prince. All of them completely reasonable, most of the time. Mother expected them all the time and rendered perfectly. Tristan nibbled at his bread while Emalynn tore hers into crumbs during this recitation.

"Were you never young?" Father asked when Mother paused for a breath.

Mother gaped like a fish. She never expected his underhanded jabs. Tristan shared a little grin with Emalynn across the table.

"You don't think etiquette is important?" Mother crushed her bread and had to set it aside.

"Of course etiquette is important." Father picked up his fork. "But we can hardly expect Emalynn to know the rules yet, and Tristan has never been one to use them when he didn't have to."

"That's no excuse." Mother slapped the table just hard enough to be heard.

"You want to worry about etiquette?" Emalynn dropped the remainder of her bread onto her plate. She turned to face Mother with an almost blank expression. "How about taking some responsibility for your actions, or lack thereof?" She kept her voice almost too quiet and held the floor against the two most powerful speakers he knew. "How about not stopping to fight in the middle of the hall so we have to find a way around you or listen in? Etiquette is about making the people around you comfortable because we are all following the same rules. Did you stop to think how your snit fit affected the cooks or servers who were waiting to do their job? How many alterations have the cooks had to make so you won't fire them for serving you something that would have been perfect if you'd just showed up on time?"

She turned to Father while taking a breath. "Or how about this? Not leaving your children stuck in a shuttle for three weeks while you plan a ceremony you can't even agree on. Oh, and while you're at it, you could have passed me a copy of the script if you were so worried I don't know how these things work."

Tristan half admired her for telling off their parents. Bonus points for making it sound civil. The other half feared this meal would end in bloodshed.

"I will not be talked to like this." Mother braced both hands on the table, turning her knuckles white.

"Treylyn." Father set his fork back in its place. "She has—"

"Don't you start." She slapped the table hard enough to rattle the plates.

Emalynn jumped to a defensive stance behind her chair.

"Sit. Down." Mother pushed herself to a stand that would have intimidated anyone except Emalynn.

Father used the same tactic on Mother, with the same effect.

"Stop." Tristan stood so fast his chair clattered to the floor. "This was a bad idea. This whole process was a bad idea. Guards, please."

He held the silence by sheer force of will until four guards came through the door, weapons still holstered but hands hovering near. Their eyes scanned the room for a threat they could recognize.

"Please escort Emalynn and me to our rooms and let the kitchen know we will take our dinners there."

He held out a hand to Emalynn. She rounded the table behind Father without taking her eyes off the queen. Tristan counted on the presence of the guards to keep Mother in check. He offered a shallow, sad bow to Father before following Emalynn into the hall.

"What was that?" Emalynn turned on Tristan as soon as the door slid closed.

Tristan waved the guards back. "It will do no one any good if you kill our Mother during our first family dinner."

He nodded to the guards to start walking. They were smart enough to keep as much distance as they could between them and the twins. Emalynn snarled but followed the guards anyway. Tristan would take this moment of calm before she ran across the next unacceptable requirement.

"Besides," he said when they were in the lift, "you're right. I've never had the guts to tell her so."

Emalynn snorted. "Will you still admire me if I do it again?"

Tristan laughed. Would he admire her? "I fully expect you to take the whole palace apart one etiquette rule at a time. I'll enjoy every minute of it."

Tristan

Tristan's rooms were exactly as he'd left them. He shouldn't be surprised. He'd only been dead four months. The surprising part was how foreign the rooms felt. He remembered all his treasures and the stories behind them. Few of them held his heart the way they had when he left. They weren't going to match the few items he'd brought back. He started pulling the things he didn't want anymore off the shelves.

"Sire?" One of the guards who stayed with him spoke up. "Is something wrong?"

He didn't know this woman. Of course not. All the guards he'd known had been on the transport.

"I'd like to be alone," he said.

"Sire?"

"That means guard me from outside the door." He waved his hands at them. "And while you're at it, make sure Emalynn's guards are outside as well."

The one started to speak again, but the other wisely pulled her away. He'd have to have a conversation with Security Chief Grouse tomorrow about how to rebuild his security force with women who wouldn't annoy him. Emalynn should be there, too.

The door chime announced the arrival of his dinner. The young server brought the tray to his table and noticed all the things he'd gathered there.

"Should I send for packing boxes?" the young man asked when he arranged the dishes.

"Not yet." Tristan smiled. "I'll call when I know what needs to be packed. Thank you."

The man looked up with surprise, then quickly lowered his eyes again. Tristan considered training this man in the ways he liked to be served but decided that would be too much for tonight. He stood aside while the man bowed himself out.

He didn't need to uncover the dishes to know they would contain some of his favorite foods. The smell of roast rigalla snuck out around the edges and tempted him. Someone in the kitchen still remembered his preferences. Fond memories and tempting scents weren't enough to overcome his clenched stomach. Yet. He'd just have to hope the little bird saved well for when he did get hungry.

He'd filled the rest of the table with things when the door alarm announced his father asking for admittance. How odd. King Levon could override any privacy setting he chose. It was a rare occasion when the king came to him anyway. Then to have him wait to be admitted suggested Tristan was dreaming. How fitting they'd gone through all that only to find he was still sitting on the shuttle, waiting for someone to decide to let them finish their journey home.

"Come." He decided to let this all play out.

Father stepped into his room, still in his formal wear from the ceremony but looking more like a real person than a god on some high mountain.

"Welcome home." Father paused just inside the door. "And thank you."

Tristan nodded to accept both and beckoned Father to join him in the seating area. It felt odd to have this kind of control when his father was involved.

"Making changes?" Father glanced at the table.

Tristan smiled and shook his head. "The changes have been made. It's just time to let them show."

"You changed more than we expected when we sent you on that trip." Father tugged absently at the hem of his coat.

"I didn't exactly go on the trip you planned." Had things worked out as planned, Tristan would still be only halfway through the itinerary of meetings with local governors and lords of the counties. Emalynn would still be working off her debt on the Pterodactyl. He'd still know less than he needed about how people really lived in the outer colonies.

"No, you didn't." Father put his hem down and smoothed it against his leg. "You've changed... in ways we could never have imagined or planned for."

Tristan nodded. No use denying it. For one thing, Mother didn't scare him like she used to. Thanking the servants for their jobs felt as natural as their being there to take care of things. "You aren't who I'm used to anymore either."

Father smiled. "No. You weren't the only one on an adventure."

They fell into silence. Tristan knew his parents had gone through a supernova with the news of attack on his transport. It didn't take a lot of imagination to feel with them some of the pain they'd felt. He didn't want to know more than that, at least not until he got over the pain of watching the transport explode.

"I remember, when I was your age, how I wanted to go on a great adventure." Father broke the silence. "I never managed even half the crazy things you've done, even before you left for your tour."

"At my age, you weren't the heir."

Aunt Celia was the crowned heir back then. Father only got the job when Celia's transport failed on their way to oversee a flood recovery project on Retensi. Some claimed the accident had actually been an assassination, but it had never been proven. Others were sure it couldn't have been an assassination because who would deliberately put a man on the throne?

"True. My plans were to find a good wife and devote myself to some art or other." Father stared over Tristan's head into some long ago time. "Celia would have been a better queen. It was all she ever wanted. I never expected the responsibility to land on my shoulders."

"At least you knew what to expect when you did become the heir."

"So do you."

"Emalynn doesn't."

Father nodded, and they lapsed again into silence. Tristan let it grow tense. He wasn't ready to completely forgive his father for putting Emalynn through all that without warning.

"Please tell me Mother isn't trying to have this same conversation with Emalynn right now."

"After your outburst at dinner? No." Father stared off into space again. "I had her drink spiked with her relaxers. If she didn't go to bed as I suggested, they'll find her soon enough."

"You shouldn't have to use them like that."

"I wish I didn't." Father turned sad eyes toward Tristan. "Your mother isn't a bad person. She just had certain expectations that didn't come to be. You can't blame her for fighting to get them back."

"I can and I will." Tristan had to look away to keep from drowning in his father's unshed tears. "Some opportunities are just gone. They aren't coming back. I'm never going to be the daughter she expected to raise, and she's never going to get the chance to raise Emalynn. She's just going to have to live with who we are now."

"Of course." Father wouldn't look at him.

"It's not like we can turn back time."

"Of course not." Now fire burned in Father's eyes. That was the power that allowed him to face off against all the women of the lords council without losing his masculinity.

Tristan nodded and sat back down. He didn't remember standing up, but that was typical of these kinds of conversations.

Silence spread between them again. This time it was a comfortable silence that said there were no more words to say. Tristan relaxed into it, happy in the knowledge that not everything had changed.

"You came to say something?" he said when the comfort wore off.

"Thank you for teaching Emalynn enough to get through the ceremony."

Tristan laughed. "That wasn't me. I had enough on my mind trying to get to know my new best friend and figuring out what you were doing putting us through a ceremony without warning."

Father slumped in his chair. "You were supposed to know about it. That was why we waited so long to bring you down to the surface."

Tristan shook his head. "We heard nothing until they tried to put another pilot on the shuttle. Someone owes Emalynn an apology for that one."

Father sighed again. "I'll add that to my list. How should I go about apologizing to her?"

"For one, don't apologize for the pilot thing. She'll know that wasn't your decision as soon as you bring it up. As for the rest, talk to her like a person. You are her father, not her king."

"I'm her king, too."

"Not if you want to apologize." Tristan leaned forward. "Out there, people are used to being flexible about power in relationships. You remember what she said about etiquette? That's really how they see it. They want their king to be human sometimes. She needs to know you are human."

"How do I do that?"

"Like this." Tristan gestured to the two of them. "Start a conversation with her and listen to what she says. Don't play games. She's not a politician."

The king laughed. "You make it sound so easy."

"It is." Tristan laughed.

Father stood abruptly. "I'll let you get back to... whatever it was you were doing." He walked toward the door, stopping just before the sensor line. "Welcome home."

"It's good to be home."

Tristan let the door close behind his father before opening the control panel. His special circuits greeted him like old friends. He toggled the door to full privacy. Until he changed it back, the door would believe it was a wall. No one would be able to enter or even activate the chime. Yes, it was good to be home.

Emalynn

The rooms were too big. Emalynn couldn't get comfortable anywhere. The lounge area in front of the media wall had seats for eight people. So did the conversation nook between the dining room and the lounge. The dining area's table could fit more than that, if there were enough chairs. There were two. Her dinner, laid out in too many dishes, didn't come close to filling the table. The same way she wouldn't come close to filling these rooms.

The bedroom was worse. Only a little smaller than the main room with a huge bed dominating the space. Really, how many people did they expect to sleep in that thing? If she had to guess, eight just like everything in the main room. And all eight of them would fit in the bath at the same time, too. The closet hid in the wall opposite the bathroom and took up the whole wall. Inside, there were more designer suits than she'd seen at a formal dance.

Emalynn wandered from space to space. These were supposed to be her private quarters, but they should have been given to a family who needed the space.

"Highness, is something wrong?" One of the guards who insisted on accompanying her spoke from her post by the door.

"Do you have any idea how much it would cost to decorate an apartment like this?" Emalynn waved her hands around the whole place. The walls that weren't media projectors were covered in dark wood cabinets or painted with gold-flecked paint. The effect was lovely, but it made the place seem even larger than it already was.

"You could ask the budget office," the guard suggested.

"I don't need to." Emalynn shook her head. "I can tell you the table right there was made with wood from Tressar. A table half its size goes for just under a thousand standard credits on the black market. If you can even find one in a legit store, you'll be lucky if it's only two thousand. That doesn't include the cost of the permit to have live wood transported across colonies."

The color drained from the guard's face. "You know your furniture."

She tried to cover her gaff with a smile.

"I know smuggling," Emalynn said. "I also know budgets. My mother… The woman who raised me rarely got more than five hundred credits for a job. That would last us three months. The apartment we shared on Roshea only cost ninety credits a month. In other words, that table would have been enough to keep us for four years. I can assume we don't have to pay for the permits either since we're royal."

"Would you prefer something else?" the guard asked.

Yes. She wanted her little cabin on Farthing Moon back, with its rough walls and not quite enough space. If she had to have a table of her own, one that showed the love of hand crafting with simple tools would suit her better.

"I want things I've earned or made." Emalynn aimed a halfhearted kick at the table leg. "Or at the very least, that I picked out."

The guard bowed. "That can be arranged."

"How?"

The guard nodded to the media wall. "Just remember, even when we aren't in the room, especially when we aren't in the room, you're being monitored."

"Ugh, that's creepy."

The guard shrugged. "It's, shall we say, for your own good."

Emalynn shuddered. She knew there were cameras everywhere. Six cameras in this room alone. More if you counted the sensors for the media wall. It would only take three audio sensors to cover the room just as effectively. In the colonies, the cameras didn't intrude directly into private homes, except almost everyone had a security system the authorities could commandeer if they needed to. She was used to that. She wasn't used to the idea it was for…

"Wait, you said you don't have to be in the room?"

Both guards shook their heads.

"Then leave."

The guards bowed their way out. Emalynn couldn't believe she'd waited this long to get rid of them. That's what she got for trying to think when she was this stressed and tired. She looked at the bed again and decided she wasn't that tired.

She came face to face with the media wall. "Well, if everything I do is monitored, let's see if the monitors have half the intelligence of the average middle school crossing guard." She spoke to the wall. It, being a computer, didn't respond until she gave it the standard wake-up command.

"Open search: Emalynn Algrian."

Screens full of links popped up, most of them to some version of the welcome ceremony.

"Limit search: advance: prior to Tristan assassination."

Still nebulas worth of information.

"Open link: separate window: Herth High School."

The high school students' page opened to her junior entry. Everything anyone could want to know about her spelled out in easy to find graphics. All pulled from her annual student questionnaire. Favorite color: purple. Favorite hair color: dirty blond. Favorite cafeteria lunch: grilled cheese with tomato soup. What your friends think you should major in: governance. Your intended major: navigations.

"Well, that was easy enough. Save window. Return to search."

She scanned over the links available. What should she make them look at next?

"Open link: separate window: inter-colony cheer competition."

A loop-vid of her team's signature build with Karen at the top started playing. Emalynn loved that build. Most teams put a boy at the top of their builds because boys tended to be lighter. Karen fit the criteria, and she was the most stable member of their team. The loop also showed one of their kick lines and Liz saying, "It's all because of Ly—Emalynn Algrian, team captain. She taught us all these different ways to kick, and they can be so beautiful."

That should give them something to think about. Would the monitors recognize the fighting style she'd added to their cheers? She'd just have to wait and see what happened tomorrow. Next up, her actual skills.

"Return to search: open link: separate window: annual navigations midterm trials."

Her record-breaking run through the simulator opened in one window, while a pair of women talked through the run step by step.

"It is possible"—the woman on the left paused the simulation run—"right here that this girl found a small glitch in the program that allowed her to alter the fuel consumption rates."

"But anyone would have been able to exploit that," the other woman said.

"True, so her record will stand." The first woman restarted the simulation. "However, that will need to be triple checked before we take anything more from this amazing run from a simulation to real navigations."

Emalynn stopped the vid. "Find similar."

There were eight more such vids. Most of them set aside the theory that it was a program glitch and advanced other theories about how a student from an outer colony could best those from the inner colonies and private institutions.

"Because we can't imagine the outer colonies would get anything resembling a good teacher." Emalynn shook her head.

Baba kept them to the outer colonies precisely because the stereotypes would allow them to outperform expectations. She said most people from the outer colonies had advantages the inner colonies could never imagine. The force of facing poverty and raids by the star wanderers forced them to think more creatively about problems. According to Baba, and most of the outlaws they ran with, this made them smarter than any inner colony-educated snob. Now everyone would have to face the uncomfortable truth that their next leader had been raised by ungraduated ruffians in the outer colonies.

"What are you going to do with that?" she asked the invisible monitors. "And what are you going to do about this?"

She called up the news reports of Baba's murder and her flight. The details, sanitized for the open news sources, still brought back the smell that assaulted her when that door opened. The sights that still haunted her dreams rose before her where the monitors wouldn't see them. The cameras wouldn't catch her choking and the tears she didn't try to keep in. All the vids named her "Emalynn Algrian, daughter of the non-citizen Baba Algrian." The news vids stopped calling her a fugitive now, but the official record still showed a reward for information leading to her arrest.

Anyone who wanted to could turn her in to the Roshea authorities now to collect that reward. Well, they could turn her in. She doubted the palace would allow her to be arrested, though that would make for a great statement. Fun politics for Karen and Dom to cover with their vids. How would it work for the princess to face court in a murder case?

She shook herself clear of that nightmare. One more test of the monitors.

"New search: demonstration vids: advance: make a table. Narrow search: advance: local materials."

The list of potential matches to her requests spilled off the wall. The top recommended vids showed high-end crafters who knew more about how to use specialized machines than Emalynn wanted to get into. She found the table she wanted about halfway down the wall on a site for people preparing to join a primitive colony (or at least pretend to). Emalynn smiled at the idea that she wasn't alone in wishing for the primitive lifestyle.

She retreated to one of couches to watch the vid from beginning to end. She imagined herself working along with the woman who explained each step from getting the raw logs to mixing the polish to keep from getting splinters during dinner. She'd had access to all the tools the woman used in the arts lab at Herth. She watched the vid again, this time pausing to copy out all the tool and material requirements for making the table.

"Now, how can I get all of that and a place to do it?"

"Request sent," a mechanical voice responded.

"Sent where?"

"Unknown request. Please restate."

"Oh, never mind." That's what she got for arguing with a computer.

She watched the vid one more time, hoping the repetition would make her sleepy enough to overcome the gut twisting feeling of facing that huge bed. No such luck.

"Where's Tristan?" she asked the computer. He would know what to say to make all this feel normal enough.

"Unknown."

How could that be unknown? Did he manage to sneak out of the palace without her? More likely, there was a privacy block on the members of the royal family.

"Where is Emalynn?"

"Suite 2234, designated for Princess Emalynn, private chambers. Security level private."

That was disturbingly specific. She got similarly disturbing responses when she asked about the king and queen. More so that they were in different suites. So Tristan had somehow disappeared or, more likely, blocked access to everyone. Great. She'd dig that out of him when she saw him in the morning. In the meantime, she was still bored, lonely, and weirded out by her own furniture. She needed a best friend.

"Where's Karen Toya?"

"Suite 3412, designated guest quarters, security level hold."

"What's security level hold?"

"Designation: guest holds low or no security clearance. Must be accompanied at all times."

Karen would love to hear she was such a security risk.

"What's my security level?"

"Undetermined. Schedule security clearance evaluation: Emalynn, Princess: ten o'clock to noon."

She had a schedule? "When were they going to tell me?"

"Request unknown. Please restate."

"Never mind." Emalynn grumbled. "Contact Karen Toya."

"Invalid request. No contact available."

Why would that be? Emalynn knew, as she started tracing Karen's status, she wouldn't get much sleep tonight. Either she could follow this wormhole or pace around the apartment, hating everything in it. Tomorrow wouldn't be the first time she'd faced a day with not enough sleep.

Karen

Karen stared at the plain white ceiling above her bed. Her mind was like a vid site that refused to close. She couldn't even push the vids to the background because she wanted to shut her brain down entirely and let sleep erase these hours from her life. Her mind had other ideas about the value of sleep. Namely that she didn't need it, because linking all these memories consciously was far more important.

Sometimes she hated her mind.

The worst of these memories involved Ly. From this afternoon's looks that only hinted at the horrors she was facing to the actual horrors the police had forced Karen to look at when Ly went missing. Karen retched at the memory of the unedited pics they showed her to convince her to cooperate. Pics that showed everything except the smell. That she had to imagine for herself. With that much detail of blood and bits, it didn't take much imagination. The shock didn't work because Karen had already said everything she knew about Ly.

Ly took her studies seriously. More seriously than her teachers most of the time. She pushed for perfection and came away with the top grades in every class. Even in governance, which she hated for reasons Karen never understood, Ly put everything she had into every assignment.

Karen couldn't shake the images of Ly intruding into every corner of the local net. Most simply reminding people she had become a fugitive. The rest accompanied by the increasingly scandalous history of Baba Algrian or whatever her name might actually be. Each new story added yet another alias. All of which told her she knew nothing about the life her best friend had lived before exploding on the scene of Herth High School. By the time Ly resurfaced, Karen had given up on her. All the void-sucking dust had convinced her Ly was as much of a fake as Baba had been.

How could she tell Emalynn about that kind of betrayal? Not just her own loss of faith, but everyone in school turned their back to her. She was gone, just like Charlie. Not exactly. No one came looking for Charlie. Officers came weekly looking for Emalynn. They pressed and pushed all Ly's friends until denying they knew her felt natural. Karen never had the heart to tell her about that. Karen couldn't turn her down when she needed help. Besides, the project sounded fun.

Ly sounded like she was having fun when she called. No, she pretended she was having fun when she called. Even then, dark clouds hovered in her eyes and voice. Those clouds had grown thicker since that conversation. What horrors did she face when the net wasn't looking that were worse than she'd seen that night?

A knock on the wall broke her concentration. She sat up, wondering what had kept Davy awake.

"Come in."

A small panel slid aside, revealing a hole into Davy's room where the internal wiring should have been. Davy moved that stuff out of the way the second day they were here. He'd also managed to tap into their security cameras to give them a little privacy, which meant he'd spent some time watching her think just now.

"What's up? Why aren't *you* sleeping?"

"I was thinking." He gave her a weak smile for the unsaid joke. "Things are going to get tough."

Karen nodded and scooted over to give him a place to sit on the bed. The one chair she had wasn't all that comfortable. This room had never been intended to make the guest comfortable. Davy took her offer and limped over to sit beside her.

"Did you mouth off again?" Karen sighed and gave him space.

"No." He winced as he sat down gingerly. "I didn't keep Tristan under control today."

Karen looked away. She hated that he took the brunt of their anger. "Emalynn went off script more, and they didn't say anything to me."

He shook his head. "They wouldn't, would they?"

Of course not. No one expected Ly to behave properly. She was a girl raised by ruffians after all. That would be a reasonable assumption, but Karen knew otherwise. They wanted her off script a little. It made a better story. If not that, Dom would take the pain for her.

"It's not so bad." Davy tried to smile.

"Don't say that." Karen reached out but stopped short of touching him. Even when he wasn't hiding new bruises, he didn't like being touched.

"No, I mean it." His shoulders sank in time with the corners of his mouth. "He..."

Karen opened her arm for him, and he fell into her embrace. She held his shoulders while they shook with the sobs that didn't make it past his throat. Karen didn't have to ask. Murphy's death hit her hard, too. No one had to say it out loud; no one did. It all came out in the sudden silences when Ly would have said his name. Tristan told his side of the story by refusing to look at Ly during those silences and refusing to change the subject to end the silence. Even more telling, Karen thought, was the way they talked of the other deaths they witnessed. Ly could speak more of the name of Tristan's protector. Tristan managed to tell them how he died, when he didn't try to say the name. They wouldn't look at each other when he came up either. In contrast, fire burned in their eyes when they talked about the children who died with him.

"It's not fair." Davy sobbed when the worst of the grief passed for the moment. "He loved her. He believed."

Karen soothed his shoulder. "What did he believe?" She hadn't noticed Murphy wanted anything more than to follow his girlfriend when she took off, not until Davy told her about the rebel group their parents led.

Davy snuggled deeper into her chest, so she felt more than heard his words. "She would be the best queen ever. All we had to do was find her."

"You knew?" Karen bounced him off her chest. "You knew Emalynn was the princess?"

Davy shrank away from her and buried the tears as fast as he could. "No. Well..." He wiped his eyes and straightened his shirt. "We knew someone was the princess, but we didn't know who she was."

He spun a practiced story about how a group of outer colony malcontents had planned a perfect revolution. All they had to do was kidnap and raise the royal heir with their values, then return her at right moment with proof of her identity, and she would become the queen and change the government to their liking without anyone knowing it. It worked, too, sort of. They found a pair of mercenaries who could infiltrate the palace and get out with the newborn princess and a royal drive with the birth and first exam on it. They didn't work alone. They were just the ones who needed to get out. The only problem was the one who took the child never got to hand her off.

"Herron got arrested for a stupid traffic violation and missed the meeting." Davy shook his head. "They should have set up a secondary meeting, but they weren't that smart. The Mercenary disappeared, and we were left to search her out."

"So you and Murphy were sent to different high schools to look for this mysterious princess, assuming she survived?" Karen wanted to kick him for being so stupid.

"What else could we do?" Davy asked. "Tristan would be crowned soon. If we didn't get her back by then, it wouldn't matter. He'd still become king."

"How many of you were there looking for her?"

"Twenty." He started twisting his fingers together. "We changed schools every semester to cover as many as possible. I hated it. We all did. We wasted our high school years moving from colony to colony, never getting the chance to make friends."

That did sound awful now that she thought about it. Murphy had pushed hard to meet as many students as he could when he transferred in. "Whose bright idea was that plan?"

Davy looked at her for a breath, then burst into tears again. This time he pulled in on himself and rocked on the bed.

She should have known. Murphy always had the most off-the-wall plans that came together in spectacular ways, even when they fell apart. The image "contest" had his hands all over it.

"He believed it worked better to leave her with the mercenary," Davy whispered. "He said she'd grow up knowing what it really meant to be below the surface. They wouldn't have to teach her anything, just find her and get her back where she belonged."

Karen felt herself start to shake. Murphy couldn't have been more accurate if he had a degree in analytics. She'd teased Emalynn about taking the governance major so often, half the time because of her resemblance to Prince Tristan. She never knew.

"Ly hates the idea."

"Any good leader does."

Emalynn

Emalynn woke in a defensive stance, facing a terrified man clutching a tray to his chest while the remnants of last night's dinner dripped from between him and the tray. She still wore parts of the suit she'd worn to the welcome ceremony.

"I'm sorry, Miss... er, Your Majesty." The boy bowed and dropped more of the plates off his tray.

Emalynn forced herself to relax. "It's fine. You just startled me."

He gasped and bowed several more times.

"It's fine." She softened her voice. "Um, you can stop bowing."

That didn't help as much as she would have liked. He stood up straight so tight he might have sprained something just standing there. His eyes showed too much white and his chest didn't move enough with each breath that came too fast.

"I'm not angry." She put up her hands as though surrendering to him. "You can relax."

He nodded but gave no sign of relaxing.

Emalynn shifted away from him slightly and moved around the lounge. She stepped slowly and carefully, trying not to scare him any more than she already had. "What's your name?"

"Miss?"

"Your name." Emalynn glanced at him but spoke as though they were sitting together in a school lounge. "What's your name?"

He hesitated. His eyes flicked to three of the cameras around the room. "Travis. Travis Hedman."

"Thank you, Travis. It's nice to meet you." She let her smile broaden slowly. She'd seen large animal tamers use these kinds of tactics on the net. She couldn't imagine what this boy thought about her. The difference between Travis and a lion from the preserve on Taghil was he could understand her words. Maybe, if she could get him to calm down enough. "Please call me Ly."

Travis dipped his head as though he were going to bow again but changed his mind.

She came through the seating area and got her first look at the real mess she'd caused. The carcass of the little bird they'd served her whole and roasted lay in pieces amid the pieces of the plate it had been served on, while the sauce had splashed almost to the cupboards and up the table legs. Most of the sauce had found his uniform, though.

"I'm sorry I scared you." She kept her eyes on the mess. "Let me help you clean that up."

"No, Miss… Majesty." He shook his head and held the tray out at her, allowing the last of the vegetables to fall into the mess at his feet.

"Please, let me help." Emalynn continued to come closer. "It's my fault. It's the least I can do."

"I'll get kicked out," he squeaked, widened his eyes even more, then hid behind the tray.

"Kicked out? For letting me help?"

The tray bobbed.

Of all the stupid… Emalynn sighed. How could she get this guy to calm down if everything she did would only put his job in jeopardy? It was her fault for not sleeping in the bedroom in the first place. If she'd been in there, he wouldn't have startled her awake and the room would have been cleaned before she knew he was there. Then she would be even more uncomfortable with the situation.

"I guess the monitors didn't pay close enough attention last night." Emalynn turned to the nearest camera and spoke directly to whoever sat on the other side. "Let's be a bit more direct, then. No one will fire, transfer, or otherwise change Travis's job without my permission. I'm claiming him as the only servant, so far, who is allowed in my apartment. Oh, and just to be perfectly clear, that means he has no other duties, even if that means he doesn't have enough work according to your charts."

She turned back to Travis, who had lowered the tray. He still stared at her wide-eyed, though now it read as surprised rather than scared. She'd take it.

"Does that work for you?"

He bobbed his head.

"Good. Now will you let me help you clean up?"

"But you just gave me all the time."

"And there are other things I want you to do, if you can." Emalynn felt plans forming in the back of her mind.

Travis pulled himself up to his full height. "What kind of things?"

"I brought some things with me on the shuttle yesterday, and they didn't make it here." She smiled at the excitement he showed now. "Also, the closet is overcrowded with clothes I won't wear. That needs to be cleaned out."

"Yes, Your Majesty." He bobbed a curtsy.

"But first, get yourself cleaned up."

He blushed briefly.

In moments, she'd managed to get him into her bathroom with a promise of fresh clothes once he was clean. The guards outside her door told her where to find a fresh uniform for Travis and the cleaning supplies, though they looked appalled that she asked. She had the worst of the mess cleaned up by the time he emerged from the bathroom. She left the deep cleaning to him and went to take her own shower after searching the closet for something she could wear comfortably.

She let the water run over her and block out the rest of the world. One luxury she could live with was this. A shower of hot water that didn't run cold before all the aches and pains of a world out to get you could be rinsed away. Once, to celebrate a successful run, Baba had rented a room in an upscale hotel for them. Emalynn stood in the steamy shower until her skin wrinkled like an old woman and all the dirt and bruises disappeared. Baba teased her that she was trying to wash off her skin.

Today, she wished it were true. If she'd been able to wash away her skin, she could be out there where she knew how things worked. Where people accepted help without fearing for their jobs. Then she remembered the debt she'd taken on.

Here, as the princess, she could change that. Karen had been right all those times she suggested Emalynn should take up governance. She still preferred navigations, but that had crossed the event horizon. Better to take what she had and make the best of it. She needed to learn the real power structure within the palace, not the government. Here is where she would have to gather the power to do what she wanted out there.

Emalynn was as wrinkled as an old woman when she stepped out of the shower. The vents kept the mirrors clear of fog and her clothes dry. She could get used to some of this. Walking out of the shower, still toweling her hair, to a strange woman staring at her from her bedroom wall wasn't part of that.

"Your Majesty." The woman bowed. "I'm Mistress Threya, head of household affairs."

"Pleased to… um… meet you." Emalynn smiled the way she did when meeting a rival team captain.

"We were scheduled to meet later today, but I need to speak with you about Travis." Threya used the camera angle on her end to look down on Emalynn the way government secretaries did when you had to get some document or other approved.

Emalynn despised these silly plays for power. Invariably, the person using them thought they had more power than they really did. Threya, as head of household, would have some real power, though, just not as much as she thought she deserved.

"Oh, good. I'm glad you were listening." Emalynn draped the towel over her shoulder. "So I know he started really early this morning, and I don't want to work him past his standard hours. What is his usual schedule? I think we may need to adjust it."

"I think you misunderstand, Majesty." Threya plastered a grin, or maybe it was a grimace, on her face. "Travis isn't eligible for exclusive assignments."

Emalynn acted more surprised than she felt. "Not eligible? Why not?"

Between Travis's abject terror this morning and this woman's haughty attitude, Emalynn began to piece together the dynamics. Any organization had its official hierarchy and the unofficial one. So far, she'd learned making Travis an exclusive servant would launch him several rungs up the unofficial chart, and that threatened Threya for some reason.

"After this morning's disaster, he doesn't have the points to be a primary."

"This morning?" Emalynn played at being innocent. "Whose decision was it to have him cleaning my apartment at five in the morning?"

Threya answered by pulling her lips into a thin line.

"From where I stand, the person who made that decision is the one who caused the mess this morning." Emalynn advanced on the wall as though she could reach through it and attack the person on the other side. "Because that person didn't ask if I wanted my apartment cleaned at that hour. That person didn't bother to check the monitors to know I wasn't sleeping in the bed. That person didn't do the basic research one should do when trying to anticipate the needs of someone you don't know."

Threya flinched at the word "you," confirming Emalynn's guess that she was directly responsible for this morning.

"Your Majesty, that is unfair."

"I don't think so."

"Regardless, you may not choose your staff."

What a funny rule. Emalynn smiled. "Really? Then I will leave it to you to warn any other server you send to me that I will reject them and physically remove them from my apartment should I catch them here." She flashed a sweet smile at the woman.

"You can't do that."

48

Emalynn ordered the wall to open a second shared window and called up the security footage of her fight on Roshea station. She let it play out, then cut the connection before Threya could say anything. The drained look on her face told Emalynn the message got through.

She went to put her towel back in the bathroom and saw Travis in the doorway to the main room. He stood as rigid as when she'd nearly attacked him this morning.

"What's wrong?" she asked.

He opened his mouth, but no sound came out.

"I'm assuming you heard most of that."

He nodded.

"And she scares you almost as much as I do."

He shook his head and showed the slightest hint of a smile.

"She scares you more than I do?" Emalynn asked.

He nodded again.

"Well, that's progress." She slipped into the bathroom to hang her towel. "So what evil things will she do to you because she can't do them to me?"

"I'll have my security clearance revoked."

Emalynn paused mid-hang. That could be devastating in a place like this, with security more ubiquitous than a mall during a school break.

"That's no good," Emalynn called as she finished smoothing the towel. "We'll have to find someone Mistress Threya respects to take our side. I wonder if Queen Treylyn would..." Emalynn rejected that idea before she finished thinking it. She wouldn't be able to convince the queen of anything today after last night's fiasco of a family meal.

"Security Chief Grouse." Tristan appeared on her wall. "Good morning, you've been causing trouble already."

"Where have you been?" Emalynn scowled at her brother.

"I've been in my rooms. I flipped security without thinking about it. Sorry." He grinned at her. "Who's that?"

"Travis." Emalynn smiled back at the servant. "He was the unlucky one to have to clean up after me this morning."

"Oh." Tristan couldn't hold the doomsday look for long before laughing.

"Stop teasing him. I think I just got him in more trouble than I bargained for."

"I'll be right over." Tristan started to turn away but turned back. "Did you give your guards any strange orders?"

"No."

He smiled and closed the connection.

Emalynn sighed. "Come on." She waved for Travis to follow her out to the main room. "I'm going to guess your day isn't going the way you expected." She smiled.

He shook his head with a grin of his own. "It will make a good story at least."

"The worst days always do," she replied. "So do the best. I hope you don't mind helping me make my place here."

The door announced Tristan before he could answer. Emalynn signaled the door to open and hugged Tristan as though they'd been separated for years.

"I'm making a mess of things," she declared as they separated again.

"As you should. It's the birthright of royal children to cause problems for the staff." Tristan laughed.

Emalynn shook her head and led them all to the lounge in front of the media wall. "Yeah, and how do we do that without ruining anyone?"

"Like Travis?" Tristan smiled at the servant who was trying to blend into a corner. "Come on over. You're going to be a part of this whether you like it or not. It's not like you can offend Mistress Threya any more than Ly already has. You might as well enjoy it."

Travis came slowly to join them. Emalynn took a clue from Tristan and let the boy get comfortable without staring at him.

"First thing, I should have warned you, is don't confront Mistress Threya directly." Tristan shrugged. "She's a vindictive, petty manager who rose to her position through family ties."

"Too late for that."

"Yeah, so now you're going to have to hit her head on." Tristan sighed. "I've never won that kind of confrontation. Of course, I'm not you, and the last time I tried, I was twelve."

Emalynn laughed in spite of herself. She'd lost battles against adults when she was that age, too. Those experiences taught her about how to win the fights later.

"Right, so what do I do about Travis?"

Tristan smiled. "Direct connect: Security Chief Grouse." He spoke to the wall.

A woman in a well-fitting security uniform with subtle rank insignia on the shoulders appeared on the wall. "You're late." She smiled at Tristan.

"I'm out of practice." Tristan shrugged.

"So this is the kind of example you're going to set for your sister?" Her bright smile never wavered.

"I really don't need to set an example for her." Tristan's grin grew as he spoke. "She's quite skilled at getting into trouble all on her own. In fact, that's why we're calling."

"Oh, yes." The woman looked down at a tablet. "I knew they had the schedule wrong when they didn't have you down here first thing in the morning. So which of you has Miz Threya in a tizzy?"

Emalynn raised her hand, though she wasn't entirely sure she wanted to be called on for this.

"I see." She glanced down at the tablet again. "So that would make you Travis."

Travis flinched.

"All right, let's get this over with."

"Wait." Tristan held up his hand. "Sorry, I'm still slow this morning. Princess Emalynn, please allow me to introduce the head of palace security, Chief Grouse. Chief Grouse, this is Princess Emalynn." Tristan grinned and nodded.

"Right. Travis, you've been fired and your security clearance through the housekeeping department has been revoked."

"What?" Emalynn squeaked.

Tristan put a hand on her knee.

"Please report to the nearest guards and ask them to escort you to Security Central." Grouse continued.

Travis looked devastated. This wasn't what Emalynn wanted. How could Tristan sit there smiling like that?

"Whew," Grouse finished. "I always hate that part. Now then, I also have an order here that a member of the royal family requested the personal attention of Travis. That sounds more like a direct employ. So, Your Majesty, did you want to hire him as a personal attendant or private secretary?"

Emalynn looked at Travis, but he was too shocked to even notice her. She looked to Tristan.

"Personal attendant," he said to Grouse. To Emalynn, he said, "You won't like what a personal secretary is supposed to do, and we don't know if he's qualified for that kind of work."

Emalynn caught the meaning—having someone follow her around with a schedule book. She wouldn't last long like that.

"All right, then. It's all settled. I'll just need to have Travis down to the security offices to get his clearance." Grouse smiled at them. "Oh, one last thing. Do you want him in a uniform or casual?"

"Um, casual." Emalynn didn't believe what just happened.

"That settles that, then." Grouse gave each of them, including Travis, a small bow. "I'll see you two at two. Don't be late."

The connection closed.

Tristan

Tristan could barely contain his laughter at the looks on both Emalynn's and Travis's faces when Chief Grouse closed the connection. He was sure Emalynn didn't notice the total freedom she'd granted them either by the wording of her first order to Travis. "Go to the nearest guards and have them escort you to Security Central." She knew what she said; she always did. "Them"—plural—would mean Tristan and Emalynn would be left without guards for a time.

It was a test, no doubt. The chief wanted to get a sense of how Tristan had changed and what Emalynn would do. She probably had several other perfectly reasonable excuses for letting them run wild if someone decided to make an issue of it.

"You'd better get going," Emalynn said to Travis. "I'll see you later."

The boy nodded and rose mechanically to leave. Emalynn watched him go with an expression that eliminated Tristan's urge to laugh. For her, this whole situation meant more than a morning of fun. She hadn't set out to tweak Threya, but help Travis. He should have known.

"What the stars was that?" She turned on him as soon as the door slid closed behind Travis.

"That was our greatest ally in the palace."

"No." She stood but walked away from him. "That part about him being fired and all that nonsense? Do you have any idea how long it took to get him to calm down the first time? Then I promised him he wouldn't get fired."

"He didn't get fired."

"Yes, he did. He got fired, his security clearance was revoked, and then he had to go find his own escort."

"Calm down." Tristan pulled his feet up as much to get out of her way as to use his knees as a shield. "He got transferred. She had to say the bit about firing so Threya couldn't countermand the transfer. And the escort thing was for us."

She stopped pacing to glare at him.

"Who are the nearest guards?" He pointed to the door. "They are going to assume we're waiting for breakfast or something and take the order literally."

"So there's no one watching us?" Her anger evaporated into something more sinister.

"There's always the monitors, but the chief just said they aren't going to do anything about it until we're late for our meeting with her."

Emalynn stopped moving entirely. He didn't see her breathe. When she did move, he missed it. She was out the door before he could get his feet on the ground. He caught up to her at the lift.

"Where are you going?"

"To get lost." She sounded more like herself. He wondered if this was how his staff felt when he took off suddenly.

"Mind if I join you?"

She shrugged. "As long as you don't try to give me directions." Then she shot him a grin filled with plots he couldn't quite read.

He smiled back. Something happened last night that didn't involve guards landing in heaps on the floor. Now that the morning crisis had been solved, he could see the change in her attitude. Not a complete turnaround where she accepted everything he'd lived with most of his life. It was more like she'd found a focus for her anger.

The lift opened and Emalynn punched in level thirty-four. Tristan raised an eyebrow at that but said nothing. She pretended not to notice.

Level thirty-four was designated for secure guest quarters. Most of the time, it sat empty, with the furniture covered with cloth to make cleaning up the dust easier if they were needed. Tristan found it boring in his youthful adventures. It had such potential, all those covered couches and things, but the doors had an unfortunate habit of going into lockdown mode when unexpected things happened.

"Did you sleep well?" he asked.

"Not really."

"Oh, sorry."

"It's not your fault." She sighed. "The apartment they gave is big enough for a family. So's the bed."

He laughed. "I felt the opposite about the shuttles and beds we used out there."

She just shook her head.

"You know..." She started when the silence was long enough to change the subject. "I spent thirty minutes last night trying to see how hard it would be to find information about me on the net."

"That's not long."

She shook her head. "That's all it took to find my school profile page and get a file's worth of images of the kinds of clothes I wear and foods I like. I also dug into Baba's history and murder. Did you know I'm still wanted for questioning on Roshea?"

Tristan looked at her. "All that in thirty minutes?"

She nodded. "And they had three weeks minimum to realize these clothes suck void."

They did. Even when she picked only the best pieces. The designers were going to be upset by what she did. They might even quit, which would be a benefit.

The lift door opened to a hall filled with more guards than he'd seen here before. The one time a room on this floor had been used (that he knew of) a single pair of guards stood outside the door of the guest in question. Today, there were two guarding the lift doors, two more down the hall, and two each in front of two doors near the end of the hall. All in uniforms that were just a little off. He couldn't tell exactly what part of the uniforms was different, though, which bothered him.

"Your Majesties?" The tall blond woman closest to the lift snapped to attention. "This floor is restricted."

Emalynn took no notice. She strode with purpose and intimidation toward the end of the hall where the most guards stood. The guards hurried to get ahead of her, leaving Tristan to follow along.

"Your Majesty. What are you doing?"

Emalynn continued past the second set of guards as though they weren't there. The guards standing in front of the rooms closed ranks to block the doors before Emalynn got there.

"Excuse me." Emalynn grinned at them. "I would like to enter."

"I'm sorry, Your Majesty," said the blond guard who'd followed her since their arrival. "These guests are on restrictions."

Emalynn finally turned with an expression so sweet it could put one in a coma. "We just want to talk to them. There's nothing wrong with that, is there?" She waved for Tristan to join her in the center of the crowd.

He slipped between the guards to stand with her, though he had reservations. He also knew if she started fighting, he would be safer next to her than between the guards and the walls.

"I'm sorry," the guard said again.

"Quit being sorry and open the door." She remained sweet in tone. "Or would you like to explain to Chief Grouse why I had to defend myself against you?" She waved to each of the four cameras around the hall.

Tristan bit his tongue to keep from asking who she was fighting so hard to see. The guards shifted uncomfortably under her watchful stare and veiled threat. Well, they thought she veiled her threat; he knew she really meant she'd provoke them into attacking the princess when they should know the cameras were active. It only took one to move aside. Emalynn palmed the door pad before any of the rest could react.

The room, darkened since it was still early morning, looked about the same as the last time he'd gotten stuck in the security settings. The only difference being the two people struggling to wake up in the tiny bed. Karen and Davy still wore their formalwear from yesterday, though it looked as though they'd gone through an air filter the wrong way.

"Ly?" Karen croaked, her voice still rough from sleep. "What are you doing here? What time is it?"

Davy looked like he wanted to hide under the covers, except the bed was still made. Tristan also noticed the access panel had been recently used.

"I came to see you. I didn't realize you have tighter security than I do." Emalynn shook her head at the door. "How'd you get so famous?"

Karen crawled over Davy to get out of the bed and embrace Ly. "It's good to see you," she said loud enough for Tristan to hear, then something more he couldn't.

Davy rose more slowly, keeping his eyes on the floor. Tristan caught the telltale signs of a night of tears. He could guess at the cause.

"Good morning." Tristan opened himself for a hug from his friend.

"Yes, morning." Davy obliged. When his mouth was even with Tristan's ear, he whispered, "There are secrets here."

Tristan nodded. "Here I thought I would have to fight my way to your room."

"Um, yeah." Davy looked over at Karen.

"It's not what it looks like." Karen shook her head at Emalynn. "Please believe me."

Emalynn shrugged with a glance at Tristan. "It looks like you were comforting a friend who suffered a loss."

That's not what Tristan thought right away, but he agreed with Emalynn. Her explanation made more sense than anything else.

"So..." Davy smiled like a host trying to restart a party after an embarrassing moment. "How was the family dinner?"

"It went as well as expected." Tristan looked at Emalynn, hoping she wouldn't go into a rant about it.

"That bad?" Karen asked.

"Nobody died." Emalynn shot back. "It's going to take some getting used to."

"No kidding." Tristan laughed. "I wasn't the center of attention."
Everyone laughed.

They fell into an easy conversation about parents and expectations. Emalynn and Karen went off on stories from their past. That time Karen came over to work on a history project and Baba insisted on testing them both as though they were facing a test the next day instead of a week of presentations. Or all the times Karen's mom tried to convince Emalynn to spend more time at their house and that Karen's brothers would make good partners.

Davy jumped in with stories about awkward dinners when he was the one being set up with his sister's friends. Tristan managed to add his own stories of awkward introductions.

For the first time in his life, Tristan knew how it felt to have friends. He'd seen these kinds of conversations in the popular vids, but he never thought he'd get to participate. His life, he'd thought, was too different. Only in the details. Parents and other adults were the same all over the galaxy. Framed the right way, his life wasn't that much different from theirs.

"Princess Emalynn." A woman in a proper guard's uniform stood in the doorway. "You are required in the library."

Emalynn looked ready to object, but Karen stopped her with nudge on her shoulder.

"Go on. We'll still be here later." Karen smiled, but Tristan heard a catch in her voice.

Emalynn nodded and rose to leave. "Next time, let's meet in my room."

She went peacefully with the guard in a way that worried Tristan. Something major had changed since this morning with how defiant she'd been about Travis and coming here.

He didn't get a chance to ask. A second guard came in to take him to his appointments.

There were more women in the hall, waiting. Davy's warning about secrets came to him as he walked by.

"You've already missed several meetings," the guard scolded when they met up with the rest of the team waiting closer to the lift.

Tristan shrugged. "So who gets me now?"

Just as before, he usually let the grownups fight over who would get his time once he returned to his schedule. That way he didn't have to fight after an afternoon of fun. In this case, they'd left early, but the principle was the same.

"Medical." The guard scowled.

Tristan stuck out his tongue. The medics would poke and prod him, looking for any change in his body. He hadn't been sickly growing up, but that didn't stop the doctors from worrying more than his father about his health. Now that he'd survived several assassination attempts and who knew what kind of dirt and other scary things, it could take the rest of the day to convince them he planned to keep breathing normally.

Karen

Karen watched the door close behind Tristan with a sense of foreboding. While they were here, it had been easy to forget. Now that they were gone, the consequences from yesterday were likely to be worse than they would have been. Veniese, the head of security, made it very clear they weren't supposed to have unapproved contact with the royal twins. She didn't want to think about what they would do to Dom for this kind of infraction.

"Get out of here," she hissed at Davy. He needed to be gone before Deliah, Veniese's enforcer, came to yell at them for all the things they couldn't control.

Davy scrambled through the hole in the wall and sealed it behind him. Karen kept her eye on the door. They couldn't let Deliah know about the hole in the wall or they'd be separated more. It would be impossible to keep the fact of Emalynn and Tristan's visit secret. They wouldn't need to keep the content of the conversation private, though Deliah would see hidden messages in it.

Karen flinched when the door opened. Since when had she become such a wuss?

Deliah stood in the doorway, hands on her hips as though that were the thing that scared Karen. Only the threats against Dom kept Karen from laughing at the clichéd pose.

"What do you think you were doing?" Deliah's scary voice had the effect she intended.

Karen's throat closed around the words she wanted to say. *Standing here waiting for you to decide what to do with me*. Ly would have found a way to put Deliah in her place.

"Miss Dominique isn't going to like the punishments you've sent her way."

Karen clamped her jaw shut. She closed off all thoughts of Dom to keep from shaking. "What do you want?"

"I want an explanation for why you had illicit contact with the princess." Deliah stepped far enough into the room for the door to close.

Karen imagined her feet were stuck to the floor to keep from stepping back. "She came here."

"You should have sent her away."

"And give her a reason to go digging into your plan?" Karen would love to do just that. Give Ly just a hint of something and she'd follow it through. She probably already had. Emalynn hadn't said a word about Dom all morning. Her whispered, "*I know. We'll fix it,*" gave Karen hope.

Deliah came closer. "Don't get smart with me, girl."

"I'm not." Karen held her ground in the face of the woman's bad breath. "Emalynn would know something was up if I sent her away, and she's not the kind of girl to just leave it."

Deliah struck faster than Karen anticipated. Pain flared in her cheek, then shoulder and knee as she met the wall on her way to the floor. A vid hero would pick herself up and strike back. A vid villain would wait for the hero to get up before striking again. Karen decided to take a smaller role and let Deliah kick her. She stayed curled up on the floor to absorb the impact the way Ly had taught her.

"Don't you dare tell me how to do my job." Deliah delivered another kick. "You are the most useless thing we could have gotten."

Karen agreed. Since she'd arrived—really since they picked her up—she hadn't been able to do one thing to ease Emalynn's position. She hadn't managed to capture even one vid to share. They'd spent two weeks teaching her how to walk properly and eat properly and bow properly. She was surprised they didn't insist she sleep properly, too. For that they left her locked up in this glorified prison cell so it wouldn't matter if she did it properly or not.

"Deliah Carter?" A woman's voice rang clear over Deliah's rant.

Karen peeked around Deliah's legs to see who had dared interrupt. She saw mostly the boots that looked strong and light the way Ly insisted footwear should be, pants that were just loose enough to prevent restrictions, and a silver case with the royal crest on it.

Deliah whipped around to face this new woman with a force that should have made the other woman step back, but she didn't. "Who are you?"

"You are Deliah Carter, correct?" The woman came a step closer and set the case on the floor.

"Yes," Deliah's growled.

"Mistress Threya wants to see you."

"Tell her I'll call when I'm done here."

Karen took the opportunity to pull herself up to sit against the wall.

She stayed curled up in case another kick came her way.

"I'm afraid that won't be enough. She wants you in her office as soon as you can get there."

Karen got a better look at her rescuer from this position. She was lean the way an athlete keeps her body. She held herself with the kind of balance required of the cheer team and perfected by Ly. She held a smile for Deliah as though she hadn't just seen the woman kicking a teenager.

"I wouldn't make her wait any longer than you need to." The woman shot a quick glance at Karen. "Rumor has it Princess Emalynn is better at tweaking her nose than Prince Tristan."

"How is that even possible?" Deliah snarled as she pushed past the woman.

Karen wanted to feel relieved. What would this mean for Dom? That woman didn't know what she'd just done.

"And you are Karen Toya." She came over to offer a hand up. "Should I call for medical?"

"No." Karen flinched. "No, I'll be fine." She forced herself to take the offered hand and stand.

"I'm Thia from the security office." The woman introduced herself as she guided Karen to the bed.

"I didn't do anything." Karen winced at how pathetic she sounded. She'd have edited that line out of a script if it had ever made it in. Her role in this vid just got worse with each passing moment. Any second, she would become the victim at the beginning of a crime vid.

"Of course not." Thia smiled. "It wouldn't be me alone here if you had." She retrieved the case and pulled the little table closer to the bed so she could set the case there. "We just noticed your security check is out of date. That would be our fault, so nothing to worry about."

Karen wanted to believe her. She wanted to think a simple clerical error had allowed her to escape the worst of Deliah's anger. That same clerical error would make Dom's experience worse.

Thia opened the case to show four scanners set in custom-formed foam. The first looked like a standard ID scanner you would see at the mall. The rest looked like something out of a sci-fi vid. Karen couldn't imagine why you would need more than one scanner to do a security check.

"You'll want to sit down." Thia picked up the first scanner. "And hold out your hand."

Karen dropped to the edge of the bed and extended her left hand. Everyone knew how this worked. ID scans happened every day. At school, they had auto scanners in every classroom for checking attendance. Thia didn't do it the way they did in the vids. She grabbed Karen's hand in hers and twisted it to the side before running the scanner over both their hands. The scanner hissed and beeped like every other scanner, as though everything were normal.

Thia checked the scanner and smiled. "That was the easy part. This next one will sting a little."

Karen tugged at her hand, but Thia's grip didn't give. For the second scan, Thia turned her hand back to the standard position but held her still. When the scanner was in position, a shock made her hand convulse before she felt the pain. Thia let her take her hand back after that.

"What was that?" Karen cradled her hand against her stomach.

"Just part of the standard security check. Well, standard for palace." Thia smiled. "You haven't been through this before, have you?"

Karen shook her head. "They scanned me the normal way on the transport."

Thia nodded as though that explained everything. "If you rub it a bit, the sting will go away." She made a show of getting the next scanner ready.

In a vid, there would be dialog to cover any real prep work that would be needed. This wasn't a vid, though Thia gave every hint of being a skilled actor. Every movement looked calculated for more than one purpose.

"What is this scan really about?" Karen asked.

Thia smiled, though her focus didn't change. "The chief wins again. She always does." Thia pulled the third scanner up and turned to face Karen. "You make vids, right?"

Karen nodded and pulled her hand tighter against her chest.

"Then I'm sure you understand what's happening now."

Karen swallowed hard. She did, but how to say it without risking Dom's life? "I wasn't scanned by a real member of the security force."

"You know more than that." Thia held out her hand for Karen's.

Karen stared at the hand. Two requests, both seemingly innocent and both potentially disastrous. The scanner would hurt her. Telling more than she already had would hurt Dom. The choice was easy. She gave her hand to Thia.

"This one will hurt." Thia's grip tightened around her still sore hand with more strength than she'd shown before. "Try not to scream."

Pain like nothing Karen had felt before exploded in her hand. Everything turned red for a moment. Then Thia lifted her head from the bed and held her like a child.

"You didn't scream." Thia smiled down at her. "And you aren't the first to pass out. How are you feeling?"

Karen lifted her hand to where she could see it. As far as she could tell, it was still a hand, attached to her arm and functioning properly. "I'm fine. I guess."

"Good. I wouldn't want to face Princess Emalynn if I'd damaged her best friend." Thia pushed Karen back to a sitting position. "Just one more to go, but don't worry. You shouldn't feel this at all."

Thia grabbed Karen's hand and ran the last scanner over it before Karen could object. As promised, she didn't feel it.

"Seriously." Karen pulled her hand back from this woman. "What was all that for?"

Thia focused on getting the scanner back in its case. "You really don't want the answer to that question here."

Karen couldn't be sure if she heard her. The microphones certainly wouldn't have picked that up.

"Now, you need your rest and I need to get on with things. Try not to worry about your hand." She checked something on her tablet. "Oh, how convenient. Davy's already alone."

She tapped on the wall and it opened for her. She ducked through and the wall closed again. Karen sat on the bed, rubbing her hand. For all the pain she'd just gone through, it didn't feel damaged.

If this had been a vid, all that shielded nonsense would have been code from the good guys trying to tell her they were on to the bad guys and she could expect rescue in short order. Only she wasn't the one in need of rescue. And vid plots didn't last in the real world. The ones who were torturing Dom were members of the palace staff, same as that woman, or so they said.

She wished she had a script and could read ahead to see if her character made it to the end of the vid.

Emalynn

Emalynn stared at the woman across the table from her. Her skin was so pale she could have been dead. The black hair framing her face didn't help. Nor did the ridiculous black robe she wore. The same as the last two women who'd sat across the table from her, trying to teach her governance as though she hadn't taken and aced that class in every school she'd been in. This woman, whose name Emalynn chose not to remember, insisted that learning the names of all the lords by memory was the most important thing she could be doing. Emalynn thought eating lunch would be a better use of her time. She made a note not to skip breakfast again.

Back at Herth, the teachers knew the importance of making the lessons interesting and relevant. In governance, they spent a lot of time pretending to be the various lords and arguing over policies. Nothing kept the attention of a class that didn't want to be there like a good argument over rare fruits when extra credit was on the line. They also knew one period of governance per day was more than enough. That principle held true for all the core subjects and most electives, too. Emalynn had never fallen asleep in class before, but she'd make an exception here.

She let her head fall back as though she'd fallen asleep and stared at the shelves upon shelves of old-style print books that decorated the library. The existence of such a collection took Emalynn's breath. They'd smuggled a single old book from Warettan to Gravil, such a short run with a tiny cargo easily hidden between two tablets. Baba booked them on a standard transport in a private cabin for the run. They lived off the proceeds for two years, the first time Emalynn got to return to the same class for a second year.

"Princess Emalynn." The woman snapped at her. "Will you please pay attention?"

"No." Emalynn closed her eyes and took a deep breath to calm her frustration.

"This is important. You must know your government if you are going to lead it."

"Really?" She sat up and glared across the table. "You mean it's more important to know that Lord Farray married Lord Regash's third son so she wouldn't have to give up claim to County Mrillet when her mother died than it is to know bananas only grow on Beralin around the equator, but are a vital source of nutrition for asteroid miners in the Calligen Belt because of a natural low-level radiation field in that region?" Emalynn impressed herself with that tidbit of trivia from the last class debate she'd participated in.

"Politics is about more than trivial facts that any aid would be able to provide you with in an instant." The woman tried to hide her frustration.

"Are you referring to the relationships between the lords of various counties and each other or the relationship between any lord and her people?" Emalynn continued. "From where I'm sitting, the latter sounds more important if you don't want the monarchy to collapse."

"It is not in danger of collapsing."

"That is the first sign it is already dead." Emalynn reached for her tablet and still didn't find it. "The people out in the colonies don't trust the government. They have no reason to. The monarchy hasn't noticed them in generations."

"I've noticed." King Levon stepped out from behind one of the bookcases, a smile on his face.

"What have you done about it?" She let all her frustration turn on him. She could blame him for everything if she tried hard enough, including her hunger and lack of sleep.

He waved the tutor out of her seat and took her place. Three more guards took up their positions around the room. So the king had to wander about his home with three guards in tow. She felt lucky to have only two, though they looked as bored with the lessons as she felt.

"Tristan tells me we're handling you wrong." Levon let his hands rest on his lap.

"No kidding." Emalynn leaned back, away from him as far as she could without moving the chair. "You're acting like I grew up here, and I didn't."

"So I've noticed." He let his eyes fall from her.

The guards, all five of them, became more alert and focused on their table. They turned toward her as though she were a threat.

"You don't need to overdo it." She sat up a little.

He grinned. "Now that is impressive."

She glanced around and realized most people wouldn't have noticed a change in the guards.

"You still have a lot to learn in a short time." He sighed. "There's no precedent for this kind of situation."

"Then you don't really know how much I need to learn, do you?" She kept her eyes on the table rather than challenge him directly. She didn't like the way the guards were looking at her.

He nodded.

"So what do I need to know that I didn't learn in school?"

"You need to know how to be a queen. There's much more to it than making grand speeches and presiding over the council." He laughed. "And most of what you really need to know you are going to have to learn on the job, just like all the rest of us."

"So since you can't give me the real stuff, I get to waste my time learning all the things they made us memorize back in grade school?"

The flash of surprise in his eyes told her more than anything he could have said about the quality of education in the galaxy. He recovered quickly with a smile. "Shall we test it, then? Tell me about Prime."

Emalynn rolled her eyes but answered his question with as much detail as she could muster. She included the statistics she'd looked up while waiting for landing clearance. Without skipping a beat, she continued on to the Trevail system, then the next colony over and the only other one in Devalin County. She added the crime statistics alongside the agricultural output, manufacturing, and population shifts over the last ten cycles. She ended with statistics about the two corporate stations that wobbled between Devalin County and Harris County on one side and Grelt County on the other. "You can't really count them in either county's stats because they don't hold allegiance with either."

He nodded when she finished. Perhaps he expected more, but that was all she had on Prime. Let him ask her about any of the outer colonies and he'd see just how much she knew about the universe.

"Well, that settles it." He leaned forward. "The educational plan is out of date. So what would you like to do with the rest of your day?"

"I'll start by having lunch with Karen, then a chance to explore without the babysitters." She nodded toward the guards who were holding up the wall.

"You need your bodyguards."

She looked them over again. They'd gone back to relaxing. Just because this was a library in the middle of the private wing of the royal palace didn't mean someone couldn't sneak in. Baba always enjoyed the challenge of hunting her quarry where they least expected it.

"I'm a better fighter than all of them put together." She swung her head around to indicate the guards.

"Nonetheless, you are the princess and must be protected."

Emalynn leaned across the table and waved for Levon to do the same. "I don't think they're protecting me. I think I'm protecting them," she whispered. "I'll prove it."

"I shouldn't allow this." His eyes sparkled with anticipation.

"If I can put them all down in a count of ten, you'll give me twenty-four hours without guards."

"That will have to wait for date change." He glanced to the side. "I'm not going to counter Chief Grouse."

"Fine, but Karen gets to come with me."

"Then you'll finish out today's schedule minus the tutors."

They nodded together and sat back.

"One." Levon said loud enough for everyone to hear.

Emalynn slid out of her chair and swept the first guard's feet out from under her before Emalynn made it to a full stand.

"Two, three..."

The second guard could have defended herself if she hadn't been in shock. Emalynn knocked her over with a simple shoulder strike and moved on.

"Four, Five..."

The third guard did attempt a defense. Emalynn slid under her arm and lifted her off her feet with a twist that landed her on her side.

"Six, seven..."

The fourth tried an attack as Emalynn approached. Emalynn let her slide past with minimal contact and added energy to her motion that sent her to the floor.

"Eight..."

The fifth guard braced herself.

"Nine..."

Emalynn had to attack against her defense in a feint. The guard took the bait, and Emalynn shifted to another move that had the woman on her back.

"Ten."

Emalynn bowed to the last guard, then offered her a hand up. The rest had already regained their feet and were ready to protect the king.

King Levon clapped three times and stood to join her with the guard. "You've won your freedom. One day from the coming date change to the following one, so long as you stay within the palace."

"Thank you."

"Sire?" The fifth guard shot the king a questioning look.

Levon nodded. "You've all just failed a test. The princess has proven we will need to review the whole royal guard. That was just embarrassing... and impressive."

Emalynn hid her smile. No need to rub it in, though the thought of having a full day in the palace without guards made her giddy.

Levon bowed to her as a master would bow to a student. "I believe the rest of your morning schedule involved tutors."

"I thought you said…"

"You are scheduled for lunch with your brother and friends in the rose dining room at one," one of her guards said, looking at her tablet. "Shall I send for your friends? It is still early."

Emalynn let her smile out. "Yes, please. Where do we get lunch?"

Levon and his guards left without waiting for her to bow or any of the other silly rituals of being a royal. Something else had changed with her guards now. Not that they hadn't respected her before, but the quality changed. Like any good fighters, they weren't hurt that she'd bested them. She doubted she'd win that kind of challenge again.

Karen

Karen decided being a side character in someone else's feature vid sucked as hard as a black hole. While Ly and Tristan were out there doing who knew what kind of interesting things, she was stuck in this little room, staring at the blank ceiling, wishing she could do something about Dom and trying not to think of her at the same time. In a moment of weakness, she wished Deliah or Veniese would come and tell her what she needed to do next. Maybe if she could just be useful enough, they'd keep their promise to return Dom to her. She didn't really believe it, most of the time. They weren't the kind of people who would keep a promise made to someone like her—a nobody from an outer colony who could be easily erased from all but the memories of a few insignificant people.

Karen kicked at her blankets with frustration. Her foot got caught in the ultimate of ironic twists. The stars must have been laughing at her. She kept on kicking until the blankets were on the floor and her foot was free of them. It didn't make her feel any better.

Her door opened just as she stood up to give the blankets one more kick.

"Miss Karen Toya?" A guard in a loose-fitting uniform reminiscent of the ones they wore at the welcome ceremony stood just outside her room.

She couldn't be one of her normal handlers. They walked in without permission, regardless of Karen's state of dress, sleep, or mood.

"Yeah?"

"Your lunch with the princess has been moved up. I've come to lead you to the dining room." The guard stepped back from the door a bit, as though she expected Karen to come out.

"But why the change?" This didn't sound good. If Deliah had plans for her, she'd be gone before she could tell her what to do.

"Orders from King Levon." The guard nodded a small bow at the mention of the monarch.

Karen nodded, too. They couldn't blame her if she followed the orders of the king. They still would, but if she worked it right, she'd be in Ly's presence when they came to yell at her about it. She ignored the thought in the back of her mind that it would just make them angrier when they did get a chance to yell at her. Karen went to join the guard in the hall with only a moment's hesitation at the door.

Another guard stood just outside Davy's door, waiting for him as well.

"Come on, Davy. You're holding up the show." Karen thought he might be more willing to join them if he knew she was here, too.

Davy came out, limping again. He also cradled his hand against his chest and sported a new bruise on the back of his neck that didn't quite hide under his hair. Karen pretended not to notice, though she hated it. Any other time, any other situation, if she saw a man getting abused, she'd be there to stand in the way; she'd council him to leave the woman or get help. In any other situation, the embarrassment would be outweighed by the possibility she could make a difference.

"It's early," Davy complained.

"That's no excuse." Karen grinned at him and offered her arm. "You don't want to keep the princess waiting, do you?"

She hoped he understood her enthusiasm. They couldn't talk openly in front of the guards or anywhere. He would have the same fears about annoying Deliah again by being gone when she came to give them instructions. They also couldn't afford to tip off palace security by defying the guards who'd come to get them. If there had been any doubt these two were legit members of the royal guard, it was gone by the time they were in the lift and heading for the rose garden dining room. These two kept their distance the same way they hadn't entered their rooms and didn't block the lift entrance once they were in. One even asked if Davy wanted to stop by medical.

He didn't.

The rose garden dining room was in the private wing on a floor with wide halls and subtle elegance. Karen could imagine trying to capture a vid here and being told it didn't look fancy enough for the palace. People wouldn't believe her about most of the things she'd learned about the palace and royal family since coming here. They'd never let her have a camera, let alone a tablet powerful enough to edit vids anyway.

The room held a large wood table with four chairs set for four, with more dishes than her family used for Foundation Day dinner when all her aunts were on planet. She couldn't imagine why each place had a stack of three plates surrounded by more forks than she could imagine using, spoons of three different shapes, three knives, and a smaller stack of plates, four different kinds of glasses, and a bowl. In the middle of the table were four silver domes and a white thing that looked like an overgrown gravy boat. All of that was surrounded by vines with little pink flowers peeking out from the green and white leaves.

"Welcome." Ly bounced across the room to join them by the door.

The guards jumped away to take up places on either side of the door. Two more guards perched in the corners on the other side of the room next to the floor-to-ceiling windows that looked out on a small garden filled with rosebushes.

"What happened?" Karen caught Ly's hug with a twist to take the impact. They spun three times before Ly allowed them to rest.

"What do you mean?" Ly asked. She quivered with excitement just like when grades came out and she got perfect scores again.

"I mean we weren't supposed to meet until one and it's barely past noon." Karen started. "Then there are the guards who are rather jumpy all of a sudden."

Ly laughed. "That would be because they don't trust I won't try to knock more of them down."

Karen didn't know what to say to that.

"You attacked your guards?" Davy stepped closer to them.

Karen caught Ly before she mentioned Davy's limp. That would be yet another topic for a time when they could talk.

"King Levon didn't believe I could take care of myself better than they could, so we ended up agreeing on a challenge." Emalynn shrugged with a grin. "I won."

Karen noticed the two by the window cringe. "What did you win?"

"Twenty-four hours without guards. Same for you."

This time all the guards cringed.

"What about Davy?" Karen asked. "What is he going to do?"

"It's okay," Davy protested.

Karen shook her head. It wouldn't be okay. Davy already took the brunt of the abuse. Leaving him alone when Deliah would be frustrated already might mean one less teenaged guest in the palace.

"What did you do?" Tristan entered with two more guards who promptly took up positions in the corners of the room. "I got a message from Father that I'm supposed to show Davy around the palace tomorrow and should probably talk to you about the way things are done in the palace."

Ly blushed.

"She proved the guards need more training," Karen said when Ly kept her mouth shut.

"You're going to hear about that when we meet with Chief Grouse this afternoon." Tristan shook his head. "And I've never missed my tablet so much. Where and when?"

Ly moved to the table with only a sly grin to her brother. "Let's see if the kitchen was paying attention."

Karen joined her, suddenly aware she missed breakfast. The boys came along as well. Ly only waited until they were all standing near a chair to lift the dome off the first dish and revealed a plate of grilled cheese sandwiches. They looked a lot more appetizing than the school cafeteria's. Karen reached for the dome closest to her and was rewarded with hamburgers. Karen's stomach reached directly for them without waiting for her mouth to start watering. She'd never seen burgers look that good on a plate—in ads, yes. Davy took his turn and opened a plate of some weird-looking things that were rolled in a white kind of bread. A spicy scent wafted up from the plate. Davy's eyes grew to the size of one of the burgers.

That left the ceramic bowl in front of Tristan, which held tomato soup.

"Oh, not fair." Tristan dropped into his chair. "You all got your favorites, and I get... What is this stuff?"

Ly laughed as she reached across to put a cheese sandwich on his plate and grab his bowl. "You don't have a high school profile to guide them." She put a ladle full of soup in his bowl and set it in front of him. "But I'm sure you'll like it."

Tristan scowled at her.

"If you don't like that, you can try one of these." He didn't take his eyes off the pile of things. "As much as I would love to, I won't be able to eat that many Burros." He grabbed one and dropped it on his plate with a little shake of his hand.

Karen picked one of the burgers and moved it to her plate. "Or you might just skip to a burger. Though it would be better with some fries."

Emalynn stuck out her tongue at Karen's insistence on the fried potatoes. She'd never liked them, and Karen couldn't get enough.

"You mean these things?" Tristan held up a smaller plate that had been hidden by the soup.

Karen stood to take the plate of fries and find a place closer to her. Then all conversation ended while they ate. Maybe she was just hungry. Maybe they really had run out of things to talk about that weren't going to get them in trouble. Karen preferred to think they'd just become comfortable with each other and didn't need to say anything. Not to mention the incredible flavor of her burger.

Tristan

Tristan led the small group of his peers to the Security Central offices. The six guards assigned to them just happened to be going in the same direction. It felt odd standing in the same lift with them while they did their best to ignore him. While the guards were ignoring him, they were more than aware of his sister. Tristan chafed that he couldn't see what they'd seen to make them all so wary of her.

The guards had pushed and prodded them yesterday. He'd been afraid they'd go a little too far with her. If that had happened, why would Father consent to let her and Karen roam the palace for a full day without protection? He wondered if anything he'd said about her last night had led to this situation. He hoped not. Then again, seeing how happy Emalynn was, maybe it was a good thing.

The lift stopped and they waited while the ID reader announced all their names before the door opened. Finally, it opened on the organized chaos of the security center. Tristan stepped out of the lift into the comfort of these offices. He remembered all the times he ended up here when the pressures of being the prince got to him. Here he could be himself without anyone saying he should be otherwise. Chief Grouse even told him why they allowed that kind of behavior, but it didn't bother him that they used it to track him better. Techani used all they learned about him to keep him happy on his trip.

He shouldn't have let that thought come to mind.

"Welcome back," Darius, a young man who apprenticed to the security department as long as Tristan could remember, bowed to him.

"Thank you." Tristan returned the bow. Normally, he would have smiled to see this boy who was the closest thing to a friend he'd had before Davy showed up. Darius's relationship with Techani would make this meeting a point of pain. It gave Tristan's heart a pause.

Darius turned to greet Emalynn, though he used a different style of bow for her. One she returned. She more than returned; she bent low enough to honor him as the one with higher rank.

"It's an honor to meet you," he said.

"The honor is mine," Emalynn insisted with more sincerity than he'd seen from her since they'd arrived in Prime. "I would like to meet with you more privately sometime."

"We'll find a time." He gave her a sad smile, then turned to greet Karen and Davy individually.

Tristan tried to catch Emalynn's attention to ask what that was all about. She avoided making eye contact until Chief Grouse joined them.

"So nice to see you both here and on time." Grouse offered her hand to Emalynn first.

Emalynn took her offered hand with a smile. Grouse then bowed to Tristan. It felt odd to be bowed to when she was willing to shake hands with Emalynn. He wanted to shake hands the way Emalynn did. He wanted to challenge Father and win a day without his guards. He wanted to get away with telling Mother she was wrong just once.

"Is there a significance to you bringing your guests to our meeting?" Grouse asked.

"We don't know how long they'll be here." Emalynn smiled with her lips only. Her eyes remained hard and calculating. "We want to spend as much time with our friends as we can before we're buried by our duties."

Grouse nodded and returned the smile and deep look. "Very well."

They moved deeper into the security offices while Grouse gave Emalynn a mini tour of the important features of the offices. Emalynn ignored all the bows from the guards and techs who were present. Grouse did nothing to stop them from bowing. Nor did she mention to Ly that the appropriate response was to nod to each. Tristan did his best to make up for her.

"You monitor everything from here?" Emalynn asked when they reached the open seating area where Grouse preferred to conduct her interviews.

"We have access to everything, but we aren't the only ones watching and we don't see everything right away," Grouse explained. "We track certain people and there are cameras we always watch."

Emalynn nodded. "So it is possible for someone to sneak through the palace."

Grouse agreed. "It's why we insist on keeping guards with the important people all the time."

Tristan had heard that explanation before. It was her standard excuse for keeping him guarded when he was younger. He was too important to risk, being the only heir to the entire galaxy and all the human colonies. He'd never found an effective counterargument. Eventually, he learned to pick and choose among the guards who were more pleasant. Emalynn would have to figure that out for herself, too.

"You're trying to talk me out of my day without guards." Emalynn interrupted Grouse's speech.

"I wouldn't be doing my job if I didn't."

They both leaned back to assess each other more.

"Ly, just accept it," Tristan said. "Just choose your guards carefully."

She shot him a look that told him he'd given in too easily all those years. "Father said twenty-four hours. Not as much time as you spent running through the back halls without your guards. She knows as well as anyone they'll learn much more about how to keep me safe if they watch what I do without them than they will in a month of keeping me under control."

The grin on Grouse's face broadened with Emalynn's speech. She'd just won the argument and showed him he was incompetent when it came to these kinds of things.

"So you'll wear this?" Grouse took a small box from Darius and gave it to Emalynn.

She examined the tracker bracelet closely. Tristan shook his head.

"A heart rate monitor?" Emalynn asked, looking at the inside of the bracelet.

"Of course." Davy leaned forward to take the bracelet from her. "Set to alert them with a sudden change in your heart rate. She doesn't know what kind of danger you're in; they'll need something faster than camera images to know if you're in trouble."

Tristan looked at his "friend" with a new appreciation of his skills. "How'd you know that?"

Davy shrugged. "If I were her, I'd make you both wear one all the time. Especially after the turmoil you caused just getting home."

"Some friend you are," Tristan grumbled.

"If you did, you'd have a stronger argument to keep your guards at a distance." Karen avoided looking at anyone.

Davy looked down when she said that, too. Tristan didn't need the expertise of the security chief or his sister to know they were dancing around a secret. Grouse tried asking them about it, but they were as silent as the void.

"I'll wear it." Emalynn took the bracelet back and slid it around her wrist. "I'll also want to select my own guards when I have to take them back."

Grouse smiled as though she'd just won a challenge. "How do you plan to choose?"

"I'm not sure yet."

Grouse nodded. "Then I guess twenty-four hours is a blessing for both of us."

Emalynn leaned back again with a sigh. She looked at the bracelet as though it were some sort of parasite she'd just invited to live off her.

"Now for you, young prince." Grouse turned on him. "We have to start rebuilding your security force as well, and we don't have a day to prepare."

Tristan's heart sank. All the guards he liked and trusted were scattered to the stars. They were gone because he'd liked them; he'd chosen them.

"Couldn't I just use the monitor?" he asked.

"That could be arranged." Grouse glanced at Darius, and the boy left. "That won't replace guards, though."

Tristan hated this. The lack of privacy and freedom were normal. He'd always lived with people watching him all the time. When the people were nice and understood what he wanted, he'd lived with it. When they treated him like a precious statue rather than a person, he fled.

"But I'm not the heir anymore."

"You're still important." Emalynn spoke softly. "If anything happened to you, I'd be compromised. So would the king."

Her words angered him, but that loving tone made him want to cry. "It's not fair."

"No, it's not." She knelt in front of him with a hand on his knee. "None of this is fair, but we can't fix it if we don't acknowledge it."

He could feel the layers of meaning she wanted him to understand. He latched onto her word "fix." They could fix it; together they could do anything. They'd survived, more than survived, multiple assassination attempts. They took the net by storm and snuck past an armada preparing to take over his home. Through it all, they managed to open relations with the Others. After all of that, making the universe play fair would be simple.

He covered her hand on his knee. "We will fix it." Saying it made it real.

That just left him describing the kind of women he wanted following him around again. Grouse came up with a short list of candidates.

"You should keep Davy with you," Karen suggested just before Tristan approved the list of guards. "He can help you evaluate them."

A look shot between Davy and Karen. More interestingly, Davy's hair shifted to reveal a fresh bruise on the back of his neck. He didn't need Emalynn's glare to realize Davy needed the protection of the royal guard more than Tristan.

"Good idea." Grouse agreed. "One last thing." She pulled out the scanner case.

Emalynn pulled her left hand into her stomach and covered it with her right.

"I just need to scan your ID chit." Grouse shifted to her motherly voice as though trying to comfort a child.

Tristan felt the pain of his ID reset surge in sympathy. Davy and Karen also rubbed the backs of their hands. Emalynn didn't take her eyes off the case.

"That isn't a scanner." Emalynn shifted as far back as her chair would let her. "It's a—"

"You're right." Grouse opened the case anyway. "And I need to do this whether you like it or not."

Emalynn jumped over the back of her chair to get away from the scanners.

Darius blocked her from getting farther away. "Perhaps an explanation, in your office," he suggested to the chief.

Tristan had never seen anyone in the office defy Chief Grouse like that. Grouse surprised him further by packing up her kit and heading to her office without comment, leaving Darius to convince Emalynn to follow. He did so simply by facing her with one hand cupped inside the other and telling her to follow the chief.

There was no way Emalynn had met Darius before today. He couldn't imagine what other connection could give Darius that kind of control over her.

"Wow." Karen breathed when the office door closed. "Who is that boy?"

Tristan only knew him as the apprentice of Techani. "He's the one who's going to have to continue the hand-to-hand training of the guards." Tristan shook his head. The guards wouldn't take it. They'd complained enough that Techani had been a man doing a woman's job. They wouldn't put up with a boy taking over.

Karen

Karen woke with regret. She'd been warm, comfortable, and able to dream of Dom without fear. She fought to stay in the dream where she could feel Dom's warm hands on her back and all the rest of her pressed up against Karen. In the waking world, all of that turned out to be the pillows and blankets of Emalynn's family-size bed.

"Come on, sleepy," Emalynn called from across the room. "The guards are really gone, and the wall says I don't have a schedule for today. I don't want to waste any of it."

Karen grumbled but rolled around to find the edge of the bed. This wasn't just a family-size bed; it was an extended family-size bed. Grandparents, aunts, and uncles could all fit comfortably in a bed like this without crowding Mom, Dad, and the kids. She managed to find the edge without falling out and slid gracefully to a stand. She considered asking for the time but thought it would only make things worse to know how early it was.

"Hey, Travis just brought breakfast," Emalynn yelled from the other room. "It's oatmeal, made right, with a variety of dried fruits to go in."

Oatmeal with dried fruit, when it's made right, was worth getting up for. Karen stumbled out to the main room to find Emalynn already dressed and dishing the oatmeal into two wooden bowls. Karen had never seen bowls made of wood before. They looked expensive. Ly handed one to her and took the other to the table where there were dozens of little containers of dried fruit.

"Are you sure it's okay to use these like this?" Karen held the bowl gingerly. The wood felt smooth in her hand with warmth that had nothing to do with the steaming oatmeal inside.

"Of course it is." Ly laughed. "I made them."

"What? When?" Karen chased Ly to the table. "When did you have time to make these? When did you have time to learn how to make these?"

Ly took her time choosing little fruits to mix into her oatmeal. She chose one more red fruit to sprinkle in her oatmeal. "When we were out there."

Karen scooped her favorite dried sour cherries into her oatmeal with a dash of brown sugar on top to keep up with Ly who had moved to the viewing area near the media wall.

"But where were you?"

Ly shook her head. "We were hiding."

"But you're not hiding now."

"The people we were hiding with are still there, and you know how much I trust." Ly smiled and took a small bite of her oatmeal.

She didn't trust. Once a secret, always a secret no matter what the person who told her it was a secret said. Ly could be trusted with anything, so long as you remembered to tell her it was a secret first. Karen never knew how many secrets that girl carried with her every day. Now it seemed she had more secrets of her own than Karen considered.

"They're really nice bowls."

"Thank you"

"So what are we going to do today?" Karen blew on her oatmeal before her first bite. It was still too hot.

Emalynn shrugged. "Explore I guess." She stirred her oatmeal rather than eat it. "I mean, I promised to stay in the palace, but this is a huge place. I'm sure there are plenty of interesting places we can get into the mild kind of trouble that will make great stories later on."

Karen nodded. It was enough of a plan to get them started. It allowed them to find the financial wing of the palace, too many dining rooms to count, gardens of all types, the throne room where Ly insisted Karen should try out the throne, and several ballrooms. It took all of that before Ly bemoaned the lack of a gym.

"There must be a gym around somewhere," Karen said. "The guards have to practice somewhere, and I doubt they'd be allowed to use that ballroom for training."

"Then let's find it."

Karen almost regretted saying anything. They were off and running. Really running through the halls, looking for the gym. Ly refused to ask for directions; she could figure it out on her own today. It reminded Karen that her friend had her demons, too. Running felt good, and they were out of breath by the time they found a gym.

"Oh, this is perfect." Ly bounced through the door.

Karen didn't know how she still had energy to bounce like that after all that running. Ly, though, looked as though she'd found heaven. Karen had to admit it was great to find this place. There were mats in the corner the same as the small gym they used for cheer practice. There were also barres stacked along the far wall and a rack of wooden weapons next to the door where they came in. Seeing Ly that excited brought out the cheerleader in her as well.

"You want to run some routines?" Ly asked.

Karen couldn't resist. They moved through their warm-up and stretch without thinking. Coach would have cut them from the team if they'd even thought about not warming up. Karen called for the first cheer, as she always did. Ly fell into position, and they ran the whole routine except for the lifts. They ran through most of the repertoire they'd developed before Ly disappeared.

"You want to see the new stuff?" Karen asked. "Not that I can show you the layers with just me..."

"Please." Ly went to stand against the wall to watch.

That came too easy. Karen took a deep breath, suddenly self-conscious with Ly watching. While Karen could make a good lineup and lead the team through a game or competition, Ly had been the better choreographer. Of course, the new routine had been Karen's idea, with help from Jose and Tina. Ly's bright smile calmed her nerves enough for her to start the routine.

Once started, she let her body remember the moves and the order. Nothing could bother her in the middle of a routine. Ly had taught her that. She should have remembered that earlier and used the routines to calm herself. She might have gotten better sleep these last few weeks.

"What do you think you are doing?" Deliah's voice shattered the routine.

Karen stumbled back, all her grace and balance lost to the fear.

"You were told not to leave your room without escort."

"Yes, ma'am." Karen dropped her eyes to the floor.

Deliah stomped her way into the gym with two of her goons in tow. "Don't you 'yes, ma'am' me. You didn't come back to your room last night either."

"Sorry," Karen whimpered. The way Deliah said it made it sound like she'd committed treason against the crown. Karen wished she could fall through the floor.

"Where have you been?"

"With me." Ly's voice caught Karen's heart just in time to stop it from beating through her chest. "By order of His Royal Majesty, King Levon."

Karen dared to raise her eyes high enough to see Ly face Deliah with all the power she could bring.

All the color drained from Deliah's already pale face. "Your Majesty." She bowed. "This is highly irregular."

Ly tilted her head to the right just a touch, adding a hint of confusion to her stern expression. "What's so odd about my friend and guest spending time with me?"

Deliah bowed again. "There's nothing odd about that. It's the lack of schedule and guards that is out of order."

"You are saying His Royal Majesty, your king, isn't allowed to make exceptions to his own rules?" Ly stepped in closer. She'd taken on her relaxed stance that could only mean she was ready to fight. "Be careful how you answer. I'm being monitored very closely today."

She was? Of course, that was the deal she'd accepted from the security chief yesterday. This situation got worse with every second. As much as she loved watching Ly give it to an adult, she still couldn't tell her not to push it any further without pulling Deliah's attention.

Deliah took the threat in Ly's voice as a challenge. "Of course he may make exceptions, so long as it doesn't allow for unreasonable risk."

Stars help me now, Karen prayed. Ly allowed a small smile to grace her lips while her eyes darkened until they made a black hole look bright. Deliah had no idea what kind of comet she was trying to catch, and Ly didn't know what kind gravity well she was walking into. Karen sank to her knees as the two women moved in, neither willing to give an inch.

"I should call for my guards to come out of hiding,"—Ly shifted into a more obvious stance—"but they would probably stop me from fighting you."

Deliah took a step back.

Emalynn closed the distance in an instant, catching Deliah's arm up behind her. "Now you can just tell me where I can find Dom."

"Who?" The tremor in Deliah's voice revealed her fear.

"Dominique Quell, my other best friend who isn't at home and isn't here."

"I don't know."

"Liar."

"You can't prove anything." Deliah snarled.

Ly released her so suddenly Deliah stumbled away. Deliah looked as though she might try to fight again, when the gym door opened. Instead, she scrambled to leave through a different door while Tristan and Davy laughed their way through the first door, followed by two guards. The guards stopped just inside.

"What's going on?" Tristan asked. "I got a sudden order to get down here. Not that I'm complaining. It interrupted a very boring lesson on colonial economics."

Ly said nothing.

"Ly said something about calling her guards out of hiding," Karen whispered. She couldn't believe Ly had managed to send Deliah away like that. Nor would she believe this was the last they'd hear from her.

Tristan turned to his sister with an expression so like Ly's when she faced Deliah it made Karen cringe. It proved they were twins, as if they needed any more evidence. Ly moved off toward the door Deliah had used, making strange gestures to Tristan. For his part, Tristan kept up with her pace and gestures.

"That was Deliah?" Davy pulled Karen to her feet. "What happened?"

Karen struggled to find her balance, leaning on Davy heavier than she should. "Ly went all scary on her."

"Scary?" Davy glanced at the twins still locked in a conversation no one else would understand even if they could hear it.

Karen nodded. "She knew about Dom. She knew about Deliah. We're doomed."

Davy pulled her into a hug. He quivered against her shaking. No doubt about it; they were doomed.

Emalynn

Part of Emalynn wanted to put off going back to the security offices before date change. The king had given her twenty-four hours of freedom, and she wanted to experience all of them. That small part of her hadn't been allowed to make her decisions for a very long time, so Emalynn led the way to Security Central, asking Tristan's guards to leave them at least that long. When they refused, Tristan smiled and said they would take the long way down. He even pointed them to the nearest lift without making her ask.

Karen followed with her eyes on the ground as though Emalynn were dragging her off to the principal's office for some great offense. Whatever that woman meant, Emalynn knew she'd just found the first link to Karen's strange behavior. Worse than that, she'd confirmed that Dom was in trouble and had been for some time. She couldn't imagine what they had done or said to make Karen act so out of character.

"Ly?" Karen choked when the lift doors closed.

"It's fine."

"No." It sounded as though she weren't breathing. "I need to tell you."

"Not here."

They rode the rest of the way in silence. Emalynn couldn't comfort her friend while she still knew so little about who they were facing. That woman had known too much about their relationship, yet not enough about what they were doing. The woman seemed at once professional and amateur.

"Princess Emalynn?" Darius greeted them. He bowed with his hands in the position of respect Baba had taught her. Everything about this boy reminded her of Baba, from the way he walked to the way he pitched his voice when he spoke to her.

"Is Chief Grouse available?" Emalynn withheld all pleasantries in the hope he would understand how serious she believed the situation had become.

Darius nodded. "She's on her way. Would you like to wait in her office?" He waved to the isolated room in the middle.

Emalynn didn't know what normal should have been. Maybe members of the royal family were given special treatment when they came to the offices. Maybe they really had been watching her closely enough to catch on. Either way, Emalynn didn't want the special treatment.

"Can I get you anything while you wait?" Darius asked before they sat in the waiting room chairs just outside Grouse's office.

Emalynn hesitated only a moment, then waved for him to join them. "Tell me about your training."

Darius blushed and hesitated to join them. "I'm not really the one to ask about the qualifications of the guards."

"I meant your training, specifically." She smiled as she remembered how hard it had been to get Baba to talk about her training.

Movement all around the room caught her attention. The guards and techs were bumping the backs of their hands while smiling. Darius saw it, too, and blushed even more.

"What was the pool and who won?" Emalynn leaned back in her chair.

Somehow, Darius managed to blush even more. "On when you would ask me about my training, and I had this afternoon." He sighed and sat across from her with all the grace one would expect of a highly trained martial artist. "And I also won against most of them that you'd notice the bet."

"And that makes you blush?" Emalynn smiled.

"I don't like to brag." He shrugged but didn't glance away.

Emalynn tried not to see Baba in every move he made. He didn't make that easy when every gesture and expression mimicked her so perfectly.

"How closely did you work with Techani Kenchi?" Emalynn choked a little on the name.

Now all the color drained from his cheeks, though his posture and gaze remained perfectly steady. Exactly the way Baba insisted Emalynn handle her emotions. Don't worry about the things she couldn't control, but show nothing else. His reaction showed a much closer relationship between him and Baba's mentor than she expected.

"Techani Kenchi is my sponsor and mentor." He spoke mechanically. Then, after a deep breath, he continued. "He is also my guardian of record."

Emalynn swallowed her shock. That was the phrase in her school record for Baba's relationship to her.

"Don't let this boy's modesty fool you." Chief Grouse walked into the waiting area. "He's Techani's second and, just as soon as we can graduate him, he'll be in charge of our physical training program. I'd love to see the two of you spar, just to see if there is someone who can put either one of you on the floor." The chief sent a warm smile toward Darius.

The boy's blush returned.

"Well, come on." She waved them toward her office. "All three of you. Although, I thought I would get a few more hours to figure things out."

Emalynn saw the look of surprise cross Darius's face before he regained control of his expression. She was pretty sure her face mirrored his. More concerning, though, was the look of dread that stuck to Karen's face. They filed into Grouse's office, past the security chief who held the door for them, as though she were the principal and they'd been caught skipping class.

Grouse shut the door with a solid click, and the lights changed to secure mode. That saved Emalynn from having to ask for the privacy. It also implied she wasn't the only one who had put the clues together.

"Well, I have to admit this is a surprise." Grouse spoke on her way to the chair behind her desk. "Tristan would have waited until his guard-free time was up before reporting to Security Central."

"I'm not my brother." Emalynn smiled to keep her voice light. "I'll admit I was tempted."

"Of course you were, but we aren't going to start with your story." Grouse sat and waved for them to take a seat. Darius perched on a cabinet while Karen and Ly sat in the two little chairs that faced the desk. "Darius, your preliminary report, please."

"It's not even that ready." He clutched his tablet to his chest.

"Before that,"—Emalynn looked at Karen—"you'd better explain the security lights."

Karen looked as though she might pass out. All color had drained from her face and her shoulders were trying to climb above her ears. She had her hands gripped together in her lap so tight her knuckles threatened to poke through the skin.

Grouse followed Emalynn's gaze. "Oh, Ms. Toya."

Karen clenched harder but looked up at the security chief.

"You can relax. I've set the security in this office to full secrecy."

Karen didn't relax.

"She means this office is cut off from all networks. No one will be able to see what the cameras see, they won't be able hear a single word, and they won't be able to call or enter this room," Emalynn supplied. "So please, breathe before you pass out."

Karen managed a weak smile and her shoulders began to descend. She went back to staring at the floor without a word. Emalynn regretted not putting that woman on her back when she had the chance.

Grouse shook her head slightly and turned back to Darius. "I need what you have. So does she." Grouse nodded at Karen.

Darius took a deep breath and poked at his tablet. "I've only been able to test about thirty percent of the palace staff so far, but of those, ninety percent have had their ID chit altered within the last year. That was enough data to start analysis of the alterations, which appear to be a harmless tracking system."

"Harmless?" Grouse challenged.

"I said 'appeared.'" He gave her a look Emalynn would never have used with a security chief, but often used with teachers who asked silly questions. "The chits report more than simple location to a node that isn't listed in the standard palace charts. I haven't located the physical node yet, though I've narrowed it to the residential section. Nor have I been able to determine the purpose of the tracking information, which includes some biometrics and vital statistics."

"Chits aren't supposed to have that kind of capability." Emalynn rubbed the back of her hand subconsciously.

"No, they aren't." Darius nodded. "And there aren't supposed to be any unmapped nodes in the palace network."

"And you aren't surprised?" Emalynn pushed.

Grouse sighed. "No. We find and remove them as quick as we can, but someone always wants some sort of inside information on the royals and governmental operations."

Emalynn wished she could be surprised. Half the primary documents they examined in governance class were recorded secretly, probably illegally, inside government buildings. The teachers didn't say that, but when the official records weren't available, they had to study the history somehow.

"You're turn." Grouse fixed Emalynn with a stare any teacher would be proud of. The kind that pinned students to the backs of their chairs. "What have you learned of the current conspiracy against you and your family?"

Put that way, Emalynn's few clues made so much more sense.

"I haven't come to many conclusions. I just have a lot of troubling questions. For example, where is my friend Dominique Quell? I know from the gossip sites before we were allowed to land that the royals swooped in and picked up both Karen and Dom in the middle of school just after the announcement of the 'winners' of the image contest. King Levon only named Karen, though, and she's the one I've seen."

A tear appeared in Karen's eye. Emalynn had to look away to finish her analysis. She'd made these kinds of reports to Baba's running mates on the smuggler routes. They never bothered her before. But then they weren't about her or her friends before either.

"I've noticed some behavioral anomalies in Karen, too. She hasn't once mentioned Dom's name since I returned. In any other context, she would have talked about her girlfriend nonstop. In school, she was the one more willing to get in trouble, but here, she's been timid to the point of fear.

"On that point"—Emalynn gestured to her friend who was shaking visibly in the chair beside her—"I wanted to investigate on my own a little more until this afternoon. I don't know who that woman was, but she couldn't have been working on orders from you or the scheduling office, since she wasn't aware of mine or Karen's schedule change since yesterday. She threatened Karen right in front of me but appeared to fear me. Either one of us should have been able to drop her if she'd attacked. Clearly, she has something to hold over Karen, and the only thing I can think of would be Dom."

Karen stifled a sob.

"I need to know where our friend is and what's happening to her." Emalynn finished. She still couldn't look at Karen without losing control of her emotions.

Grouse nodded. "That will help." She nodded to Darius.

Darius poked at his tablet. "I think I can trace some of this back through the records. It might give us a lead."

"She isn't here." Karen sobbed. "She never arrived on Prime."

Grouse relaxed into her chair. "What happened?"

Karen gasped for breath before starting the story of how they'd been tricked. Dom disappeared the second night on the cruise ship, and Deliah appeared to "train" Karen in how to manipulate Emalynn.

"She was that blunt?" Grouse asked.

Karen nodded. "If I didn't cooperate, she showed me images of Dom with bruises and cuts."

Emalynn fought the tightening of her stomach. She couldn't allow her anger to interfere with her ability to fight. If she did find this Deliah woman again, she wouldn't hesitate to send her to medical in critical condition.

"Has that continued since you've been in the palace?" Grouse looked relaxed, but her voice betrayed her tension.

Karen nodded. Her mouth worked to say something, but her voice died in her throat.

Emalynn took several deep breaths to bring herself back to balance. "Was that woman Deliah?"

Karen nodded. "But..."

"She's only the enforcer," Darius said. "Is Veniese the leader?"

Emalynn looked at him with surprise. So did Grouse.

"It's a fake name I found in the coms list," he said. "I haven't been able to link it to a real identity. But I have linked both Deliah and Veniese to Davy as well. I'm guessing he's supposed to manipulate Tristan."

"Good luck with that," Emalynn muttered.

"I don't think anyone knows what you two are capable of," Grouse said.

Emalynn agreed. Whoever this Veniese woman was, she was in for a surprise when Emalynn found her.

"Well," Grouse said, "for now, I'm reassigning Karen's living quarters to your suite. I trust you can keep her safe."

Emalynn nodded. It's what she would have asked for.

"I'm also assigning Darius as your personal guard. You can work with him to trace this conspiracy to its source."

"What?" Emalynn and Darius said in unison.

"You need someone you can trust to watch your back and fill in the details you don't know about the palace and royal life. And Dare, you need an excuse to leave all your other duties for this investigation. Until I say otherwise, you are her only guard."

Emalynn and Darius looked at each other. He gave her a curious gaze that matched her confused feelings. She didn't want any guards at all, and a boy, at that, would be insulting. Except she could imagine them as friends, and he was the only one here who might be able to hold his own against her in a fight. Then there was his connection to Techani and her last connection to Baba.

"Dare, make sure they each get a tablet with appropriate security clearance."

The lights returned to normal and the door lock clicked open.

Tristan

Despite Grouse's orders to keep Davy by his side at all times, Tristan couldn't deny his mother a second attempt at a family dinner. He also couldn't afford to leave Davy alone, even in his chambers with guards. He'd seen the bruises, in all stages of healing. Fortunately, someone knew the conundrum and placed six chairs around the table in the family dining room. Tristan insisted Davy sit closer to Father and took the seat closer to Mother on his side of the table.

Father and Mother joined him shortly after he arrived, separately again. Mother gave Davy that assessing look she used from the throne when she didn't like the lord or whoever came before them. Father at least tried to make polite conversation about their latest lessons. Davy stumbled through that part while Tristan tried to keep Mother from noticing how late Emalynn and Karen were.

"Sorry we're late." Emalynn bowed at the door to both Father and Mother. It wasn't the kind of bow Mother expected, but more than Tristan thought she would give.

Karen bowed as well, much closer to what Mother would have expected from Emalynn. Behind them came Darius, who joined the other guards along the wall. He bowed as expected of a guard. Except he wasn't in a guard's uniform. In fact, he was in civilian clothes that made him look like a fashion model. Tristan couldn't imagine what would have gotten that boy out of his uniform; he'd been so excited when they finally gave him one.

"Emalynn." Mother began in her stern voice. "We expect you to be on time to every event on your schedule."

Emalynn smiled at Mother and sat across from Tristan. "How was your day?" she asked.

"Normal," Tristan said. "Mostly filled with tutors and advisors."

Emalynn nodded. "I really need more variety. I mean, I know I can't actually finish the navigations major, but can't I continue with the advanced physics?" With that last, she'd turned toward Father.

"Emalynn," Mother snapped. "We were talking."

"I'm sorry." Emalynn turned to the queen. "I thought you were lecturing, and I've had enough of that for today."

Tristan cringed and wished he could cheer. This dinner wasn't going to turn out any better than the first one if Emalynn kept on like that.

"Who else has been lecturing you?" Father asked before Mother could get too mad.

"The tutors." Emalynn turned to answer his question. "It wouldn't be so bad if they stayed on topic, but three of them complained to me about Chief Grouse's orders that I keep Karen by my side. I really don't like being told my friends are somehow less just because they were born on an outer colony."

Karen hid a giggle behind her hand. Tristan had heard the same rants all day. He wondered if they'd seen the same tutors.

"I'm sure they didn't mean to insult you." Father glanced at Karen. His expression changed in response to her biting her lips.

"Oh, they were quite clear about it." Emalynn shifted in her seat. "They were a bit more subtle about how little they thought I'd learned in my outer colony schools."

The servers entered then with their dinner, and all conversation ceased. Tristan watched the servers move in perfect choreography so they all set the plates in place at the same time. He hadn't noticed how carefully they had to move before. Having seen the chaos of meals in other settings, he wondered why they insisted on this kind of precision here. He found the answer in his mother's expression. She also watched the servers, but with a critical eye.

All of that left his mind when the silver cover disappeared. His plate held a mass of noodles in a red sauce with something brown mixed in. Tristan had no clue what that was, but the rule about not serving him new foods at family dinners should still apply.

"Lasagna casserole?" Karen's face lit up with delight. "I thought you said I'd have to eat things I couldn't identify."

Emalynn laughed. "I guess someone got the hint to do a little research." She hurried to put her napkin on her lap and grab her fork.

Davy and Karen weren't far behind her. Tristan bit back his tantrum and got ready to eat. Father hesitated only a moment before joining suit. Mother stared at the mess on her plate as though it might eat her. They were supposed to wait until everyone was ready to eat before starting. Mother wouldn't be ready until the dish cooled too much to know what it was supposed to taste like, so Tristan took the plunge and stabbed a noodle with his fork. It fell back to the plate before he got it in his mouth.

94

Davy laughed. "Try scooping them up."

"Like with a spoon?" Tristan asked. He needn't have. The girls were demonstrating quite clearly.

Father managed to get one of the noodles to his mouth first. The change in his expression said everything Tristan needed to know. It might look like a mess, but the flavor would be worth it. When he succeeded, he knew this would soon be one of his favorite dishes. It reminded him of the blended flavors of the stew they always had on Farthing Moon. Of course, it took all the work out of building a bite to have all the right flavors in it. Just as the stew did. It didn't matter which bits you had on your spoon; all the flavors came with it. Mother poked at the noodles with her fork.

"So this is common?" Father asked when the silence grew too long.

"Yeah." Karen sighed. "I wish they'd serve it more, but that's just me."

"This is your favorite?" Davy asked.

Karen nodded and sent the question back. Father encouraged them to give details about the food. Then more about what they did in school. That side of the table became warm and friendly as Davy and Karen warmed up to the topic. Emalynn watched them with a small smile one her lips.

"You call this food?" Mother pushed the noodles around more.

"Try it," Tristan said before Emalynn could react. He could feel Emalynn's frustration and knew Mother wasn't its source. Still, the two would end up fighting if Mother didn't learn to put her prejudices away quickly.

"Tristan." Mother glared at him.

He flinched, despite himself. He should be old enough not to worry about her sharp tongue.

"It may not look all that fancy," Emalynn spoke to her plate, "but you shouldn't worry too much about what your food looks like."

"What?" Mother slammed her fork down.

Emalynn pushed another bite into her mouth with a pleading glance at Tristan. He didn't know what she thought he could do.

"I've had enough of your insolence." Mother glared at Emalynn. "You will look at me when I'm talking to you."

"Stop it." Tristan slammed his fork down exactly the way Mother had. "How can you expect her to treat you with respect when you won't return the favor? She's lost everything she knew of her life. Is it so much to ask for the foods she's used to, or are you going to take that away, too?"

He forced his hands to release the tablecloth and returned them to his lap where he could hold the hem of his shirt without the danger of pulling dinner off the table. The grip on his hem did little to quell his shaking. He'd never stood up against his mother like that before, outside of fantasies.

"Tristan, you should know better than to behave in such a shameful fashion." Mother had her hands on the table, ready to push herself to a stand.

"Do you know why I was taken?" Emalynn's quiet voice cut through the atmosphere like a laser. She had returned her fork to its place beside her plate and sat with her back as straight as Mother could have wanted. Her eyes were focused somewhere behind Tristan.

"They say the royals have been gone so long they don't know anything about the colonies anymore. The people of the outer colonies study the governance of the galaxy as though it were something foreign. Governance classes are structured the same as ancient history and Others studies. In elementary school, we had to make a plan for how to improve some part of our government. Half the projects ignored the central government completely, because the kids thought there wasn't anything that could be done. The other half suggested taking someone from an outer colony and letting them be princess." Her eyes refocused on him. "Sorry, Tristan, no one thought you were going to make a change when you took the throne."

Until recently, he would have agreed with those kids.

Emalynn turned her gaze to the king. "The teachers weren't surprised. They might have encouraged that kind of thinking. In high school, they were more careful to keep their political thoughts to themselves, and still, we saw no hope of being relevant. Those who looked into the governance major had local ambitions. They wanted to be a mayor or possibly join a colonization mission. A few thought they could use governance to take a position in a corporation. Kids who wanted to make a difference went for communications or sciences. The really ambitious kids found their way into engineering. For us, the government was only an obstacle to achieving anything. We had to learn how it worked so we could get past it."

Father accepted her speech with the same straight-backed position she used to deliver it. Tristan couldn't read anything in his father's expression. There was no sign if he even understood what she was telling him.

She gave him a slight nod, then turned to Mother. Her expression remained calm, almost blank. Her voice didn't rise in volume or tone, but somehow it took on a deadly aspect.

"I was taken because the only way to get into this level of government is to have the right genes. They intended to raise me as a peasant, then send me back when I was ready to lead the way they wanted. I was taken because you are so stuck in your ways that you can't even be bothered to taste the food I grew up with. I am one of them, and I'm a member of this family. Our laws are clear. The only way you can deny me is to kill me. I was taken to make a difference, and I intend to do just that."

Inside, Tristan stood and cheered for her. No one, including Father, had ever spoken to Mother with so much hard truth. Nor had anyone managed to keep Mother from interrupting a speech like that.

Mother hadn't moved through the whole thing. Her expression, however, had hardened to something beyond deadly.

Emalynn picked her napkin off her lap, refolded it, and laid it over her plate. She stood gracefully and turned to Karen. Karen rose from her chair with only a little less grace. Together, they bowed to Tristan. Emalynn added the hand gesture she used when she bowed to Darius. They turned and bowed to Father. Darius met them at the door, and they were gone.

"Well—" Mother started.

"Don't start." Father interrupted.

Tristan wasn't hungry anymore either. Davy copied his movements as he returned his napkin to the table and left. He couldn't keep himself from bowing to his mother, but he kept it shallow while giving Father his full respect.

"You are growing into a fine leader, Tristan," Father said when Tristan had one foot out the door.

He stopped but didn't turn back. "I'm not the heir."

Emalynn

"Are you sure about this?" Dare asked again when they got to the gym. "This isn't the most defensible place."

Emalynn was tired of this argument, but she couldn't release her anger enough to yell at him without risking losing control. "I'm sure."

In the gym, she could run the forms until she calmed down enough to think without risking damage to things that weren't meant to be used physically, like her friends or the furniture. Something tugged at the back of her mind. Something she should be able to see if her head wasn't so clouded by her mother's prejudice.

"We could all use a workout anyway." She smiled at them over her shoulder.

Karen nudged Dare to help her set out the tumbling mats. She muttered something to him when they got far enough away that Emalynn would have to strain to hear. It was probably some sort of explanation about how this was what she really needed right now and to just "let Ly do what she needs to do."

Emalynn ignored her muttering. If they needed that kind of explanation, leave it to them. Anything that would keep them out of the way while she worked through the thoughts that wouldn't form clearly in her mind. She finished warming up and stretched before checking that they were engaged in an activity of their own. They'd set out the mats, and Karen was still in the middle of her routine of stretches. She couldn't tell what Dare was doing, but he seemed content enough to stay on that side of the gym.

The first few moves of the first form took all her thoughts. Every synapse focused on pushing her body to perform each move perfectly. Slowly, her body took over, sliding into the perfect balance of the moves. Still, it didn't release her mind until the fourth form. Between thoughts of hand positions, images of the queen crept into her mind alongside images of Baba. No surprise there.

How could the queen live up to the mother Baba had been? She'd

99

never known hardship or the desires of a young girl who had nothing but love. How could Baba live up to the woman who became queen? She'd never known a day that promised to become tomorrow. The two women who both claimed to be her mother couldn't have been more different if they'd tried. Baba's pale skin belied the blood connection she didn't share with Emalynn. Her hair, had it ever been allowed to show its natural blond, would have given proof to any station guard that Emalynn couldn't have been her daughter. Looking at Queen Treylyn was like looking in a mirror.

It should be obvious that Emalynn is the queen's daughter. Then things like this evening happen, and it's clear as day they have nothing in common.

She stumbled in the sixteenth move of the tenth form and had to refocus. Shift and move, slide the hand into place. Every muscle in the right state of tension, just enough to put her bones in the right places and leave her open to change directions as needed. Focus on the feel of her body; the speed of her heart needed to match the speed of her moves.

Shift and move. Feel her weight. Imagine Dom and Karen teasing her about the slow-motion exercise she preferred. The two of them were always together except when the office insisted they needed different classes. The one time they had two classes in a row in different rooms, they still made the time to meet again in the halls every day. Anyone who wanted to control one would have to control the other. Karen said as much in Grouse's office. The question came down to who here on Prime would know that much about these girls.

King Levon invited Karen to the palace. Queen Treylyn, though, didn't like the idea. No matter what words they used in the fights and lectures, Emalynn could see the tension between the monarchs centered around Karen.

Emalynn stumbled again. Only a few moves from the end of the cycle and she'd just found a thought that took too much of her mind. This would take more time than she'd anticipated. She refocused enough to finish out the cycle and start again.

"Slow down." Dare stood beside her in position.

"Please, leave me be," Emalynn grumbled.

"It'll work better together." He dropped form to turn to face her. "Your mother taught you this technique. Did she show you the tandem version?"

"We practiced together all the time."

"No, I mean the mental exercise you were doing."

How had he seen that?

"Baba didn't teach me that. I figured it out for myself."

He froze. Three deep breaths later, he reanimated. "Using the forms to help you think makes sense."

"Then let me do it."

"It's not working, is it?"

Darn him for being right. Dust this whole situation.

"What can you do for me?"

He smiled. "I lead the form. You follow. It will keep you on track while your mind unravels whatever it is you need to unravel."

It was worth a try. They started again from the beginning. She let Dare set the pace and size of the moves. His choices would stretch her more than she expected, but it was worth it for how quickly she was able to let go and delve into her thoughts. She started right in on the queen's focus on Karen.

Treylyn's animosity centered around Karen and clipped Davy only in the ways Davy and Karen were the same. There were the obvious parts about them being common and born in the outer colonies. If that were the standard, Davy should have been the more reviled for having known connections to the rebel group Alecti. Karen's life held less exciting elements. She chose cheer as her school sport and looked to be heading for a communications major. Harmless except for her ties to Emalynn.

Why didn't the queen focus her anger on Emalynn, then? She was born noble and raised lower than peasant. Baba never graduated. She dragged Emalynn from one illegal job to another until she was able to leave the child alone for long periods of time. Each new job carried more risk for both of them until that risk caught up with her. Karen had nothing to do with that, and anyone who knew Karen well enough to know her connection with Dom would have seen that, too. The queen's anger with Karen wasn't about her connection to Emalynn; it was about her connection to Dom.

The simple answer to that wouldn't fit either. Sure, there were people who hated anything other the procreative relationships between women and men. More often, they turned their hatred toward the men. Historically speaking, that made sense; men healthy enough for sex had been rare at one point. The mere idea that they would waste any of that energy on other men would have had dire consequences for all of humanity. That wasn't true anymore with birth rates hovering near the fifty percent mark over the last two centuries, but traditional hatreds and fears died hard. That same sentiment encouraged women to find pleasure in each other, so it wouldn't explain Treylyn's reaction to Karen.

Only one explanation made sense, but not really. The queen had to know something about Dom. She didn't need Karen to manipulate Emalynn into proper behavior; she could do that directly and would be seen more favorably as a mother for doing so. If she knew the threat against Emalynn, it would be in her best interest to quash it. That left only one path that would make sense: Treylyn suspected someone of manipulating Karen but didn't have enough to do anything about it.

"I got it," Emalynn whispered as they started the thirteenth form.

"Finish the cycle." Dare continued to move from stance to stance with the grace of a cat.

She wouldn't think of stopping. Now that the big things were loose and ready to be handled, she could worry about the little things, like how to decorate her room so it would be hers and what to do with all the clothes she wouldn't wear. By the time she bowed out of the last move, everything that could be fixed just by thinking about it was.

Karen clapped for them. "You two looked like you were dancing. I'm not sure fighting is supposed to look so beautiful."

"Thanks." Emalynn flashed her devious smile. "Ya wanna learn?"

"Still no." Karen huffed. "How many times do I have to tell you I'm not a fighter?"

Dare bit his lips together while Emalynn let her laughter ring out.

"Fine, we'll start tomorrow. I want a shower and my bed." She led them out of the gym, then realized she still didn't know her way back to her room and let Dare take over.

He also took deft control of the conversation and kept Karen talking about the nothing kind of rumors from school that used to feel like everything. That left Emalynn with her freshly untangled thoughts and plenty of time to notice the details of their surroundings. The halls were strangely empty of guards, though they passed several pairs of patrols. They'd been in the gym until late, almost date change, so perhaps this was normal for late night in the palace. Most people would already be in bed, so the public areas should be deserted. She expected a change when they got to the private wing.

Pairs of guards stood outside every door. Darius noticed it, too. Half the rooms on this floor were unused, so they shouldn't have guards outside them. Her door should have been unguarded as well; she wasn't there and Dare was the only member of the security department she'd accepted so far.

Without even a look, they shifted their places to put Karen between them. Karen, bless her, continued the story she'd been telling in the lift. The first two pairs of guards they walked by without incident. Then came the ones standing outside her door.

"We should check in on Tristan," Emalynn said as they came to her door.

"Won't he be in bed already?" Karen played the innocent so well.

"No." Emalynn could feel him in that space in the back of her mind. "He's just as upset about dinner as I was."

They moved past her door.

"Darius." One of the guards stepped out to stop them. "I'm here to relieve you."

Emalynn disarmed her and had her on the ground before the other guard could join them. Darius pushed Karen out of the way to confront the second guard. The rest of the guards in the hall left their posts, most drawing their weapons. Emalynn pulled the laser pistol from the guard's hip and shot three times. Three guards went down. More shots behind her were followed by the thuds of bodies hitting the floor.

"Run." Dare's command voice was low and calm. He gave no room to question the order.

Tristan

Tristan stared in horror at the vid Davy called up. The figures, all obscured with masks and lighting tricks that couldn't be undone with clever computer hacks, ranted on about the horrible things they claimed the monarchy had done to them. Tristan believed they had suffered, but not that his father's government had done anything to make it happen. Davy had shown him thirteen different groups that all had similar complaints.

The two guards who'd taken up a stance near the door snapped to attention, forcing the media wall to pause.

Tristan stood to complain. Then he heard the distinct hiss of a laser pistol just beyond the door.

"Take cover," the guards ordered, pulling their weapons.

"Stand aside." Emalynn pushed a second weapon into the guard's hand.

Darius followed seconds later with Karen. "Lock that door. That's an order."

His guards complied just in time for more shots in the hall.

"What?" Tristan looked at Karen cradling her arm and Emalynn still in a fighting stance.

Emalynn shot him a quick look. "Get dressed. We're leaving."

The part of her he could feel had a strangely calm composition. The look in her eyes told him not to argue. He and Davy ran for the bedroom. Their clothes from the day were still piled in the corner.

"I fell wrong." Karen's voice filtered through the door.

That didn't look like an ordinary fall. Davy's fading bruises reminded him of the threat against them. He grabbed the first pair of pants that came to hand and pulled them on. The shirt didn't match, but that wasn't a problem.

"More importantly," Emalynn's voice pierced his ears when Davy opened the door, "we have to keep Karen safe."

"Karen?" Darius remained as calm as ever.

"She's the one in danger."

"But…"

"They want to manipulate me, and they'll do anything to her to get what they want."

Davy's back stiffened. "What about Dom?"

"That's why we're here." Emalynn glanced at Dare. "Tristan told me all about his ability to skip the security systems. We need to get out of the palace."

"I've never left the palace," Tristan complained as he rejoined them.

Emalynn scowled. "What were all those stories you told me in the shuttle?"

"Little adventures." Tristan shook his head. What had she done now? "I didn't want to get out. I just wanted to get away for a little while."

Emalynn turned toward the door when something banged against it.

"What's going on out there?" Davy shivered.

"Fake guards in real uniforms," Darius growled.

The real guards in the room glanced at each other with a fatalistic look. Great, more people willing to die for him. Losing his place as heir should have taken that off his shoulders.

"We have to leave." Emalynn fixed him with a stern stare.

"She's right." Darius turned to him. "If you can get us to the garage without alerting security, I can get us out."

Tristan ignored Darius and met his sister stare for stare. "Security is tight." He put his hands in the question position.

She smiled. "There's always an Other way." Her hands were in affirmative.

"Communications." Question.

Affirmative. "Security." Negative.

Tristan sighed. They had relied on the Other too much, yet she was the best chance they had of getting around palace security. "Grouse?" Question.

Negative.

"I can get us to the garage, but not in it." Tristan moved toward the main door. "And we'll be short on time if they know we've gone." He popped the panel off the door and toggled the switch to make the door think it was a wall. He disconnected the main communication line, too, and put the panel back up.

The second panel in the bedroom took a little more work to convince the wall it was really a door and open into the back halls for him. The lights there were dim, but the dust told him no one had been through since his last adventure. "Ly, leave the monitor on the bed."

Emalynn, to his surprise, complied without hesitation or argument.

Darius ordered the guards to stay in the room for one hour before contacting Grouse and telling them what happened. They argued until he told them it was an order. Then they simply glared at him.

None of this would be good. When they got back from this adventure, he'd lose more than half his tricks for getting away. Possibly more. One look at the panic that threatened to engulf Karen and Davy told him it would be worth it if they could just get through tonight.

Emalynn led the way into the unused hallway beyond his wall. Karen, Davy, and Darius followed her quietly, looking as grim as he felt. He slid through and let the wall close behind him. At some point, this must have been a legitimate route through the palace, but he couldn't imagine why they would allow it. On this side of the wall, he didn't need to pop the panel open; he could just grab the control wires and yank. That section of wall would never open again.

He slid past the rest of the group to lead them down through the miles of dark hallways into the servants' passages near the kitchen. They had to be careful; the early shift would be coming in soon. Normally, he wouldn't worry about that. The cooks and other early staff would just try to feed him sweets while they alerted Grouse about his location. The sweets wouldn't be bad, but the part about alerting security would be.

He heard people coming and pushed them all into a women's changing room. How did Emalynn keep her breathing so steady in times like this? He could feel the air scratching his throat with each shallow gasp. They hadn't been running or anything. He'd be willing to bet becoming the heir again that Emalynn had found somewhere to run her forms before diving into his room, claiming there were fake guards chasing her.

"Here." She pushed some fabric into his hands. "Put that on."

"What?" He held it up and found a woman groundskeeper's uniform. "What for?"

"A few extra seconds before someone recognizes you." She smiled and pushed him deeper into the room where Davy and Darius were changing into similar outfits.

A few seconds didn't seem like much. Then he thought about the ten seconds it took her to drop five royal guards in the library. If anything leaked onto the general net, that would be a good clip. Any vids of him sneaking through the back hallways in a gardener's uniform should be deleted as soon as possible. They moved on, looking like a strange crew that would never happen, so hopefully no one would see them.

The garage sat next to the loading dock. He'd been there only once and realized there were too many different kinds of transports for him to ever think of being able to pilot them. That's what staff were for.

"Who has pilot's licenses?" Dare asked as he palmed his way into the garage.

"I've got my permit for small planet side," Karen said.

"Same." Davy raised his hand.

"I'm licensed for small and medium skippers, surface to orbit shuttles, and intra-system small passenger craft," Emalynn said. "I also have my permit for interstellar passenger and cargo craft."

Tristan joined the others in staring at her with his jaw on the floor.

"I did mention we were smugglers." She shook her head and walked into the garage ahead of Darius.

Then it was her turn to stare with an open mouth at the sheer number of vehicles in the garage. Tristan didn't tell her they couldn't see all of them from here.

Darius shook off his surprise and took the lead again. "Well, we'll have to stay planet bound. I don't have the access codes for any of the craft that go above the atmosphere." He led them to a humble-looking craft that would fit them all with little room to spare. He unlocked the hatches but slipped around to the navigator's side to enter.

Emalynn stood outside the pilot's side with a question on her face while the rest of them took their places in the passenger compartment.

"Hurry up," Darius called through the open hatch. "You're the one with a license. I only have a permit."

Emalynn got in, her demeanor fully professional again. "File a plan to a remote part of this world." She snapped her safety harness on and brought the control board to life.

"How remote?"

"Deserted island." She turned to Darius with just a hint of a smile.

They weren't going to stay on plan, but every search plan out there suggested starting with the intended destination. He couldn't tell where she was going to take them, but it would take more than a couple of seconds for Grouse to figure out what they were up to.

Emalynn had the craft up and gliding between the rows of other craft. Tristan marveled at how smooth the craft's movements were. He almost missed Darius directing her to the main hatch. The hatch cycled open as they approached, and Emalynn slid out into the night-running lanes of the city.

"Here's your flight path." Darius pushed the navigation to Emalynn's console. "That's going to alert someone soon."

"How far to the city's edge?"

Tristan sank back into his seat and let the ones who knew what they were doing take over. He just enjoyed the ride and the thrill of leaving the palace almost unescorted.

Davy nudged him. "Do we have a med kit in here?"

Tristan saw the strange colors Karen's arm had become. Her gasping breath wasn't from running through the palace. He reached under Emalynn's chair and found the emergency kit. The only bottle he recognized held an analgesic that would knock her out. Still, he handed it over just in time for Emalynn to increase their acceleration into the darkness away from the city.

Karen

Karen drifted among the clouds, chasing a unicorn. No, that wasn't right. It wasn't a unicorn. They only had one horn and no one believed in them anymore. Besides, Karen wasn't a virgin. Didn't unicorns kill non-virgins?

"Karen."

The unicorn knew her name. And sounded a lot like Emalynn. Oh, that was Ly floating through the clouds, too.

Karen tried to wave, but something bit her wrist. The dog looked up at her with fire in its eyes. What breed of dog would need to burn its own eye?

"Karen."

Ly loomed in her face. She was so close. Why didn't she stop the dog?

"Karen, wake up."

I am awake. Only you've taken us someplace totally weird.

"What did you give her?" Ly sounded angry now.

Davy muttered something in the distance. Davy would see the dog. He always believed her.

Karen drifted down from the clouds into the forest. So many animals here chattering away to each other. Squirrels always had a lot to say.

"We can't go to a hospital." Ly the unicorn silenced all the little critters.

No, of course not. Squirrels can't go to a hospital. They aren't citizens.

Ly got in her face again. "Karen. Karen, you have to wake up."

Karen tried to focus on Ly's face. It seemed serious.

"I wae."

"What happened?" Ly wouldn't let her move the hand the dog bit.

Karen tried to think. The dog wasn't real. She looked down for where her hand should be, but the clouds rolled in and covered it with too many colors.

"Karen, focus."

Karen turned back to Ly. "Fall."

"Crud." Ly turned away. "Is there a scanner?"

Pain pulled her focus to her wrist. She wanted to look, but Ly would be mad if she looked away again. The more pain, the less she could focus on the forest around her. There were other voices, but she only understood Ly.

"Hold still." Ly jabbed something into her arm. "Tell me when you notice the pain fading."

Pain. All she could think about was the pain in her arm. "Happen?"

"You broke it." Ly filled her vision. "Hold still."

Karen felt herself falling, but she couldn't reach for Ly to keep her up. Pain shot through her mind like black lightning.

When her vision cleared, Dom sat beside the bed, looking down at Karen with tears threatening to drip from her eyes.

"I'm so sorry." Karen reached for Dom with her other hand.

Dom brushed her hand away. "You failed." Bruises began to appear on Dom's face.

"I tried. I really tried. You have to believe me."

Dom's right arm bent at a funny angle. "I believed in you. You could always convince people to do anything. As Ly's best friend, it should have been easy. All you had to do was get her to act like a proper princess."

Tears spilled from Karen's eyes. It wasn't fair. She'd done everything they'd asked of her, and Ly figured it out on her own.

"If you'd really wanted to, you could have."

"It's Ly we're talking about." Karen couldn't stand to see Dom like that, but she couldn't look away. "Since when could any of us lie to her?"

"You shouldn't have lied." Blood dripped from the tip of her nose and pierced Karen's forehead. "You should have done as you were told."

"It's not fair."

Dom became transparent.

"It's not fair. They don't know her."

"You failed," Dom whispered as she faded away.

"You failed." A new face shrouded in shadow appeared.

"No!" Karen screamed and closed her eyes, but the shadow followed her into the dark. "You failed us and you know the punishment."

Karen fled deeper into the darkness, trying to outrun her own shadow. She ran until she couldn't breathe. The shadow crept closer, hiding among the other shadows. Karen grabbed the first thing she could find and threw it. She grabbed and threw again. The shadow followed her through everything. Never quite where she thought it was.

"It's not fair." She whimpered as she crawled toward something that sounded familiar.

The sound called her out of the darkness where the shadow couldn't follow.

"It's not fair," she muttered again.

The sounds were voices. She knew those voices. They were the voices of her friends.

"We just don't know." Darius's voice sounded far off.

"There has to be a way." Tristan was a little closer.

Pain returned as a welcome reminder of life. Her thoughts were clearer when she focused on the pain. Part of that pain came from her eyelids that warned her it was bright out there.

"What are you doing?" Dare grumbled somewhere in the distance.

"Talking to the one person I know I can trust." Ly had a distracted tone.

"That's not a person."

Karen cursed her curiosity and cracked an eyelid. They must have landed in the sun. Her eyelid slammed shut and added a headache to her list of pains.

"Hey, you," Davy screamed in her ear.

She flinched, and something heavy and hard hit her head.

"Now don't beat yourself up." This time he didn't yell, but pulled her arm away from her head. He dropped something else over her face that cut back the light that leaked through her eyelids. "It'll be better if you open your eyes now."

She tested his assurance and found the light more bearable. He'd covered her face with a scarf so everything looked a little hazy. Or it could have been her brain was still scrambled.

"Mmm app'n" She glanced down at the brace around her right arm.

"You broke your wrist."

She shifted her gaze up to him too fast and nearly blacked out.

"Watch it." Davy grabbed her head and held it still. "The amateur medics gave you a bit too much Cethadine."

Karen groaned.

"The good news is you're alive and will heal."

"Ba news?"

"You don't have any secrets left."

Karen tried to glare at him. She still had secrets. She couldn't have told them everything.

"You still sleep with a stuffed bunny named Eva." He laughed. "Dom gave her to you."

She didn't have any secrets left.

"There's more, um, good news." Davy glanced over his shoulder. "You keep Dom's ID code in your locket."

Karen reached for the locket around her neck, but it was gone. She tried to sit up, but something held her down. She reached for the safety restraint release.

"A little help," Davy yelled.

Tristan appeared beside him. "Shush," he whispered. "It's going to be fine."

Karen glared at him. That locket was her last link to Dom.

"Ly'll give it back," Tristan said. "She needed the code for the pilot."

Pilot? Ly was the pilot.

"Got it," Ly called. "What are you doing?"

"She wants her locket back."

The boys disappeared from Karen's sight, but she still wasn't able to find the release for the harness holding her down.

"Lie still." Ly's voice took control of her muscles. "Here's your locket." A small metal something pressed into her hand.

Karen lifted it up to see the locket with Dom's picture in one side and hers in the other. There were no bruises, cuts, or blood on the picture. The locket was supposed to update the picture when it could. The picture hadn't changed in so long.

"She's dead." Karen let the tears fill her eyes and blur her vision. She didn't want to see that static picture anymore.

"She's not dead." Ly came into view. "I just found her."

Ly's smile, sad and soft, didn't allow doubts.

"She's dead. I saw."

"You were drugged."

Karen tried to sit up again. This time, the world shifted instead, but she was able to see they were still in the little vehicle they'd taken from the palace garage. The front window had converted to a communications screen filled with blue and red shapes over a background of browns and grays. One of the red dots pulsed like a heartbeat in the bottom of one of the blue boxes.

Ly shifted back to sit closer to the screen. "That's Dom, showing her heartbeat. At least that's what I think the pulse means. At any rate, the chip wouldn't send any signal if she were dead. That's definitely Dom living up there."

The background moved, and Karen saw the Other pilot watching them. Ly had talked about the Others as people before. Did she really know how to talk to them?

"She's sure the code from your locket is there." Ly pointed to the pulsing red dot.

"Where is there?" Karen didn't understand what the red and blue were supposed to be.

Ly looked up and pointed to the sky with a wry expression on her face. Karen followed her gaze and realized they were going to have to find a way into orbit. This little craft wouldn't make it halfway through the atmosphere.

"Are there farms?" Karen asked.

She could feel the boys thinking she'd gone dark again. So she did still have a few secrets. She'd spent many summers on the farms of Roshea.

"Small communities will have a transport shuttle to get the crops to orbit. The smaller the community, the less security on the shuttle port."

Tristan

They flew in low over the fallow field and landed just behind a tree line. Tristan still marveled at the ease Emalynn had with any sort of flying machine. She wasn't suited to be the heir any more than he was, but she'd probably handle it better anyway and turn the whole government on its axis while she was at it.

"I can't condone this," Darius muttered one more time when the flitter rested on the ground.

Emalynn sighed. "You don't have to condone it. It's the plan we have and it's the one we're going with." She'd said the same thing every time he'd protested since they came up with this plan.

Tristan understood Darius's objections. They should, according to the palace, contact the palace and have either the security force or space defense force attack the ship. Emalynn and Karen insisted they'd kill Dom if anyone even hinted they knew who they were or where they were hiding. Karen was still half convinced just leaving the palace was enough to kill Dom for. Davy admitted he didn't trust government agents to get it right. Tristan hated leaving Darius on his own, but he agreed with Emalynn.

"I get it." Darius turned to Tristan. "You want your adventure, but don't steal the shuttle. You have the authority to commandeer it legally."

"And alert the entire net that we're out there again?" Tristan shook his head. "We'll fix it when we get back."

Emalynn shot him a glare. They still had to deal with the shuttles they "borrowed" to get back to Prime.

"Let's go." Karen tapped Tristan's arm. "Distraction team goes first."

"Are you sure about this?" Tristan opened the hatch but hesitated to step out.

Emalynn laughed. "Oh yeah, as long as you don't say anything, they won't believe it's really you, but they won't be able to take their eyes off you. Happens to me all the time."

"Didn't you just say you didn't want to alert the net where you are?"

Darius grumbled.

"They won't alert the net." Karen giggled.

Emalynn laughed along. "They'd get laughed at if it turns out not to be him, and most people will assume it's not."

"So you are trusting that people can't tell the difference between Tristan and a lookalike?" Dare crossed his arms over his chest and leveled a hard stare at Emalynn.

"Nope." Tristan remembered how many people commented on how much he looked like the prince when he was traveling as Trevor. They looked right at him and didn't notice.

"Context is everything." Karen grinned at him. "Now would you just relax?"

She pushed Tristan out the hatch and they headed off through the trees. She started in on the silly stories she'd promised as soon as they were in the landing field. He didn't believe one word of what she said, but allowed her to make him laugh until he had to lean on her shoulder to keep walking.

"This really worked for you?" He gasped as they approached the hangar door.

"Most of the time," Karen admitted. "It was the cheapest way to get into the clubs. The bouncer spent more time looking at Ly than paying attention to me until she would decide to let us in just on the chance it really was you."

"But I am me."

"So concentrate on not looking like yourself." She pulled the door open and waved him in.

The hangar office had everything it needed to be a shuttle port. There was a chest-high desk directly across from the door, silly plastic waiting chairs, and a security pass-through. He could walk all the way around the pass-through without touching it. So much for security here. It didn't even beep when he passed the entrance. Probably not turned on.

Karen walked up to the counter and knocked. A woman half covered in grease came out wiping her hands on a dirty rag. Tristan became fascinated with a fake fern between two sets of chairs.

"Hi." Karen became all bubbles. "We were just wondering if you had anything we might be able to rent for the parade?" She moved to block the attendant's view of Tristan.

"What parade?" the woman asked with a heavy rural accent.

"Ya know. The parade. We just want to make a float that's going to blow away all the others this year and maybe get our town on the map for something other than our potatoes."

The woman tried to object that she didn't know what Karen was talking about, and Karen got more and more detailed without ever naming the parade they were trying to best everyone in. The more they talked, the more Karen sounded like the woman's daughter. Tristan moved on from the fake plant to the brochures about the latest in farming equipment. According to one, there was a new hover tractor available that would cut the time for fieldwork by twenty-five percent. Impressive.

"We are planning a tribute to Prince Tristan."

Tristan looked over at them but shrugged and went back to examining the brochure rack. At the back, he found one that listed all the tourist attractions for this little town. Not much to recommend it, though not as boring as he would have thought. There was a small museum about agricultural history and the oldest diner on Prime.

A high-pitched whine warned him Emalynn had what they'd really come for, but the attendant didn't seem to notice. Karen kept talking about how great it was to have the opportunity to honor the prince now that he'd returned from his traumatic travels. Karen's skill at telling tales rivaled Emalynn's at fighting. Between the attendant's curiosity about him and Karen's flamboyant explanation, she didn't notice the shadow of her shuttle chasing across the field and over the trees.

Tristan joined Karen at the counter. Time to end the distraction. "Don't tell her everything. Do they have what we're looking for or not?"

The attendant looked at him in disbelief. "Are you...? I mean, you look just..."

"Prince Tristan? I get that all time." Tristan laughed lightly as though responding to some elder's idea of a joke at an official dinner. "No, I'm not him."

Karen laughed, too. "Like he would ever go anywhere without his escort. Especially now. We're just lucky to have such a good lookalike."

"Knock it off." Tristan sighed. "We need to find a base for the float."

"Of course." The attendant laughed, too, but it sounded forced. "What were you looking for?"

"Something to build a float over." Karen started her description of the float again. Somehow she managed to remember what she'd said the first time well enough to nearly copy herself word for word.

"Never mind." Tristan smiled at the attendant. "Sorry to bother you." He tugged Karen's sleeve to get her to leave.

Karen wrapped her good arm around him in a possessive way as they walked out. Tristan felt creepy letting that woman believe he was just a simple boy who happened to have the most enviable face in the galaxy. Maybe she would tell the tale of how she'd almost met the prince. He hoped she wouldn't open herself to that kind of ridicule. Either way, she was about to realize the shuttle was gone, and she'd blame them.

Darius's objections to this plan made more sense now.

They were halfway back to the tree line when a flitter hummed overhead. The shadow it threw over them dwarfed the flitter they'd come in. For two seconds, Tristan hoped it hadn't spotted them. Then it turned and circled back.

"Run."

They took off for the cover of the trees.

Emalynn

Emalynn watched the other flitter fly overhead and make a tight turn over the field. Her heart dropped when she saw the royal insignia on the side.

"That's not a royal flitter." Dare pulled her behind the shuttle.

"It looked royal." Emalynn regained her balance and took a defensive stance against the shuttle.

Dare mimicked her stance.

"The royals never put the insignia on the side of their vehicles." He pointed to the one they'd taken from the garage.

It was the same blue as that flitter circling overhead, but no insignia. Come to think of it, she hadn't seen any insignia in the garage.

"Then why?"

"Computer generated graphics," Dare said. "Security protocol, to make sure assassins and other crazies don't know which vehicles to blow up."

That made sense in a way she could appreciate. The flitter up there took its cues from the net, just like everyone else.

"Who knows?" she asked.

"Only those who need to know." Dare glanced at her. "I don't think your father knows."

Davy poked his head out of the shuttle. "What's—"

"Get back inside," Emalynn ordered.

Davy ducked in.

"We have to distract them." Emalynn stood up to check where the flitter was now. "It's not looking for me."

Dare nodded. "You have a plan?"

"You aren't going to like it." She watched the flitter glide over the tree line again. Please let them be under the trees. As soon as it was out of sight, she took off for their little flitter. She made it into the little vehicle before the larger one overhead came back into view.

"Emalynn." Dare ran after her.

She waved him off and locked the hatches. She opened the autopilot and laid in a simple course that would take the flitter out of sight as quickly as possible, dodge around the little town, and back here to land, since this was the only place she knew enough about to land safely with the autopilot. She added a ten second delay and scooted over to the navigator's side. Opening the pilot's hatch would disrupt the program.

Dare pounded on the pilot's hatch. She could only hope he'd catch on before it got dangerous. When the other flitter came back in sight, slower than before, she hit the run button and unlocked the hatch just long enough to jump out. She lay where she landed, wishing to all the stars their followers weren't smart enough to infrared scan. She didn't dare look up, so she could only guess by the sounds of the two flitters what happened. Since neither made landing, crashing, or weapons sounds, she assumed her plan had worked.

"Emalynn, you stupid—" Dare yelled.

"I'm right here." She pushed herself up from the mud. Now she looked even more like she should be piloting that shuttle.

Any further chastising from Dare was put off when Tristan and Karen emerged from the trees at a dead run. Emalynn and Dare took off, too, in a race for the shuttle. So much for airing it out.

The four of them jumped through different hatches close enough to the same time that it wasn't worth worrying about who won. Emalynn kept running right to the pilot's seat, where she started the launch sequence before engaging her safety harness.

"That was brilliant," Davy crowed while the rest of them huffed and puffed.

Dare just shook his head as he buckled in. He leveled a glare at Emalynn but kept his thoughts to himself. He'd have plenty to say later, and she'd take it. They were already way beyond what he'd agreed to and too far to turn back now. She could only head for orbit as fast as this shuttle could handle and hope the inspection certificate from a month ago was accurate.

The shuttle handled as well as she could expect. The dingy exterior and smelly interior belied a good solid shuttle. Just like the practical equipment they had on Farthing Moon. Why pay for luxuries when you could get something that would survive the hard use? The smell wasn't so bad either; it reminded her of the barns.

"You are crazy." Dare didn't sound as mad as she expected.

"Sane doesn't survive below the citizen line," Davy answered. "What's next?"

Emalynn laughed to herself. Every last one of the plans she'd been involved with growing up could have been considered crazy if you didn't know all the details.

"We have to sneak onto a ship where there are thugs and worse." Karen sighed.

"I don't think we can sneak." Emalynn sighed. "There's nothing remotely sneaky about this craft. I think we can get an invitation."

She outlined her plan to act as though this shuttle were as untrustworthy as it looked. She could adjust the thrusters to make its orbit unstable and other indicators that it wasn't stable enough to reenter the atmosphere. Dare could be the voice since he was, as far as their enemies were concerned, unknown.

"They won't believe I'm a solo pilot," Dare complained. "I look too young."

"You're flying a farm shuttle," Karen said. "Where do you think young pilots start?"

"All the more reason I need one of you as a navigator."

Davy raised his hand. "I'll navigate. This group isn't likely to know what I look like."

"How's that?" Emalynn asked. She would have thought he and Karen were in the same kind of situation.

Davy hushed Karen and took a couple of breaths. "My transfer to Prime was overseen by Queen Treylyn herself." He wouldn't look at any of them. "She made sure I knew she was on the transport."

Emalynn glanced back just in time to see Tristan's nod of confirmation. He intended that to mean they were all safe, but Emalynn saw the possibility that their mother was involved. She kept that thought to herself and accepted that part of the plan. They didn't have anyone else to try, and they still needed to figure out how to hide the rest of them. It wouldn't do them any good to get on the ship only to face their security head on.

Tristan found an access panel with enough space for him to fold himself into. Karen crawled into an unused built-in storage compartment that smelled of rotten hay. She was able to get deep enough to hide in the shadows, especially after dirtying her uniform with the slimy remnants of that hay. Emalynn steeled herself to slide into the undercarriage storage bay where they shoved the inevitable results of carrying live animals into space. She'd have little time once she landed the shuttle to get in there deep enough to not be seen. Unless the stars were against her, security wouldn't look too hard at something like that.

"This had better work." Dare breathed as they set the plan in motion.

"It will be just like in the vids." She grinned at him while the shuttle lurched and shuddered. "They wouldn't dare ignore a distress call this close to Prime. The laws are enforced here."

"You believe that?"

She swerved to put them on a collision course with the transport. "Nope, but they will believe the laws of physics."

"You're crazy."

That might be true, but it worked. Dare played his part perfectly, and she guided them into the ship's landing controls. She dove for her hiding place before the shuttle touched the bay floor. If they were as paranoid as she expected them to be, the shuttle would remain in the tracer field until the bay had been refilled with atmosphere and security ready to board. She wasn't disappointed.

"Oh, thank you, thank you." Dare greeted the security women who came aboard through every possible door.

Emalynn cringed at the sheer number of footsteps she heard above her. The women's voices didn't come through the floor clear enough to make out what they were saying, but Davy and Dare kept their responses loud enough to give her an idea of what was happening right up to them being cuffed and taken from the shuttle. These women were more paranoid than she'd anticipated. Or they were doing more than they knew was worthy of being hidden.

Great, now they would have more people to rescue while they were here. With any luck, they would take Davy and Dare near where they were keeping Dom to make things just a little easier. It wouldn't be that farfetched. As promised, this was just like in the vids. They succeeded in their primary goal, and the antagonists bent their plans just a little. She just had to be patient and the security goons tromping around would grow bored with their duty on the little craft. More likely they would grow tired of the smell and step out for a breath of recycled and filtered air.

Emalynn wished she could step out for a clean breath of air.

Footsteps retreated down the ramp one after another as they finished their search and lockdown of the shuttle. Eventually, even that wasn't far enough from the smell, and they sealed the hatches. Emalynn pealed out of the outer layer of her clothes as she emerged from her hiding place. No need to track more of that muck around than she had to. She tripped the manual locks to ensure their privacy before alerting Tristan and Karen that it was safe to emerge.

"This is bad," Tristan complained as he stretched the kinks out of his body.

Karen struggled out of her outer layer as well. "We needed Dare for this."

"We still have him." Emalynn pulled her tablet out from under the pilot's seat. "See, we can track them."

Dare's and Davy's IDs moved away from theirs and closer to Dom's.

Now that they were aboard, she could get a schematic and follow them through the hallways.

"This isn't going to work." Karen folded herself on the floor. "They are going to kill Dom before we even get there."

"Stop it." Emalynn's voice was sharper than she intended. "We aren't lost yet. Not so long as one of us is free to cause havoc."

Tristan glared at her. "What can we do? If we even think of stepping off this shuttle, those guards are going to catch us as easy as they took Davy and Dare."

"So little faith." Emalynn sighed. Someday they would laugh about this, possibly with their grandchildren looking on in wonder.

She set the tablet aside and returned to the pilot's seat. She brought up the base functions and found the ship-to-ship interface. As expected, the goons here didn't think about this kind of security. Just because they had triple checked safety for one of them to open the shuttle bay door, the ship's computer didn't. Better than that, the alarms were completely unshielded. What harm could she do with access to the alarms?

The bay filled with the klaxon warning of imminent exposure to the void. The guards ran for the exits and the safety of airlocks. Spacers trained to never ignore or question the warnings of a breach. Not one of them noticed the vents weren't sucking in the atmosphere. It gave her a thrill the same as the first time she'd cleared a bay for the crew.

"What's going on?" Tristan leaned over her shoulder to watch the clearing of the bay. "We just got here."

Karen also came, this time with a smile on her face. "You just pulled the fire alarm to get out of a test."

Emalynn shrugged. "They guard the front hatch with lasers and goons. They remember to close the back hatch. Some remember to put sensors on the main windows. No one thinks to guard the plumbing."

"You could have been so much more trouble in school."

"And risk getting expelled?"

Tristan looked back and forth between the girls, then shook his head. "Now what?" Karen asked.

"Trick the air locks into thinking there's no air over here, then find a hatch we can trick back and we'll be in."

Tricking the airlocks wasn't hard. She'd done that just as often as she'd cleared a bay. Smuggling crews didn't generally care about getting off the bay, only in getting cargo from one shuttle to another without being seen so they could pass inspection.

Karen punched her shoulder. "This isn't a school prank."

Emalynn rubbed her shoulder. "It never was."

Karen had a point. The stakes here were higher even than a smuggling run. If caught, the brig would be the least of their worries. She sighed and dug deeper into the background functions that were unguarded.

"Of all the stupid..." she grumbled as she altered the ships ID to her own ID number. That would get the attention of a certain chief of security who just might give her points for creativity.

Karen

Karen tried to see what Emalynn complained about. She really should have paid more attention in computer systems. All she could tell was Emalynn was playing with base commands.

"Your ID?" Tristan asked.

"Would yours catch her attention better?"

Tristan shook his head. "You're right. She'll be watching for you."

"Who?" Karen asked.

The Other filled the screen before either twin could answer. Moments later, there were blue dots and red dots in two pyramids covering her image. Then one of the blue dots in the second row changed places with one of the red dots.

"What's that?" Karen asked.

Emalynn sighed. "The Other wants an ambassador, I think."

"Tell her yes," Tristan said.

He had to be crazy. They couldn't do that. Emalynn said as much when she finished giving him a sour look.

"We're the heirs. Father will have to honor our commitment." Tristan smiled. "Besides, I want to go."

That boy was totally crazy. "Why would you want to go with them?" Karen asked.

Tristan shrugged. "I've been fascinated with them since I was little. Now that I'm not the heir, I'm going to need something to do that isn't being the most eligible bachelor in the universe."

Karen laughed and shook her head. "I don't get you."

"What's not to get?" Tristan asked.

"You're fine with giving up the most envied position in the galaxy and, more than that, leaving humanity behind to go hang out with…" She waved at the screen. "That."

"I never asked to be prince or heir or any of that, and it's not as fun as the vids make it out to be."

"It's not just the vids that make it look fun."

"Oh, right. Running for my life across the galaxy is exciting until you actually do it." He rolled his eyes. "And when I'm not doing that, I'm sitting with one tutor or another who's trying to convince me governance is the only subject I need."

"Come on, you two." Emalynn jumped up from the pilot's seat. "Those alarms aren't going to last forever."

"What did you do?" Tristan asked, looking at the now blank screen in front of them.

"I think I told her you'd be the ambassador if she could get permission from Grouse." Emalynn grinned at her brother. "She's as tenacious as they come. I'm sure she'll find a way to get through."

"How do you talk to those things?" Karen glanced at the blank screen.

Emalynn didn't answer. She just walked to the side hatch and opened it. Tristan followed on her heels, leaving Karen to scramble after the twins. What they said about twins having a language of their own proved true with these two. She could see how they managed to slip through every net cast to catch them without effort. They just didn't think like the rest of the universe, so who would be able to predict where they'd go?

"Now we take over?" Karen caught up to them near a bank of lockers.

"Let's start small," Tristan said. "Take the shuttle bay."

Emalynn nodded. "If Murphy…" Her voice caught and the thought died unsaid.

Tristan also stumbled a moment. For the first time, Karen had seen their connection fail, and they looked away from each other.

"We're going to need to keep those airlock doors closed." Karen tried to restart the conversation.

Neither twin was willing to give up the dark cloud that had covered them.

"If we can disconnect the atmosphere sensor," Karen quoted Davy, "the airlocks will rely on the failsafe and refuse to open."

Emalynn turned to her with a strangely haunted look. "How did you know that?"

Karen shrugged. "Will it work?" She wanted more than anything to ask what had happened out there, but if she did, she'd lose Emalynn completely. Murphy had been the only boy to break through Ly's defenses. More so than Karen had thought. Something crazy must have happened out there.

"Yeah." Ly shook herself. "We only need to break one and the doubt in the system will make this bay so isolated it might as well be another ship."

"On it." Tristan ran to the nearest airlock.

Emalynn moved toward a bank of lockers. "And we'll need to find different clothes if possible. Then poke a hole in our own defense so we can get out of here."

"How will we do that?"

Emalynn shrugged.

The lockers held work safety suits in all sizes. Karen had seen such things only in vids. Emalynn showed even more of her history in the way she related to these suits and even knew how to get them out of the lockers. She chose one for Karen, then handed a second to Tristan, who joined them as though he'd been there all along. She stepped into hers in the time it took for Karen to figure out where it opened. Tristan managed to get his on and sealed up to his neck with little difficulty.

"You hid your past from me," Karen complained when Emalynn reached out to help her get the suit on and sealed.

"Would you have believed me if I'd told you?"

"No." Karen sulked.

Emalynn gave her a tight-lipped smile and a nod. Karen looked away. Seeing this side of Emalynn made her feel as though her entire life had been a thin veneer. What kinds of secrets would she find if she dug into Dom's past? Or Murphy's? She already knew Murphy had been a spy for some kind of rebel group. Maybe she shouldn't be surprised by that. He'd transferred to Herth because his parents had sent him to live with his aunt who didn't look a thing like him. The transfer was for "behavior problems," but he'd never done anything to warrant that kind of label.

"Are we even friends?" Karen asked.

"Of course we are," Emalynn said. "I've never lied to you."

"You didn't tell me any of this."

"You never asked."

"Girls." Tristan stepped between them. "You can fight about this after we've rescued Dom, Darius, and Davy."

Karen turned away. He was right. They were here for Dom. She could hate then forgive Emalynn later.

Tristan

"There it is." Tristan pointed to the entry hatch for the maintenance tubes. According the map he'd found, one tube connected to the whole array of tubes, intending to let repair crews bypass safety seals.

"Great." Emalynn came over and did something to the monitors on his safety suit. "Can you find a route to the galley?"

"The galley?"

"We'll need weapons, and no one thinks of guarding the galley." She grinned at him over her shoulder before bending to open the hatch.

"Weapons?"

"Knives, forks, anything heavy or sharp."

Tristan sighed. While he'd been learning which fork to use first and how to sit at a state dinner, she'd been having real adventures. Of course, he'd known that all along, so the flash of jealousy took him by surprise.

"If I'm setting the course, shouldn't I go first?" He moved to get ahead of her.

She shifted to make it easier. "Only if you also want to be the first line of defense."

Tristan backed down and let her climb into the hatch. He had to wait for her to cycle through the mini airlock before following her. They waited for Karen to join them, then crawled off toward the galley.

"How long before they notice we're here?" he asked.

"They already know." Emalynn continued crawling without pause. "We have to hope they haven't figured out how to track us."

"If they have?"

"We won't make it to the galley."

He put all his spare thoughts into hoping they weren't being tracked. He did his best to move as quietly as Emalynn did and keep up with her. So much for all those grace lessons. Being able to navigate a crowded ballroom with his tablet balanced on his head didn't translate to moving through these little tunnels. Apparently, cheerleading did. He could only hear his own thumps and bumps as the three of them moved along. By the time they came to the hatch in the galley, Tristan couldn't believe the place wasn't full of guards who'd followed them by listening for him.

He stepped into the galley expecting something more like the castle's main kitchens. The three of them took up most of the space in this little room. All the cooking paraphernalia was hidden in drawers or cabinets. Emalynn found the table knives easy enough and hid almost all of them somewhere in her safety suit. Karen found the serving spoons and slid several of them into her belt. Tristan emptied a small canister of salt into his pockets under the assumption he was more likely to hurt someone else with the salt than have them turn it on him.

"Hey." Emalynn tossed a thin cloth and ball of string to him. "Make some pepper puffs."

He thought of make up powder puffs the publicity people slapped in his face before official events when the cameras might get close. Those were sneeze worthy. Fill one with fine ground pepper and... He did just that, leaving long tails on the little balls to give him more range. Maybe he wouldn't sneeze himself to death.

This time, Karen clinked a bit as they moved through the service tunnels. Emalynn, however, could have been a hologram for all the noise she made.

"Where are we going?" Tristan asked when they came to an intersection.

"The bridge," Emalynn said. "It'll be the quickest way to take control, and they won't expect that."

"Unless they're listening," Karen whispered.

"Oh, thank you," Tristan grumbled.

"Hush." Emalynn held up her hand.

Tristan held his breath. His heart drummed against his ribs. If he could have willed it to stop, he would have. He could just hear the women in the standard corridor running.

"They know we were in the galley," Emalynn whispered. "We have to hurry."

Tristan didn't have time to consult his tablet for the route, but Emalynn moved through the tubes as though she'd lived in them her whole life. He wondered how many times she'd used service tubes as a smuggler. It didn't matter, so long as she knew where they were going now. Then he noticed the marks at every junction. The bridge would be the starting point for any numbering system on board. They just had to follow the numbers down. The closer they got, the more often Ly stopped to listen.

She stopped just inside the hatch for the bridge. Tristan strained to hear any of the normal sounds. There were the beeps and blips of systems, but no voices. He didn't spend much time on ship bridges when they were in stasis orbits. Emalynn's expression had become blank and her body looked almost limp.

"Wait here." Emalynn disappeared through the access airlock.

Tristan shrugged at Karen, who rolled her eyes back at him. They'd have to wait for the door to cycle back to follow her anyway. The sounds of Emalynn fighting reached through the walls intermittently and only in the form of bumps as large objects slammed into the wall. He could imagine her moving through the bridge, dropping the whole crew faster than if she'd been in a vid. Emalynn didn't worry about making sure the audience could see her moves the way actors did. Only this fight had a lot more thuds and bumps than he expected.

Karen moved back down the tube away from the bridge. She had a ladle in one hand and a long serving spoon in the other. Tristan pulled a pepper puff out of his pocket and wound the string around a finger so he wouldn't lose it.

The hatch cycled open just as something else hit the wall hard enough for him to feel it. He threw the puff before he saw the woman's face.

"You breech-born brat." She brought her hand to her eyes. The sneezing took her before she could reach Tristan.

He hit the puff against the wall before following Karen back down the tube. The pepper got up his nose and he had to pause for a sneeze before he caught up to her. A fatal error, as he felt her hand on his ankle. He kicked and connected with something, but she didn't let go.

Karen had made it around a corner and out of sight.

He tried to throw the salt, with no effect. The woman dragged him back to the hatch and shoved him in. Another woman waited on the other side. She got a face full of pepper too. He didn't see the other two until they had his arms twisted behind him. The pepper continued to attack of its own accord. He slipped the grip of one guard when she sneezed several times in rapid succession. The other caught his free hand before he could throw the salt again.

"Can we just space him?" the one holding him asked.

"Idiot." A woman who sounded very familiar stepped forward and grabbed his chin. "Killing the prince is still a death penalty offense."

Tristan looked up into her face but still couldn't place her. The name Veniese came to mind, but that didn't help much. She couldn't be one of the lords or even in a noble family; his tutors drilled those names and faces into him every time they met. She must be a high-ranking employee somewhere, though not in the palace. In one of his aunts' families maybe. He had too many aunts to be sure.

"You just had to come on one of your adventures, didn't you?" The woman's grip on his chin was painfully tight. "Now what am I going to do with you?"

"Let me go." Tristan kept his voice steady.

The woman holding him twisted his arms tighter.

"What are we going to do with them?" another woman asked.

Tristan twisted to look in her direction and saw Emalynn unconscious on the floor. How? How could they have...? There were so many of them, and she wasn't the only one on the floor. She didn't even have the worst bruises.

"Put them in the brig for now, full security," the woman he almost recognized ordered. "I'll have to think of something before that breach of a security chief figures out where these two have run off to this time."

Tristan gave into a fit of sneezing rather than show his smile. Grouse would find them soon enough, with all the messages Emalynn sent. Darius wouldn't have gone this far without sending at least one hint her way. By his count, he'd already been off task longer than she'd allow. He could hardly wait to tell her what these women thought of her security. She'd laugh. She'd probably also laugh about the pepper puff.

He sneezed in the face of the woman, Vanise. He couldn't help it. She was right there, and the other woman had his hands behind his back. That trick earned him another twist to his arms as the woman holding him pushed him toward the door.

Karen remained free. Tristan held on to that one small ray of hope. He didn't know what she could do. He had to hope that any friend of Emalynn's would be at least as creative.

Karen

Karen folded herself as tight as she could against the wall of the service tube. Tristan put up a good fight full of sneezing and swearing until he was shoved in the hatch. She felt guilty for leaving him to fight on his own. She really should've gone back and defended him. Some hero she would be. When it came to it, she was cowering in a service tube while the prince fought for his freedom. They weren't going to be making any vids about her life.

The guard continued to sneeze. Karen continued to hold her breath and grip the spoons she'd taken from the galley. At the time, she could imagine herself fighting off the goons who'd taken Dom. Perfect fight choreography and all the special effects she could think of. She hadn't imagined the fight would happen in the service tubes.

"I know you're there," the guard called between sneezes.

The sneezing made it easier to track her movement. That just made her approach scarier.

"You can't hide forever."

So cliché, and so not helping her cause. Karen wanted to tell her those kinds of lines didn't work, but that would make them work. Instead, she forced herself to loosen up. Ly always told her you can't do anything if your muscles are already working. She separated from the wall just enough so it wouldn't limit her movement. She reimagined her fight scene, this time without the special effects and in the tube.

The woman's head came around the corner, and Karen swung. She got a solid hit on the woman and swung again. The third swing went over the woman's head. The woman collapsed to the floor. Karen swung a few more times just to be sure.

It took more than a few deep breaths for her to calm herself enough to deal with the body lying before her. Blood oozed from several places on her head. Maybe she wasn't dead.

Karen reached out and touched her neck. She wasn't dead. Which meant she would wake up at some point. Karen should probably be gone before that happened. She backed down the tube, watching the woman for any signs of movement, until she got to the first junction. She ducked to the right and crawled as fast as she could. At the next junction, she went left, then down then left again. Right, left, down, down again, and right.

Running randomly through the service tunnels couldn't last forever. Her wrist throbbed with all the crawling, and she needed a lav and a nap, not necessarily in that order. The adrenaline she'd been running on was wearing thin, and she was lost. She couldn't be sure she could even find her way back to the bridge if she tried. Time to look up a map.

She reached for her tablet, but it wasn't there. This safety suit didn't even have a pocket for it. She'd lost the tablet they'd given her, and it had been an expensive one. What would the royals do to her now? She couldn't believe how much trouble she'd managed to get into in so little time. Her mother would have a fit when she found out about this. Losing a royal tablet must be worth at least ten years of extra chores and no parties.

But that wasn't important right now.

Now she needed to figure out where she was and where she needed to go. There had to be some sort of navigational aids, like room numbers or something. There were markings all over the place, only none of them meant anything to her. Numbers and letters all mixed together at every junction, more labels along the walls with a different pattern.

"With two patterns pointing to the same answer, it should be relatively easy to figure out," Ms. Hawth, her advanced logics teacher, told them every chance she could. Karen just needed to remember how the rest of that lesson went and she'd be able to find her way, or at least know where she was. Then she just needed to figure out where the brig would be and she'd be halfway to a plan to get them all free. It wasn't so bad then.

The brig, she reasoned, must be somewhere toward the lower back part of the ship. That's where it always seemed to be in the vids, so there had to be a reason for that. If its location were plot driven, it would move around more. Did they need a long walk from the bridge to the brig or perhaps many obstacles to get there? If the plot needed it to be quick and easy, it would be close to the bridge, but it never was. It was always somewhere down and away.

Then she had the evidence the Other had given them. The little red dot inside the box that Ly said was this ship. The dot started in the middle but moved to the lower back end. Ly took that to mean Dom was in the brig.

Karen followed her logic all the way to the farthest end of the ship. She found a hatch and promised herself there wouldn't be anyone on the other side. Still, she clutched a spoon in her hand for protection.

The hatch cycled open to a semi-dark room filled with pipes and huge canisters. She'd found the engine room, not the brig. She knew it wasn't safe to be out where the standard cameras could find her, but it felt so good to stand up. She didn't want to get back into the service tubes. Besides, part of the plan was to take over the ship. They could do that from the engine room, at least in part. Enough to keep the goons busy until someone figured out one of Ly's messages.

"Hey!"

Karen swung her spoon as she turned. The bowl struck the woman on the side of her head. Karen almost dropped the spoon from the impact. The woman in a ship's uniform stood for a moment before she crumpled to the ground.

"Breach," Karen whispered. This whole situation had gone way past the event horizon. She checked to be sure she hadn't killed this woman. With a sigh of relief, she felt her pulse. Now she had to worry if there was anyone else who would come before she could... do whatever it was one did to take over a ship from an engine room.

Whatever it was, she should hurry about it. If they hadn't noticed her yet, they would shortly. Or at the very least, someone would miss that woman. The vids always showed some sort of control desk in the middle of the engine room. Since this room could have been a set from one of the major productions, she figured they were pretty accurate about that kind of thing. If only she'd paid more attention, she might have known where to find that desk.

She crept slowly around the canisters and pipes, half expecting to meet another crew woman or worse. All she found were more canisters and the control desk.

This was too easy.

She slid the spoon back into her belt. The vids made this part look easy, but then it could be assumed the characters had more than a passing knowledge of how ships work. Karen didn't. She stared at the panel, amazed at how many controls there were. The center of the panel had a dozen sliders all set at different levels. There were more buttons around those and an input board off to the side.

A creak made her jump out of her skin. It was probably just the engine doing engine things. Or it could be the sound of a whole army of goons slipping in to surround her.

She didn't have time to worry about things she hadn't paid attention to in school. She reached her arm across the panel and pulled all the sliders to zero.

Emalynn

The first thing Emalynn noticed was the pain. Everything hurt, especially her head. After the pain came the memories. So many women on the bridge, as though they were just waiting for her. Still, she'd managed to put several of them down. That thought took some of the sting out of her defeat.

When she opened her eyes, she only confirmed she was in a cell again. How many times did that make now? Baba had made it clear that ending in a cell just wasn't a good option. Now here she sat again, just like...

She jumped off the bench to get away from those memories.

The cell had uniformly white walls all the way around. No window wall meant they were using reactive glass. So the guards could see her, but she couldn't see them. It also meant she didn't know anything more about this brig than that it was a brig. Which wall faced the command center or how many cells in the pod? Knowing that much would give her something to plan with.

She also needed to know how many pods there were and if there were other prisoners, and if so, who were they? She didn't even know if she was in the same pod with Dom or Dare. She could only hope Tristan and Karen were still out there figuring a way to get the rest of them out.

What would Baba think of her now? After all that training and learning, and here she was stuck in a brig, waiting for a couple of untrained kids to get her out. Or she was waiting for the chief of security to notice her messages and come get her out. Either one would be bad. If Grouse came to get her, she'd never get this kind of freedom again, and Dare would lose his position in the guard. Great, she'd gotten them all into more trouble than she could get them out of. Now she understood why Baba never wanted to take more of a crew than she had to.

She started the warming meditations to ease the pain in her muscles. Breathe in, breathe out, and stretch. Breathe in, breathe out—and everything went dark.

A moment later, the emergency lights came up and everything looked different. The wall in front of her had become clear, revealing the observation desk for the pod. There were only five cells in the pod, and directly across from her stood Dare. In the cell next to him, someone was curled into a tight ball on the floor. The next one down held Davy. In the middle were two guards with stunners drawn pointing them into each of the cells in turn. They were well trained but caught off guard.

"Ly." Dare knocked on the glass. "Leaning donkey"

"What? Oh!" Of course, the strongest press in the forms. She set herself near the wall and pressed. The reactive glass bent under her strength, but not enough. She pushed her toes into the glass and tried again. It creaked a bit and caught the attention of the guards but still didn't break. She turned her foot so she could get even closer and pushed again. A few cracks appeared in the glass. Now one guard had her stunner pointed directly at Emalynn, as though that would scare her. The other had hers aimed at Dare. Emalynn grinned at Dare and shifted her front leg to an awkward angle to get her hip as close to the glass as she could and pushed again.

The glass shattered outward, forcing the guard to cover her face. Emalynn used her momentum to attack. Things went weird when gravity disappeared. She was able to snag the woman's uniform and pull her toward the ceiling with more force than the woman could control. Dare had the other guard unconscious by the time Emalynn regained control of her floating.

"Hey, let us out, too." Davy tapped at his window.

Emalynn pushed off the ceiling, aiming for the control desk.

"I didn't do anything!"

Dom's scream pulled Emalynn's attention enough that she missed the desk and bounced off the floor. She caught the edge of the desk on her way back and was able to spin herself around to face it properly. With only emergency power, there wasn't much she could do.

"Look for the manual release." Dare floated down to join her. "It'll be a lever, probably—"

"Found it." Emalynn pulled at the lever that was hidden under the desk. "It's stuck."

Dare put his hand over hers and braced his knees against the edge of the desk. Emalynn took a similar position. Together they were able to unlock all the cells.

"I didn't do anything," Dom cried. She had uncurled herself and was trying not to float out of her cell. "I didn't do anything."

Emalynn looked for Karen and Tristan. She found Tristan in a tight ball, with his face buried in his knees, floating about a foot above the slab in his cell.

"Tristan." She pushed herself toward him. "Tristan, I'm here."

He didn't respond. He didn't even flinch when she ran into him. She managed to turn just enough so she hit the wall first.

"Tristan, it's all right," she whispered to him. "I'm right here."

He started shaking but loosened his grip on his knees.

"I'm here, Tristan. I'm here and there's no bomb." She reached up to push them away from the ceiling. "There's no bomb. No one's going to die."

"You're dead," he whispered so quietly she almost didn't hear him.

She had to swallow hard to keep from laughing. "Not yet. They haven't killed me yet." She spoke just as softly as he had.

She could feel him relax as her words broke through the horrors he'd imagined. She held him while he came back to reality and let his tears drip out into the room.

The lights came back on. That's all the warning they had that gravity would return. Emalynn landed on her back with Tristan on top of her. Glass shards rained down around them.

"Are you okay?" Dare asked while helping Tristan up.

Emalynn brushed the glass away before levering herself up. She thought a quick thank you to the stars that they were in artificial gravity. She didn't need any more bruises than she already had. A second thanks for the safety suit when she saw how much of the glass she'd landed on.

"I'll be fine when we get out of here."

Dare smiled at her. "How injured are you?"

"Nothing's broken and I can walk on my own." She winced as one of the bruises flashed with pain. "I'm good enough to keep moving."

He nodded. "Do you have a plan?"

She shook her head. "For now, get out of here."

They all looked like they could use a good hot shower and a soft bed. Davy had his arm around Dom's shoulders, leading her as though she couldn't find her way on her own. Or maybe she wouldn't follow them any other way. Emalynn's stomach twisted around the thoughts she refused to think. She'd seen that before, but now wasn't the time to deal with it. Just keep her moving and get her help when they could.

"Where's Karen?" Davy asked.

Good question. "In the middle of the chaos, I hope."

Karen

Karen was wedged between two large pipes with a mass of wires still clutched in her left hand. It took some effort to open her hand and let the wires fall away. She could still see the open panel on the control desk for the main engine where she'd grabbed the wires. The broken ends were still dangling out.

"Heh, this ship isn't going anywhere for a while." She smirked.

Score one for the amateur, though she could maybe have chosen a less painful way to sabotage the ship.

Karen unwedged herself from between the pipes, feeling like she'd been through one of the hardest practices Ly could think up and forgot to stretch after. She stretched out the worst of the kinks.

"Karen." A voice she didn't recognize echoed around the room. "We know you're in here."

No, you don't. Karen backed against the pipes she'd just pulled herself out of. The gap between them wasn't so narrow if she went in sideways.

"Enough fooling around. Come out before you get us all killed."

Karen slid between the pipes. She could hear several people moving around the room, but not where they were. All the pipes and things made the sounds bounce around. On the plus side, it would make any sounds she made equally hard to trace. She just had to stay out of sight long enough to find a maintenance hatch.

"Spread out and find her."

Karen slid between more pipes, for once thankful for her slight frame and less-than-voluminous breasts. She slid between more pipes, farther from reach. The goons Veniese liked to employ wouldn't be able to reach her, even if they found her. It would still be better if they didn't find her.

She came to the end of the maze of pipes. Naturally, there would be a limit, but on this end, the room didn't get good lighting. She must be at the edge of the room. She could see the hatch she wanted a little farther from the pipes than she liked. She slid back into the pipes to consider her options.

"We know you came to find Dominique." The voice continued. "We can take you to her."

By the void, they knew how to tempt her. So cliché yet so true. They weren't lying; they'd take her to Dom, but she'd be their prisoner. As a prisoner, she wouldn't have to lie to Ly or try to make her do things she didn't understand. What good did it do be there? On the other hand, she couldn't be sure they'd keep them together or even alive.

Karen put her faith in her friend. She made a dash for the hatch. She didn't feel safe, so she crawled as far and as fast as her battered body would take her. She'd gotten herself lost again before the adrenaline wore off. She found a nook where she could curl up out of the way and think. She needed to find Emalynn or for Emalynn to find her, but anything she did could lead the goons to her as easily as her friend.

She wished she could contact the Other and have her tell Emalynn where she hid. The problems with that were many. Contacting anyone would lead the goons to her. She didn't know how to contact the Other. Even if she did, she didn't know how to talk to her, and on and on. It was all just a fantasy.

She had nothing to go on. She didn't know where to find the brig. If that was even where Dom would be. They'd kept her locked in an ordinary room on the cruise ship to Prime. For all she knew, they were doing the same to Dom. Dom might not want to be rescued.

"I didn't do anything."

Dom's voice came from everywhere at once. Karen sprang to full alert. The first real proof that Dom was alive, and it could be just a figment of her imagination. No, she'd really heard her and other voices much too quiet for her to identify.

"I didn't do anything," Dom cried again.

Karen bit her lips to keep from yelling back. Dom wouldn't be yelling like that if it were Ly with her. She had to tell herself she couldn't do anything for Dom if she were captured, too. She wasn't sure if she believed it. She curled up in her little niche and tried not to think about all the ways she could make things worse.

She woke swinging, but Ly caught her wrist and put a hand over her mouth.

"Come on. We have Dom," Ly whispered.

Karen nodded and pushed Ly's hand away from her mouth. "How did you find me?"

Ly smiled. "We traced your ID chit. It's amazing what Davy can do with a computer."

Karen rubbed the little bump on the back of her left hand. It had been there for as long as she could remember. "It's that easy?"

Ly shrugged and started crawling away. "If you know the code."

Karen followed. She had so many questions and no words to ask them with. She tried to be as silent as Emalynn moving through the tubes. How did she do it? More importantly, she wanted to know about Dom. She needed to know her lover would still love her and any damage would heal. She needed to know they would be able to resume their lives when all this was over, even though she knew that would be impossible.

"Karen." Emalynn stopped beside a hatch. Her voice had that soft quality of someone about to say something painful.

"Don't tell me she's dead." Karen could feel every muscle in her body tighten as she thought of the worst.

"She's not dead." Emalynn slid over to put her arms around Karen. "She's alive and will stay that way, but she's not well."

Karen felt like all the air had been sucked into the void. Everything went cold.

"Listen, Karen." Emalynn pulled her close. "She will get better. Right now, all you have to do is love her."

Of course she loved Dom. She always loved Dom.

"Don't try to talk to her."

Don't what? "What's wrong?"

Emalynn gave her a squeeze. "She's just not ready to talk yet. We're going to have to ask you some tough questions, though. Try to stay calm."

"What are you saying?"

"I'm saying, for her sake, you have to hide your emotions." Ly looked way older than she should.

Karen wanted to kick and scream and tell her to make it all better. She wanted to cry that this was all her fault. If she said it, Ly would believe her, and it wasn't true. Ly didn't invite them to the palace; King Levon did. She didn't torture them; that was Veniese.

"Promise me she'll get better." Karen barely breathed the words.

"I promise."

"And when we get back, you tell me everything."

Ly gave her a sad grin. "I'll answer all your questions."

It wasn't quite the same, but close enough.

Karen nodded her agreement and Ly opened the hatch. Karen crawled into the little space and waited for the doors to cycle her through. She held her breath the whole time as the seconds stretched into years. She wanted to see Dom, of course she did, but she was scared by what Emalynn had said.

"I didn't do anything." Dom had her arms around Karen's neck before the hatch cycled all the way open. "I didn't do anything."

Karen let Dom pull her from the hatch and hugged her back as hard as she could. "I'm here. I love you." Karen reveled in her lover's arms.

Dom pushed her back by the shoulders. "I didn't do anything." She looked directly into Karen's eyes, searching for something.

"I know," Karen whispered and leaned forward to kiss her.

Ly said not to talk, but there were more ways than talking to tell a lover they were missed and you were sorry for everything, even the stuff that wasn't your fault.

Karen lost herself in feeling Dom's presence. Her hips, her hands, her lips all argued against this being just a dream. If it was just a dream, Karen didn't want to wake up. She would never let Dom out of her sight again. When she had to close her eyes, she'd have an arm wrapped around her.

"Enough, you two." Darius pulled her back. "We aren't safe yet."

Karen tore her eyes away from Dom to glare at the boy.

"He's right." Emalynn pulled her attention. "This room won't stay off the sensors for long."

The room, it turned out, was a small office, with several terminals around the walls and a main desk in the middle. Davy and Tristan were huddled under the desk, doing something to the wires. They had pulled out a tangle of colored cables and circuits, but unlike her, they were carefully disconnecting them and reconnecting them in different configurations.

"We have to know what we're dealing with." Dare waved to an oversized chair.

Karen knew they were right. "I don't know what to tell you."

"Sit." Emalynn pressed them closer to the chair without touching them.

Karen kept a tight hold of Dom as she shied away from their friend. She didn't like Ly in this guise; she was too much like the goons out there who didn't think anything of kidnapping and torture of underage kids. She hated that she was two months older than Ly and felt like a kid to her adult.

"What do you know about the woman who took you?" Emalynn backed away as soon as they were seated.

"I didn't do anything," Dom yelled at Ly.

Karen pulled her in closer. "Only that her name is Veniese."

Emalynn and Dare stood in almost identical poses and waited.

"Deliah, the one who told me what to do, answers to her. She's scared of Veniese. They all are."

"Why did they need you to control Emalynn?" Dare asked.

Karen shrugged. "They never said anything about why. Just that if I didn't get Emalynn to do certain things, Dom would suffer."

Again they waited. Ly had that way of just standing there, leaving the space for people to think more about their answer. Karen never thought she'd seen anyone else able to match her the way Darius did. Void, it worked.

"Veniese isn't the one in charge. She answers to someone else, but I've never even heard her voice." Karen remembered Deliah's threat once that if she didn't comply, someone worse than Veniese would get involved. "She, the one really in charge, must have real power or money or something. The way Deliah and Veniese relate to her is like a lord in some overwritten vid plot."

"Those plots aren't as overwritten as you think." Tristan poked his head up from the desk. "Anything else you know about this lord?"

"I thought we stopped Lord LeBlanc." Emalynn dropped her silence as power stance.

"He's not the only uncle who didn't like that I was heir."

"Well, you aren't heir anymore."

"Yes, thank you."

"So who liked you as heir?" Emalynn asked.

Tristan shrugged. "Almost as many as who didn't like me."

"I hate our family," Emalynn grumbled.

Karen couldn't blame her for that. She had some less-than-admirable aunts and uncles that she didn't like seeing at family gatherings, but none that had tried to have her killed or worse.

Emalynn

Emalynn forced herself to stop glaring at Tristan. It wasn't his fault their aunts and uncles were all power-hungry black holes ready to eat the galaxy and everyone in it just to increase their control. Worse than that was their habit of using that power for expressly evil purposes that left those without with even less than they'd had before the most recent power play. How many poor people were harmed in their attempt to stay alive?

Full power came back online with a blare of warning sirens.

"What is all that?" She turned to the boys who were still digging into the wiring of the control desk.

"Sorry." Davy reached up and hit something. The noise died except for the ringing in her ears. "I didn't expect them to get the power up so quick." He flashed a quick grin at her and ducked back below the desk.

Emalynn sighed. They still didn't have a good plan to get off this ship. Their enemies had better repair skills than they anticipated. What more could go wrong?

The security locks on the door slammed into place, sealing them into this room with a deadly final sound.

"What just happened?" Karen cried. She and Dom had panicked looks on their faces.

Davy and Tristan laughed. "It worked," Tristan cried.

"What worked?" Emalynn did glare at him this time.

He ignored her anger by continuing to giggle with Davy.

"We just..." Davy laughed. "Told the ship it's infected. We sent it into biological lockdown."

They fell into each other's arms laughing. Dare shook his head and rolled his eyes for her benefit. Karen and Dom had gone back to snuggling.

"How is that going to help?" Emalynn asked.

This time, Tristan controlled his laughter enough to answer. "It's a fake reading that we'll be able to change at every door. We'll be able to move about, but they'll be stuck unless they have a hacker who can figure out what we did."

They were laughing again.

"Crud and double crud," Emalynn whispered. So they were all locked down in a ship that would broadcast plague codes and was otherwise as useful as an empty can of soup.

If she were honest with herself, this would be perfect if they had a plan and a place to be to get off this death trap. With a sigh, she went to one of the other terminals and tried calling up the ship's schematics. The main shuttle bay would be off-limits. That would be too obvious. If the goons had managed to get in, the shuttle would be totally disabled by now. There had to be another way to get off safely.

Dare looked over her shoulder. "Call up the heat signatures."

She did and found there were a lot more people in this floating can than she'd imagined. No wonder she'd been taken by surprise on the bridge. Still, she needed to work on her crowd fighting skills. In the meantime, all the heat signatures were stuck in small spaces.

"How widespread is that biological contamination?" she asked of the giggling boys.

"Ship wide." Davy gasped. "I didn't know where we might want to go."

Tristan gasped as he pulled himself together. "Also, it was the best way to disrupt them."

"This will affect the maintenance tubes?"

That sobered them up fast, which was all the answer she needed. If they could convince one door at a time that the contagion had been neutralized, or never existed, they would be able to get an escape pod to release. She just needed to find the larger pods and the fastest route from here to there.

"What do we have for weapons?" she asked Dare over her shoulder.

"Just the two stunners from the brig," he responded.

Not much. Assuming they used every shot with effect, they could down maybe twenty women. The shortest route to a crew-size pod had at least twenty-two women between here and there. They could handle two women without the stunners, but that assumed all the rest of their shots would be fully effective.

"Emalynn." Dare's quiet voice caught her attention more than his hand on her shoulder. She looked up, then followed his gaze to where Dom sat petting Karen's hair. Karen had fallen asleep on Dom's shoulder.

Dom put her finger to her lips. "I didn't do anything."

Emalynn nodded. "That gives us a little time." She spoke quietly to Dare. "We need more weapons."

"Or another way to drop those women." He grinned at her.

Another way? He couldn't mean fighting. As an exercise, that kind of challenge would be fun, but in real life with women who were willing to kill was something else.

"Do you have access to environmental controls?" Dare asked the boys.

They dove into the control panel with the same zeal they'd had when she gave them permission to pull the wires from under it. A few minutes later, they offered their plan.

"We could give the ship a fever," Tristan announced. "We can't control the environment directly, but we could add some specs to the biological database to make it think raising the temperature is the appropriate way to counter the infection."

That might help. If they could convince the ship to raise the temperature high enough...

"Can you raise the humidity, too?" Dare asked. "That will make the heat more effective."

They poked at the control panel some more. "Done," Davy announced. "Every infected area of the ship will be experiencing a humid heat wave."

"This room isn't infected," Tristan said. "The next room is, though, so the locks are still in place."

Wonderful. Now they just had to wait for the heat to take its toll. She watched her own screen. Soon, the heat signatures faded into the background temperature. They'd be running blind. It would take time for the heat to take down trained mercenaries, and these women had that kind of training.

She leaned against the wall and slid down to sit on the floor. She could use a nap, too, if she could stop worrying about her friends and what they were going to do. She'd led them into this, so she'd get them out. A look at Dom cooing like she always did over a Karen who'd stretched herself past her limits summed up the whole situation. They all should have been normal teenagers, and not one of them could be again, if they ever were.

Dare slid down to sit beside her. "It's not all your fault."

She sighed. "I'm still responsible."

"I could have stopped you." He leaned back and closed his eyes. "Grouse expected me to keep you out of trouble."

"I'm sorry."

"I'm not." He leaned forward and looked at her. "Would you feel any less guilty if I'd kept you on the planet even after you knew where Dom was?"

He had her there. Not only would the guilt have still been there, but she'd have hated him. "If you'd done that, we'd be back at square one in finding a compromise about my security."

He smiled. "We wouldn't want that."

They sat in companionable silence long enough for her to drift beyond consciousness. She could imagine them fighting their way section by section through the passages of the ship. Even in her imagination, they didn't make it to the pod.

"Grouse isn't stupid," Dare murmured.

"Hmm?"

"She knew you'd try something like this." He snorted a little laugh. "Not this exactly; she's not that creative. She knew you would figure out where the threat was coming from."

What a strange thing to say. "Is that supposed to make me feel better?"

"Did it work?"

"No."

"Then no."

They lapsed into silence again. This time her imagination had them being mistaken for part of the crew when palace security showed up to rescue them. She shook herself. When had she become such a pessimist? She pulled herself up to sit straight and opened her arms to meditation position. She could feel Dare doing the same beside her. He took his position as her personal guard a little too seriously.

She calmed herself the way she used to when Baba took her on a run and they were about to land. Not much you could do when port officials were doing their thing. Let the pilot handle that. All thoughts were useless. Push them down deep inside. Breathe clear and steady, letting all the tension sink into the floor. Hold only enough energy to keep her position. Only when her body and mind were completely empty did she relax control over her mind.

The ship shook hard enough to bang her head into the wall behind her.

She didn't need to look at Dare to know he was ready to fight, too. They were on their feet before the ship regained stability.

"I didn't do anything." Dom's panicky cry summed it all up.

"It's time to go."

Tristan

Tristan jumped when Emalynn announced it was time to go. He'd barely managed to wake up when the ship rocked like that. Her decision to stop waiting told him he was right to worry. Whatever had made the ship rock so hard they could feel it like that couldn't be good. He wondered if some part of the ship had blown up, but there weren't any warning sirens. Or maybe they'd managed to screw up the ship's systems so much it wouldn't notice a hull breach.

"All right." Emalynn took on her leadership stance. "Let Dare and me lead into each new section. Does everyone have a weapon of some sort?"

Karen still had her spoons, which she shared with Dom. Tristan could find a pinch of salt still in his pockets, but the pepper puffs had been taken. Davy only shrugged. He never had a chance to get anything. Emalynn glanced at Darius, who only shook his head and held up the stunner he'd taken from the guard.

Emalynn produced a pair of steak knives from somewhere and handed them to Davy and Tristan. "Hopefully you won't need them."

Tristan took the knife gingerly, not really sure what to do with it. His defense lessons never covered knives or any of the other weapons Emalynn had made up. He'd taken up laser pistols, but only as a hobby. He could hit any target he aimed at, but he'd never aimed at another human. Even that time...

The knife clattered to the floor. His ears rang and his vision went fuzzy.

"There's no bomb." Emalynn's voice broke through the din. "Tristan, look at me. There is no bomb."

His eyes focused on hers. They were tired and bruised. He could see a hand-shaped bruise forming on her left cheek.

"Everyone is safe. You're safe."

He nodded. This was different. He had to remember this was different. She was here with him. They weren't arrested. So many things were different; he had to focus on that. Focus on the differences.

"Are you here now?" She kept his focus on her eyes.

He nodded.

"Good." She put the knife back in his hand, only this time with the blade running down his wrist. "Hold it like this, then fight like normal if you have to."

Fight like normal. He laughed a little. He didn't fight. He always had guards around to do that kind of thing for him. He'd learned the stances and forms, such as he did, as much to block the panic of being out of his world as to please first Techani and then Emalynn. If it came down to it, he'd rather run and hide than fight.

He let her pull him to his feet. Darius was leading Davy through a few basic moves. Karen and Dom were dueling with their kitchen spoons. How long had he been taken by the panic?

"Now, go explain to that door that it can open." Emalynn nodded to the door to the main hallway.

Tristan nodded. They had a fake biological infestation to deal with. Davy broke away from his training to join him at the panel beside the door.

"This should work," Davy said as he popped the cover off the panel.

"Of course it will." Tristan said with more confidence than he felt. They'd stumbled on the codes to start this mess in the first place. They'd had to rewire the control desk to give it more authority than it was supposed to have. They couldn't undo it at the control desk, which would have been easy, or they'd release the whole ship. He pulled the sensor chip and disconnected the inputs.

The locks clicked into place. That wasn't right. Weren't they already supposed to be in the locked position?

"Don't worry." Davy had the control mechanism open. "Put the inputs here and here." He pointed with his pinky while holding several other wires in place with the rest of his fingers.

Tristan saw it now. Bypass the sensor chip and the control panel would see what they wanted it to see. The hard part was getting the little wires into the tiny panel with Davy's hands already there. He tried four different positions before he was able to get the inputs where they needed to be.

The locks thudded open, but the door remained closed.

He could feel their eyes on them. He pulled the inputs out and the locks reengaged. Crud.

"It's going to be manual." He told them. "When you hear the locks go, open the doors."

"Crud and double crud." Emalynn grumbled as she put her stunner in her belt.

"No, we'll get the door." Karen stepped forward. "You need to be ready."

It would be a full group effort, this escape. Just like in the vids. Vid writers used everything they put in. If one of the hapless heroes happened to be a juggler before the adventure started, by the end, juggling would be required to get through one of the troubles. Real life rarely happened that way. Council lords rarely suffered the consequences of their votes. Hapless adventurers usually didn't make it out alive. The only fame they had was when their bodies were found by the rescue agency and the news sites descended on their families.

Here they were, two fighters, a hacker, a prince, and a pair of lovers with serving spoons. Out there were too many trained mercenaries to count in a ship that was falling apart surrounded by the void of space.

"How'd we get so lucky as to be in the right adventure for us?" he mumbled.

Davy laughed. "Find? We made this adventure."

Tristan put the inputs in place and heard the locks thud open again. Karen and Dom pulled the doors open. Emalynn and Darius poked their stunners out into the hall and moved forward with caution.

"It's clear," Emalynn called.

Tristan dropped the wires and jumped through the door right behind Davy. Karen and Dom managed to get through before the door slammed shut with a final sounding clang.

No going back, then. They'd passed the point where they could back out of this a long time ago.

"That way." Emalynn pointed to the safety barrier.

The whole ship had been divided into places no longer than about twenty feet. "How far do we have to go?" Tristan asked.

"About four hundred feet in that direction and then down two decks." Emalynn took her position by the barrier. "Then that way about a hundred feet to get to the escape pod."

Divide all that by twenty. This process would take a while. Tristan took a deep breath and went to join Davy at the panel. He pulled the leads and waited for Karen and Dom to signal they were ready. The only difference between the door and the safety barrier was the door was lighter.

The mercs on the other side of the barrier had plenty of time to notice they were coming, and Emalynn still got off the first shot. One more shot before they called "clear." Tristan didn't expect to see four mercs laid out on the floor.

"The fever worked." Darius clapped him on the shoulder.

The fever, that was why he was feeling so warm. They should have toned it down a bit before they left.

Emalynn

They made good progress through the ship. They'd been able to pick up more energy packs for the stunners from the mercenaries they disarmed on their way through. They used fewer shots than Emalynn'd expected. The fever had taken its toll on the crewmembers far better than she expected. Mostly because the mercenaries were too stubborn to take off their gear and suffered more because of the environment. Emalynn had already abandoned the safety suit. She'd die instantly if there really was a hull breach, but she'd take her chances that the hull was sound. If it wasn't, that safety suit would only delay her death by a few hours anyway.

Baba would hate hearing her think like that. She would hate that Emalynn had gotten herself into a situation like this where she would have to worry about whether she could make if off a failing ship before a hull breach. She wasn't really happy with all of this either. Nor was she happy with the fever. Despite the progress they were making, they were beginning to fail from the heat.

"Come on. Let's keep going." She gasped. "The next section should have the level shaft."

Something banged on the other side of the seal. Emalynn could feel the fear in her companions. It mirrored her own.

"What was that?" Karen had her spoon held up in front of her as a defense.

Emalynn could only shake her head. She'd been listening to the sounds of the ship all along. People were trying to move through the ship. Others were just trying to communicate. These sounds were different. Not the wild flailing of the mercs who were stuck in their own ship. Darius's shrug didn't help either. She found herself gripping the stunner too tightly.

"Ow." Tristan jumped away from the control panel, shaking his fingers.

Davy dropped his part of the operation just as fast. "Dusted thing is overpowered."

"How is that possible?" Emalynn asked.

The locks on the seal thudded open before he could reply. Emalynn pushed Karen and Dom behind her and aimed her stunner at the point where the seal would open. Dare had done the same with Tristan and Davy. What a sight they were, half naked, trying to defend themselves against a hoard of raging barbarians with kitchen implements. Someday this would be funny.

The seal began to shift and all thoughts of anything other than what or who was on the other side. She had to remind herself to breathe slow and even. Time slowed with every breath. By the time the seal opened far enough for her to see the boots of the women pulling it open, she was sure she'd aged at least ten years.

Darius put up a hand to keep her from firing as soon as she got a clean shot. She didn't know what he saw that gave him doubts about their attackers. He didn't alter his aim at all, or relax in anyway. So he only had doubts.

She had her doubts, too. They didn't have the strength for a real fight. Whoever they were, they'd be stronger than her little group. The only chance they had to remain free would be to surprise their attackers.

Surprise is a funny tactic. There were many ways to pull off a surprise, but each would only work once. Anyone could think of shooting before the door was all the way open. Any good commander would expect that tactic and have trained to counter it. So far, the only weakness she'd seen in these women was their creativity. They followed orders the way adults do without thought to the other ways things could be done. For example, opening this seal. It should have been done by now.

Or her sense of time had stretched from the adrenaline, heat and stress.

She refocused on the opening of the seal, and time returned to normal. The seal slid back into its slot, revealing three women in black full dive suits with laser rifles pointed into the room. A fourth woman had her rifle over her shoulder after opening the seal.

"Identify," Dare ordered without lowering his stunner.

The stunners would be useless against dive suits. Those things were designed to protect you from the vacuum. So either the ship was in worse condition than she thought or these weren't members of the crew.

The women lowered their weapons. The one in the middle opened her palms to Darius before slowly raising her hands to open her helmet. Emalynn followed Dare's lead and didn't move. The face she revealed didn't tell her anything other than she was willing to expose herself to the environment.

"Your Majesty." She turned her attention to Emalynn. "I'm Captain Corsain of Prime Guard. We received your message."

Emalynn kept her stunner trained on this woman. "I sent my message to Chief Grouse of the palace guard."

"Of course." She still had her hands turned palm out. "The palace guard doesn't have jurisdiction in orbit."

Naturally, Emalynn held in her sigh. Politics and jurisdiction would be as much a way of life here as it was a game in the outer colonies.

"Are you here to rescue us, then?" Emalynn let her voice drop just enough to show her annoyance. She could play this game if she had to.

The woman paused before answering. Her eyes flickered just shy of actually looking toward Dare. "We've come to offer assistance."

Emalynn relaxed and let her stunner drop from firing position. "You are law enforcement?"

The woman nodded.

"I would like to report a crime." She tried not to smile at Dare's failure to keep a straight face as she described the actions of the crew in legal terms.

Emalynn took all her words and phrases from the most popular of the police procedural vids. She talked mostly about what had been done to Dom and Karen, pulling out all her best vocabulary words like "coercion" and "unlawful detainer." She couldn't look at Darius through the whole thing, because she might burst out laughing.

Captain Corsain wasn't much better with her looks of disbelief. Clearly, Grouse hadn't told the Prime Guard everything.

"Thank you for your report." Captain Corsain kept her lips in a tight smile. "We'll investigate this thoroughly. In the meantime, would you like to get off this ship?"

Emalynn could play up the sarcastic princess bit, but getting off the ship sounded like a better idea. The heat of the fever was getting to her.

"We should maybe find a way to reset the temperature controls." Tristan came forward. "I don't want to kill anyone."

"You did this?" One of the other women had removed her helmet so she could speak. "How did you gain access to the environmental controls?"

"Rosa!" Captain Corsain yelled.

"It's fine." Emalynn stopped the dressing down before it could annoy her. "We didn't. They're too well guarded for good reason. They"—she waved at Tristan and Davy with a smile—"found a loophole in the biological data-base and told the ship it had an infection and the only way to clear it was to raise the temperature."

She let all her pride in their accomplishment show through. The Prime Guard mirrored that pride with their own reassessments of this mission. Captain Corsain's expression said, *I don't know if I want these kinds of people running loose on my ship.*

They said nothing more about it as they led them through a series of disabled seals. Emalynn saw wedges shoved into the doors to prevent them from resealing the ship. It seemed odd if the guard didn't know about the fake biological. The crew mercs they saw along the way were left to lie where they fell. With each new body, Dom complained louder that she hadn't done anything.

Tristan took it all in stride, as though it were all normal. Maybe it was. People treated them with undue respect and care just because they were royal. Dare, however, had slid into his ready stance as they walked. His eyes shifted from one guard to another, all but ignoring anything else in the room.

"How many soldiers are with you?" Emalynn asked.

"Majesty?" Captain Corsain asked.

"How many?"

"The four you see, two more guarding the access hatch." She clipped her words short.

Dare gripped his stunner and shot her a look of worry. It matched her thoughts. Something felt off about this, but they didn't have any other options. This ship, if they could get it back to healthy, was filled with mercenaries out to destroy them. The guard ship would at least be space-worthy and pilotable.

"Just six soldiers?" Emalynn asked lightly. "You thought that would be enough to take on a full transport?" She glanced at Tristan. "You have some faith in your people."

The guards at the access panel jumped to attention when they came around they corner. The self-contained environmental controls of their dive suits would be strained by the fever. Those things were designed to keep you warm in the cold of space. They weren't as far gone as the mercs, which could be a blessing or a curse. She couldn't tell if she should trust these women, or were they more mercs taking advantage of a situation? If they really were Prime Guard, she had a problem with their assumption that she would just follow them because they said so.

Tristan would. He still hadn't really learned the hard lesson that he couldn't trust people just because they wore a uniform he recognized. He would step into that transfer tube in those clothes that wouldn't keep him warm in a properly regulated ship if they told him to. She grabbed his arm before he did that just because the guards bowed to him.

"Did you bring dive suits for us?" Emalynn asked of the captain.

Of course she hadn't. She sent two of the guards through first to bring back enough suits for all of them. The rest took up perimeter positions around the youths.

"Trust." *Question.* Tristan looked at the Prime guards around them.

Negation, Emalynn responded. "Pilot." *Affirmative.* She pointed to herself.

Affirmative.

She nodded with a smile. "There's a panel. You should probably reverse the fever."

"What—" Dare cut himself short when she shook her head.

She looked at the captain, who smiled back at her. When the captain looked away, Emalynn turned her grin on Dare. She could only hope he'd follow along.

"No." She spoke louder than she needed to. "I'm flying or I'm not getting on that thing."

Dare grinned at her for only a second, then set his face in a frown. "You flying is what got us in trouble in the first place."

"Me flying got us here in a craft that probably needed another couple months of maintenance."

"You need to learn to trust us."

"You?" She advanced on Dare in a way that would have intimidated anyone else. "You're part of this?"

He backed down. She would have to praise his improv and acting skills later. "They're not going to let you pilot."

"They will if they want the honor of bringing me home." Tristan threw over his shoulder. "She flies or I don't go either."

"I didn't do anything." Dom stood next to Emalynn in defiance of Dare.

"I'm with her." Karen took her place on the other side of Emalynn.

When did they all learn to improv like that? They had the attention of the captain now.

"So tell her." Emalynn nodded at the captain.

Dare puffed himself up and turned to the captain. "By order of the palace guard in service of Princess Emalynn, for her safety and the safety of all around her, Emalynn will pilot your ship to the ground."

The captain laughed. "Boy, you don't have the authority to make such an order."

"And you don't have the authority to reject it." Dare lost all his meekness by the end of that sentence. "Let me introduce myself. I am Commander Darius Kenchi, second in command of the palace guard."

Emalynn watched the woman swallow that bitter pill.

"You really ought to pay more attention to the popular vids." Dare continued in a lighter tone. "You'd know Princess Emalynn is an expert pilot and far more paranoid than any member of the palace guard."

She wasn't so sure about that last part. He gave her a good run on paranoia. She didn't mind being known as paranoid, not by the people who thought it was their job to protect her. Or by the people who thought she'd be as easy to manipulate as any other lord.

"I'll let my crew know," Captain Corsain grumbled.

Just then the guards came back with dive suits. She couldn't be the last one off the ship, as she would have preferred, but she wasn't first either.

Karen

Karen gripped Dom's hand and watched the crew of the battle shuttle. Dom gripped back and muttered, too. If you didn't listen to her words, she could have been having a normal conversation. Dom, like Emalynn, didn't trust the women of the guard. Well, not all of them anyway. Dom's focus stayed on the pilot and the captain. Karen's worry focused on a couple of the guards who'd come to get them. The women who'd never taken off their helmets until they were well underway.

"Brace for atmospheric entry," Emalynn called from the pilot's seat.

Nothing happened. The tension around the cabin increased with every passing second. No one dared to move until they were through the turbulence of entering the atmosphere.

"All clear," Emalynn announced. "Estimated time to touch down: fifteen minutes."

Karen let out her breath. She hated atmospheric reentry; that's when most disasters happened.

"That's not possible." A woman in a crew uniform but sitting among the guards jumped out of her seat. She opened something on one of the auxiliary terminals. "Holes, we are in atmosphere."

"Told you." Another woman burst out laughing. "Didn't I tell her to watch that vid of the princess' navigations run?"

"That's not real," the first woman complained.

"It's real." Emalynn kept her focus on the board in front of her. "Please return to your seat."

Karen would have thought Ly would be happier about her grade in navigations. It was the only class she passed because she missed the second half of the semester. All because of that now famous run on the simulator. She probably noticed some little flaw that could have gotten her a better time or better fuel usage factors.

The crew and guards continued to argue whether Ly really was such a great pilot until someone suggested a test... one they could bet on. A plastic tumbler and marker appeared. They passed them around, still joking and arguing about it, but each woman who got the cup made her mark and passed it along.

Emalynn huffed a great sigh and got up. She marched over to the crew's pilot and snatched the cup out of her hand. The whole crew fell to silence until Emalynn made her mark at the rim.

"No fair letting someone else win for my perfect landing."

When it got to Karen, she made her mark at the bottom.

"I didn't do anything?" Dom shoved the cup back at Karen.

"If someone has to win for a botch, better it be her friends." Karen let Dom make her own mark before passing it to Dare.

Someone filled the cup with water and set it in the middle of the floor. Surface tension kept it from spilling from the normal vibrations of a ship in motion. Karen couldn't take her eyes off the cup, even when Ly announced the final approach. The dome of the water jiggled and waved but didn't break. Ly spoke to the control tower with all the confidence of a veteran pilot. All the while, her hands glided over the control panel, and the rest of them felt nothing.

She made it look so easy. Someone should make a vid about Ly's talents that had nothing to do with being princess. Karen felt a wave of jealousy wash over her at the thought of someone else making such a vid.

The only sign of their landing came when the dome of water on the top of glass bounced enough to send a drop of water up. When it landed, the resulting wave washed out enough water to deny Ly her win. The guards surrounded the cup to determine the winner, well not all of them. The captain and the guards who made her queasy gathered by the exit. Tristan and Davy had their heads so close together they might have been kissing. Ew, what a thought. Dare had taken up his post beside Emalynn. Ly bowed her way out of the pilot's chair in deference to the pilot.

"I didn't do anything." Dom pointed to the group of four by the exit. "*I didn't do anything.*"

Sometimes, Karen could understand. Sometimes. Not this time. She watched those women as they conferred with the same kind of low, heads-together fashion as Davy and Tristan. One expected that of boys, especially when surrounded by so many buff women. But grown women, who probably had husbands at home waiting for them, gathered like gossiping boys meant they were plotting something.

Karen tried moving closer to them, hoping they wouldn't notice with all the commotion. They stopped and glared at her before she got close enough to hear anything. She'd shown them she knew what they were about. Only she didn't.

164

"Hey, Karen?" Emalynn grabbed her elbow. "Are you okay?"

"I'm..." The scene had changed. The celebrations and congratulations for a mission accomplished were done, and the crew was beginning the job of prepping the ship for its next mission, and the guards were lined up on either side of the exit. "I'm fine."

Emalynn gave her a knowing smile. "You're tired. You didn't get to rest in a cell."

"Aren't you happy about that."

"All except the part where you're too tired."

"Are you going to send me to bed without dinner?" Karen grinned.

"I'm going to send you and Dom to our suite, and you can argue with Trevor about the dinner part." Emalynn pulled Karen into a deep hug. "Don't forget about that huge bed."

Karen laughed. "And what are you going to do? Take all the blame? You're going to go tell Chief Grouse that it was all your idea."

Emalynn stiffened at the truth in Karen's words.

"We were all involved." Karen tightened her arms around her friend to keep her from backing away. "We should all be there. Dom included. We succeeded. That has to count for something."

"It does." Emalynn squeezed her back. "Please trust me. Dom shouldn't face a cranky Chief Grouse."

Karen stiffened then. Ly should know better than to use Dom against her. That just wasn't fair. When she pushed away, Ly's expression hit her harder than her words. The dark voids in her eyes threatened to drag Karen into some form of hell.

"Take care of her," Ly whispered.

Karen nodded. She couldn't form the words of a question. All the reasons she'd had for not trusting the guards, especially when Emalynn wasn't there, vanished into that one uneasy feeling.

She felt a little easier when she realized the women on the ship stayed with the ship. They were escorted into the welcome center by a different set of women in the same uniforms, then handed over to palace guards inside. So many different guards they couldn't have passed along any messages. She knew that wasn't true.

"Miss Karen, Miss Dominique." A red-haired guard came to them with three more in formation behind them. "You'll come with us, please."

Karen looked at this woman. Like all the guards, she intimidated simply by standing there. Unlike the other, Karen felt no sense of trust for this woman. The women behind the lead guard gave Karen the kind of look a gazelle might see on a lion.

"Ly?" Karen turned to see her friend already surrounded by other guards, chatting or giving orders. "Ly!"

"Miss Karen." The red-headed guard stepped between them.

"I didn't do anything. I didn't do anything." Dom pulled Karen away from the guard. "I didn't do anything."

Karen pulled away from Dom just enough to look around the guard at Emalynn. Everyone looked to see what the princess would do with this commotion.

"Hey, Ly," Karen put her hand out in the sign they used at competition to signal a problem. "Let's trade."

Ly responded with the same sign and a big show grin on her lips. "So you want me to take Dom to bed and you'll go talk to Chief Grouse?"

There were smiles most of the way around. Trust Ly to shift things to the ridiculous and make her play the straight role.

"I was thinking more about a mix and match." Karen bobbed her head at the red-haired guard who hadn't quite given up on blocking their conversation.

"I see." She shrugged. "Could be fun. Hey, Tristan, wanna swap guards?"

"Yeah." He nodded with the same nonchalance she used. He set about lining up the guards with a kind of joy she hadn't seen since middle school, when the arts teacher let them loose in the classroom filled with supplies.

Most of the guards took to the game with resigned indifference. They didn't care what group they were assigned to. A few looked miffed. The red-haired guard scowled so deep it made Karen want to cringe. All the more reason to think the woman had unknown motives that might have kept her and Dom from reaching their destination.

She hated this as much as Ly hated anything to do with politics. Of course this was part of politics. No wonder Ly hated it so much. She'd never had much time for people she couldn't trust.

"Sorry, Your Majesty, but you can't change the assignments of the squad leaders," a dark-haired guard told Emalynn.

Emalynn scowled. Karen held her emotions in check, though she wanted to scream. "It's fine." Karen smirked back at the redhead. "I'll take her for her." Karen swapped a dark-skinned, light-haired guard for a dark-haired, light-skinned one. "That keeps things nicely balanced."

Ly shot her a funny look and made a couple more swaps before declaring she thought the teams were now even.

Tristan shook his head. "Really?" He made one last swap that didn't seem to do anything, as the women could have been twins.

Davy took his time perusing each set of guards. "Well, they're as even as can be with what we have."

Many of the guards rolled their eyes. Let them think they were just silly teenagers. The one who mattered saw what had happened. Karen could only hope they'd disrupted her plans enough.

On the lift, it became clear they hadn't. The red-headed guard punched in a section that wasn't part of the residential wing. Before she could object, the last guard she'd picked touched her lightly on the arm and shook her head. Karen held back but couldn't hide her concern.

"Is there a problem?" the redhead asked.

"She's scared." Karen pulled Dom against her side.

The lift door opened into one of the office floors she'd explored with Emalynn. This one had a garden off one of the main rooms. They'd joked about the way the cameras were blocked. Karen didn't find it so funny now. Blocked cameras made the space great for many things that weren't trysts by moonlight. Karen's mind turned to all the horrible things that could be done if no one saw. She thought of all the things they might have done to Dom, all the things they did to Davy when they were sure no one saw.

What would they do to her now, if they were in that garden and knew they were unwatched? She would find out soon enough. Just as soon as the guards bullied her into that garden, as they were doing. Two of them were doing all of the bullying. The other two stood back subtly, cautioning Karen against any sort of protest.

"Once you've identified Deliah, get out of here as fast as you can," the dark-skinned one she'd chosen whispered as they were pushed into the garden.

These women knew where they were and what they were doing. The instant they were past the last working camera, all pretense dropped. Red grabbed Dom away from Karen with her laser pistol jammed into Dom's side. One of the other guards pointed her pistol at Karen's face.

"Hello, Karen." Deliah appeared ahead of her. "I've been wondering what you were up to."

"She was—" Red started.

"I know where she was and what she was doing." Deliah snarled.

Karen stared at that pistol. Heroes in the vids could ignore a pistol in the face. She was reminded yet again how much she wasn't like a vid hero.

"So, Karen..." Deliah pushed the pistol down and took its place in Karen's vision. "Did you have fun up there?"

"No," Karen said.

Deliah laughed. "Did you keep the princess under control?"

Karen shook her head. Deliah loved these little games, and there was nothing Karen could do about that. Play the game until she could find a way to get Dom out. That had always been her strategy.

"Speak up, dear."

The guard said to identify... "Deliah, you know what happened."

Dom squeaked when the guard holding her dropped from a laser blast. The only thing that saved Karen from doing the same when someone pulled her back suddenly was that her throat was already so tight from facing Deliah. She found a stunner pistol in one hand and Dom's hand in the other. Everything else was moving too fast for her to make sense of it.

"I didn't do anything," Dom whispered.

Karen nodded. "Let's go." She pulled Dom with her back into the main hallway of the offices. She tried to remember all the things Ly had pointed out about security.

Tristan

Tristan followed his guards to his suite. He even let them inspect the rooms before entering himself, despite the deep mistrust Emalynn and Karen had displayed. The game had been fun, but it made it too clear they weren't trusting. Specifically that Karen had a reason to distrust. That should have been clear from the adventure they'd just been on. Grouse would have figured out what they were up to by now. In any other situation, Tristan would have trusted her choices.

"All clear." The lead guard was one Tristan had seen around but didn't know well.

"Good, then you can set up sentries in the hall." Tristan bowed her out of the suite.

She didn't follow his bow. "Sire, you are to be closely guarded."

"Not that close." He waited for her to take the hint. "I'm planning on taking a shower."

Davy hid a smirk. One of the guards had the decency to blush.

"We won't be in your bathroom." She bowed to him to cover frustration.

"Of course not, because you'll be in the hall." He smiled his best I'm-only-faking-it smile.

She stared at him in silence, trying to out-stubborn him. How foolish.

"If you want me to come into the suite, you and all your guards will have to leave. If you don't, we'll just take ourselves down to Security Central and have a nice chat with Chief Grouse."

She pulled her lips into a tight line and bowed to his logic. When they were all accounted for, Tristan bowed Davy through the door and entered himself. "Oh…" He poked his head back out before closing the door. "You'd better check your women. At least one of them is a traitor."

He let the door close but didn't set the lock. The fastest way to get them back in here would be to lock them out.

"How did you know there was a traitor in that group?" Davy stood staring at the door.

"I don't." Tristan laughed. "But with all that's been going on, it's a good bet." He shrugged. "Besides, now they'll be watching each other as much as us and we can have a little privacy."

Davy smiled. "You are very sneaky."

Tristan only shrugged.

They stood there in silence for a while. Tristan wasn't sure how friendship worked, not with peers who weren't angling for his position in the family.

"So I was telling you about code 58." Davy looked away again. He couldn't talk about it while looking at Tristan.

Tristan felt it was his duty to pay attention. He'd known, when he told... When they'd given Davy those instructions that it wouldn't be easy on him. Tristan never imagined half the things Davy could only hint about.

"It wasn't all bad." Davy looked up, though still not at Tristan. "I mean, I got to meet your mother."

"You met my mother in the prison?" Tristan asked.

"I wouldn't call it a prison exactly. It was a room at the end of a long hall that I wasn't allowed to leave." He moved around the central seating area, touching each of the chairs. "That's where she came to see me."

"My mother, Queen Treylyn, came to see you while you were being held on code 58?" Tristan found it hard to believe. His mother didn't seem the type to get into the dirty aspects of her role. He wasn't even sure if checking on the validity of code 58 was her responsibility.

Davy paused. "A lot of people came. I wasn't exactly lonely in there." He clipped the end of his sentence.

Tristan shuddered at the implication. "You're not talking about my mother?"

"No, no, not her." Davy shook his head. "There were others. I'm pretty sure they were sent to make Deliah look good by comparison."

Tristan rubbed his hands over his face. He'd only been gone a few months, yet everything he thought he knew about his life, about palace life, changed. Before, the thrill in slipping his collar was just that—a thrill. Now, it became a survival skill in a place where he couldn't know who to trust. Davy, who he'd only just met, admitted to being coerced into a scheme to manipulate him and Emalynn. Davy recognized some of the women on the rescue shuttle from code 58. Now Tristan knew more about what it meant to be held for evaluation than he wanted to. Conspiracies were a part of life. They always had been, but they'd always been in theory.

"Look." Davy paused in his pace to face Tristan. "I don't mean to say they were all corrupt, but..." He pulled his arms tight around his stomach. "They weren't all there to check my code 58 status."

It was Tristan's turn to give in to the agitation. He stayed by the dining table, circling it and touching the back of each chair as he went around.

"Some of that had to be legitimate." He took a deep breath. "Some but not all. Then there's this whole conspiracy with you and Karen. I get that. You were an easy target." He tapped his way around the table again. "What I don't get is... why there are four chairs at my table."

"What?"

"Four chairs." Tristan counted them again. They weren't the style of chair he'd had before either. These were high-quality Inglehart chairs that only came to mid-shoulder. Even the carving on the back was the kind he liked. He would have picked them, but last time he'd picked furniture, this design hadn't been available.

"What's so 'huh' about four chairs?" Davy blocked him from counting the chairs again.

"Because I only have two chairs. If I want to meet more people for dinner, I go to one of the formal dining rooms." Tristan put his hand on the nearest chair. "And they wouldn't change my furniture without a reason."

"You didn't give them a reason." Davy pulled the nearest chair out and started running his hands along the carved wood of back.

"Other than running off again? No. And that would have been a good excuse to leave me with no chairs, not four."

Davy laughed and moved his hands down below the seat. "Who would have thought of no chairs?"

"Father."

"So this isn't his idea." Davy ran his hand along the table. "Is this the right table?"

Tristan looked carefully. The grain looked right. It was also Inglehart, so the chairs made sense. It would be hard to tell. There, he found the scratch he'd put in it just before he left for his tour. He'd been mad about something Father had said and threw a plate cover in frustration.

Davy pulled out the next chair and ran his hands all over it. "If your father would leave you with no chairs—which is funny, I hope you know—who would think you should be punished with more chairs?"

"Mother probably," Tristan guessed. "She's always the opposite of Father."

Davy examined the third chair. "And her point for the extra chairs?"

"To hold the guards assigned to make sure I don't run off again?" He laughed. "At least until I make the guards miserable enough to beg for reassignment and Grouse can convince Mother I don't really need to be that closely watched." Tristan played up the ridiculousness of it. He hadn't needed guards in his suite since he allowed security to add cameras to the main room to watch him remotely.

"It's silly really." Tristan continued when Davy's face showed the surprise of having found something. "I wouldn't eat with the guards holding me in my room. I'd eat first and let them have the table after. Or more likely insist they go down to the staff rooms to eat and get a sub for the time they're gone. At that point, one guard is just like another."

"Not all the time?" Davy asked.

"No, there are times when you want the ones who really get it."

Davy stopped pawing the chair to raise his eyebrows.

"There are some who get that being guarded all the time is heavy. I mean I already know that I have absolutely no privacy. You get used to the cameras and microphones everywhere and they just fade into the background until you do something stupid. But having someone there so you can see them watch you, well it changes things."

"So who are the ones you like?"

Tristan sucked in a deep breath as the transport exploded over the city in his mind. "Dead." He'd insisted that all his favorites come with him. Such a silly thing to have a temper tantrum about.

Davy pushed the third chair in and had to bump Tristan out of the way to check the fourth one.

"There are none that you like? What about the ones who just pulled our skin out of the fire? Some of them have to be worth something."

Tristan laughed. "They're great for the rescue. I just don't know any of them well enough to say if I want to have them following me around all the time."

Davy grabbed his hand and pulled it under the seat of the chair. Tristan felt where Davy put it. It was rough where the upholstery met the frame. Except for one tiny dot that was smooth.

It didn't feel like a microphone, and a camera there wouldn't make any sense. Whatever it was, it had to go.

"Let's give the extra ones to the people your mother intended them for." Davy nodded at the main door.

Tristan liked the way he thought. They each picked up one chair and brought them out to the hall. All six guards were still there, arranged more for an argument than guarding the door. Davy set his chair next to the door on one side, and Tristan put his on the other. They didn't need to say anything. The two who knew about the chairs revealed themselves by their reaction.

Emalynn

Chief Grouse must have learned her parenting skills from Baba. The lectures about safety and thinking before you act were just as Emalynn remembered. Right down to the small hints of pride for what she'd accomplished while putting so many people in danger. She added a bit about not ditching her security team.

"But I had Dare with me." Emalynn winced at the whine in her voice.

"Dare is not a team."

In the end, all the exhilaration and adrenaline had worn off and all Emalynn wanted was a shower and a warm bed. She wasn't going to get either anytime soon. All of that yelling was for show. The real meeting started when Grouse closed the doors and the privacy lights came on.

"What did you learn while you were out there?"

Emalynn smiled. "That I shouldn't consider myself immortal and take a few more guards with me on my next adventure. Oh yeah, and planning is a good thing."

Grouse gave her the exasperated parent look for a few heartbeats before she gave in to the smile. "And now for the real information."

Emalynn explained about Vanise and that she wasn't the one in charge. She gave all the details she could remember about the number and training of the mercs. Grouse looked impressed with her description of the kinds of damage they were able to inflict. "And I wasn't kidding about that planning thing."

"I understand that you made quite the mess of that ship."

"So I did mention the planning thing. Remember that." Emalynn sighed and got to the real story about how they'd thought it would be so easy to just sneak in, grab Dom, and sneak back out. "That sounds really stupid right now."

Grouse just smiled and waved for her to continue.

She went on, detail by detail, until they got to the bridge. That's when Emalynn's memory failed, probably because of the lump on her head. "I woke up in the brig. I don't think I told them anything they didn't already know."

"Like what?"

"That I'm an expert at being a snarky teenager." Emalynn grinned.

Grouse matched her grin. "I think you've made that perfectly clear."

The security chief only cared about public relations when it made her job harder. To her, the trouble the PR department had with Emalynn provided entertainment.

"How'd you get out?" Grouse prompted.

"They didn't catch Karen," Dare said. He'd sat so silently she'd forgotten he was there. "And they didn't plan for the kind of chaos that happens when you put a stressed out teenage girl in an engine room."

The look on Grouse's face was a horrifying mix of pride, mirth, and fear of what could have happened. Emalynn knew that feeling too well. Now that they were safely within a planetary atmosphere, she could think about all the ways they could have been killed when Karen shut down the engines.

"Holo-walls are weak without power." From here, she could appreciate the beauty of the rain of glass. She could also imagine how it could have been worse when the gravity came back on.

"Sorry to interrupt, Chief," an older woman called through the door. "You need to see this."

Grouse grumbled and opened the door. "This had better be good."

The woman handed over a tablet. There were a couple of indistinct voices, then laser fire.

"When did this happen?" Grouse handed the tablet back to the woman. "Who took point?"

"Thia. She's still out searching."

A crowd of guards circled the chief.

"Monitors?"

"They're taking back passages and other unusual routes."

Emalynn had a bad feeling they were talking about Karen and Dom, but they should have been safely in her suite by now.

"Do we know why they were there?" Grouse kept her voice tight, but Emalynn could see her frustration.

"No, Chief, we're still investigating."

Grouse touched the bridge of her nose with two fingers and sighed. She took a deep breath before turning back to her office, nearly clipping Emalynn in the nose with her elbow.

"Darius."

Dare jumped to attention. "Yes, Chief."

"Please take Princess Emalynn back to her suite. I want you no more than two inches from her hip at all times."

174

"Yes, Chief."

"And you..." Grouse turned to Emalynn. "Keep him close even when you go off on another adventure. And remember that thing about planning you were talking about."

Emalynn nodded. "Karen didn't trust the redheaded team leader you sent."

Grouse whirled on her so fast Emalynn jumped to a defensive stance. "What?"

"In the welcome center." Emalynn glanced at Dare for confirmation. "She wanted to trade guards."

"The team leads claimed you ordered them to do whatever the princess said, except change the lead with each of them," Dare confirmed.

"Oh, breach." Grouse growled. "Get back to your suite, and let Thia do what she does best. Forget about going on an adventure this time."

Emalynn bowed to the security chief and let Dare lead her out of the office.

"What was all that?" she asked when they were clear of the center.

"Not yet, but I've never seen her that adamant." He looked grim.

They'd underestimated the number of their enemy, again. Worse than that, they'd underestimated their penetration.

Dare grabbed her hand. "I know that look. Please don't go running off again."

She opened her mouth to object, but he was right. "Fine." She twisted her hand so she was the one holding his.

They walked in silence, neither one of them noticing the looks on the faces of people in the hall.

"Can I ask you something?" She lowered her voice to keep from being heard too easily.

"Sure." He smiled.

"Why does she treat me different?"

"What do you mean?"

Emalynn stopped walking to look back. "With her, I feel like a normal kid again. Like the way she lectured me back there. No one else does that."

"Would you feel better if I lectured you, too?"

"No."

He laughed but pulled her arm so she had to turn and walk with him or shake him off. She stayed with him.

"She's good at her job."

It wasn't much of an answer. Of course she was good at her job; that's why she was the chief. Emalynn should have known he wouldn't be able to tell her something like that. It was just another piece of this stupid royal puzzle.

"For her," Dare continued in slow phrases, "that means being the one that can tell the king when he's making her job harder by his actions or giving Tristan the codes to lock his door even against her. For you, it means treating you like you expect to be treated. Just enough respect for the fact that you lived alone with a bit of mothering."

"Why?" Emalynn twitched her arm to get him to let go but stayed close. "Why does she do those things?"

Dare stopped this time. Emalynn took two steps before she realized he wasn't beside her. She turned to confront him, but he spoke first.

"Had she asked in any other way, would you have walked out of that office with me willingly?"

She turned and walked ahead to give herself some chance to think. She hated the idea of being stuck with security. It was like she had done something wrong or been caught on a smuggling operation. Guards, cops, whatever were there to prevent you from doing something they didn't like. They were the opposite of freedom, heavier than any collar.

He caught up and walked beside her. Next to her, not ahead to tell her where to go or behind to make sure she didn't stray. He walked beside her like a friend.

"Probably not." She admitted with a sigh. "And not with anyone but you."

He blushed just in time for the lift doors to open.

"That's why she does it that way. She really does care. It's not just an act."

Emalynn looked at him. "Again, why? She's doing her job. Why does it matter if she cares?"

"Because people who care do their jobs better." He turned and caught both her hands so she had to face him directly. "She told me you will make a better queen than we've had in generations because you are who you are. Trust that she will get you to that throne."

They walked in silence past the door that used to be hers to Tristan's. There were six guards standing there with a pair of chairs sitting beside the door. Dare snickered as they passed.

In her room, which was now a whole apartment worth of rooms, she found her wood plates set out in the dining room. There was a small kitchen, though no pans or ingredients. It was ridiculous to give that kind of impression merely as a decoration. She'd ask Trevor how to change that in the morning. It reminded her she liked to cook sometimes, especially when Baba...

Dare was bent over one of the chairs, running his hands over every surface. He held up one hand to prevent her from asking. He waved her over and put her hand on a small button on the bottom of the second chair. Of course, the chairs outside Tristan's room must have the same buttons on them. She took the chair out to the hall and positioned it carefully beside the door with a quick wave to his guards. Dare followed her out with the second chair.

Emalynn went to take her shower while he searched the rest of the suite for more such devices. As if she needed any more clues that she was still a target and always would be. Becoming princess hadn't made her life any safer. It could be argued she was better off being the daughter of an assassin than a member of the royal family.

"Ly," Dare called from outside the bathroom as soon as she shut the water off.

"Did you find more?"

"Yeah, but it's what I didn't find that's the problem."

Emalynn wrapped a towel around herself and opened the door. "Don't scare me like that."

"Karen and Dom aren't here."

Emalynn pushed past him to the second bedroom, hearing the clipped conversation between the guards and Chief Grouse again. She'd let herself forget for a moment. "We have to find them."

"No." Dare caught her by the shoulders. "We have to stay here and wait for them."

"What do you know?"

"That a very trusted member of security is out looking for them."

Emalynn fought off the urge to push him away and go find her friends. Instead, she leaned into his embrace and let him hold her still. Whoever was behind all of this, she promised herself, would suffer scar for scar all the damage they had done.

Karen

Karen could spot the security cameras now that she knew what to look for. In this part of the castle, they were mostly placed to keep track of what the office workers did. Only the ones in the corridors and outer offices were wide-angled to catch people moving about, and they were focused on entry points. Karen had learned how to make her own entry points out there. They slipped into a service panel to use the maintenance passages to slip between sections in the office wing, but couldn't get far that way. Fortunately, the workday had finished so they were able to slip into an inner office. By staying low to the ground, they were able to squeeze under the desk without, she hoped, being seen by the camera.

Dom stopped muttering once they were out of sight of the guards. She stayed as quiet as a mouse listening for a cat and as obedient as a well-trained dog. Dom, who had been her partner in all things, had become little more than a well-behaved child. Karen filled herself with the hope that it could be fixed and lived in that. She pulled Dom close and told her to go to sleep. She didn't know how long it had been since they landed, but that was already too long without sleep. They couldn't stay too long; the office would open again in the morning.

"Karen?" The voice brought her fully awake with the pistol in hand.

Dom still slept on Karen's stomach. Karen caught her breath and listened. Had she heard the voice or was it part of her nightmare?

"Karen Toya?" Yes, a woman's voice from the other side of the desk. She froze.

"Karen? My name is Thia Regayo. I've been a member of the royal guard for sixteen years."

Karen remained still. You couldn't make noise if you weren't moving, and maybe she was bluffing. The name sounded familiar, so did the voice.

"Chief Grouse is worried you won't trust any of us. I'm alone and unarmed."

Easy enough to say. Karen gripped the pistol tighter. This woman should just go away.

"The wall behind you is a media projector. In a moment, Security Central is going to take control of it and show the security feed from this room. You'll be able to see for yourself."

The wall came to life, first showing a standard work platform with the royal seal in the middle. That faded and the screen broke into for sections. Two for the two cameras in this room. One showed a woman with medium-brown hair from the front, and the other showed the same woman from the back. Karen recognized her as the one with all the scanners. The third section showed the video feed from the outer office. It was grainy and dark, but Karen could see the shaft of light from the door to this office. The third showed a heat registry image. There were two warm spots in the room, one about twice the size of the other. Oh, for stars. She hadn't thought about that way of tracking them. The royal guard probably watched the whole stupid run and laughed at them.

"Karen, will you please come out?"

Karen shook her head. She had used the blind spots from the camera in the outer room. A whole team of brutes could be out there and not shown on the camera. Thia herself wore a skintight white shirt with short sleeves, revealing her tattoos, tucked into equally tight black pants. That outfit wouldn't hide a nail file and showed just how well muscled the woman was.

"How do I know you won't just arrest us?" Karen asked.

Dom woke with a start. "I didn't do anything," she whispered.

Karen stroked her hair to keep her calm.

"I can't offer any proof," Thia admitted. "But I promise I won't. My only orders are to walk you back to Princess Emalynn's suite."

"How can you keep us safe, then?" Karen pulled Dom in closer. The last guards were supposed to do exactly that.

Thia laughed. "That won't be up to me. You have a pistol, right?"

Karen nodded, then realized she couldn't be seen. "Yes."

"Then here's the deal. You come with me, and if you see anyone in the halls, you are authorized to shoot them."

Dom tugged at Karen's arm but was looking at the media wall. Thia stood there, with her arms open wide. "*I* didn't do anything."

Karen needed to get Dom somewhere they could feel safe, and Ly's room was the only place in the palace she could think of.

"What if I don't want to go to Emalynn's room?" She watched the front image of Thia for any signs that would tell her if she could trust this woman or not. She didn't have a clue what that would look like.

Thia paused for a moment before answering. "Where would you like to go?"

"I want to go home." Karen said it without thinking. She wanted to go back to the mundane life of fighting over the bathroom in the morning and worrying about whether she got all her homework done.

Thia tilted her head as though listening to something Karen couldn't hear.

"Who are you talking to?" Karen demanded.

"Security Chief Grouse." Thia's answer came so fast it couldn't have been a lie. "She says sending you home tonight isn't possible, but she'll start making arrangements as soon as we know you are safe and comfortable."

Safe and comfortable? "Do you consider a cell comfortable?"

"Not really." Thia's voice fluttered with amusement. "I wouldn't call them safe either, not after your recent adventure. Though there are sleeping rooms in Security Central if you prefer. I'd think the bed in Emalynn's room would be more comfortable."

Karen remembered that bed. Emalynn had mentioned it as well—to convince her to go with that traitor of a guard. She couldn't believe Ly was one of the traitors, which meant she didn't know who all the traitors were.

"Why is it so important to get me back to Emalynn?" Karen demanded.

Thia's hands dropped to her sides, no longer actively showing they were empty. Her shoulders slid back and her chin rose just slightly, giving the impression she had become more formal. Her expression lost all signs of mirth.

"You are her friend. It's why His Majesty called for you." She stopped to take another deep breath. "We are all sorry for what happened, but hiding under that desk won't make it any better. I'd tell you Emalynn will be out of control until you are back with her, but that isn't really true. She will be focused on you until we can show her you are safe. Exactly as she has been since she arrived."

"How can you know I'll be safe with her?" Karen demanded. Ly wasn't focused on her, was she? She was. That was why she'd led them out of the palace and found where they were keeping Dom.

Thia let her head droop toward the floor. "We don't. We're actually sure you will be in danger wherever you are. We would prefer you are surrounded by guards at all times, but that didn't work. Now the princess will only trust herself with your protection until we can clear this threat."

Dom tightened her arms around Karen. "I didn't do anything." She spoke in the soft tones she used when trying to convince Karen to do something.

Karen returned the squeeze. They were right; hiding under this desk would only last so long.

"It's a long way from here to Ly's room." Karen shifted to make it easier to get out from under the desk. "How are you going to keep us safe?"

"I won't," Thia said. "I'm just here to guide you. My team is clearing the way. You won't see them or anyone. If you do, use that laser pistol."

How did she...? The guard who gave it to her would have reported it. That guard had proved loyal.

"How can you trust me to shoot people?" Karen gripped the pistol. She'd never used one before.

Thia smiled. "I don't. I trust my team to leave you with no targets. Anyone who breaks through can't be trusted."

That made sense. Karen wondered if that was a sign she was still dreaming. Either way, following this woman back to Ly was the only way to get a good sleep and maybe some good dreams. She slid out from under the desk, pistol first, and stood to face Thia. Karen pointed the pistol at her.

"You have the safety on," Thia said. "May I show you how to turn it off?"

Karen nodded.

Thia stepped closer to the desk, not around it, and reached out to push a small black button on the side of the weapon. It hummed with a rising pitch until a small light on the back lit up.

"This model needs time to recharge after each shot." Thia stepped back. "It also has automatic targeting. It will make minor adjustments to your aim." She stopped suddenly, her eyes losing focus for a moment. "I won't take it away from her, now or later. Schedule lessons."

Dom jumped at Thia's sudden tone change. Karen stiffened as well, keeping the gun pointed at Thia, though she wanted to shoot whoever was on the other end of that connection.

Thia smiled and relaxed. "Are you ready?"

Karen nodded and pulled Dom closer to her side.

Tristan

Tristan woke feeling more tired than when he'd gone to bed. The room lights were on full, which meant he'd missed the gentle wake up and might even be late for something. He didn't even want to know what was on his schedule this early. He rolled over to see Davy holding the pillow over his head.

Funny. Before his fate-filled journey of the past few months, he thought he would have to get a bigger bed before he could sleep with another person. Then he learned how everyone else lived. Now the same bed felt huge, and he hadn't even noticed Davy sleeping beside him all night. He did notice how many other things he'd been used to were jarring now. Servants sneaking around his room at night to make things perfect for his morning. Someone had gathered his clothes from yesterday and set out a fresh outfit for both of them. It felt like an intrusion now.

This new attitude of his would get him in trouble. He gathered up the clothes and returned them to the closet. He'd pick for himself later.

"Hey, breakfast is probably waiting in the dining area." Tristan nudged Davy. "I'm going to shower."

"Ugh."

"I didn't set the lights, so someone is probably coming."

"I'll hide right here." Davy fluffed the blankets up over his head.

Tristan wished he dared to do the same. His new attitude came with limits. He couldn't just ignore the schedule without fear of Mother's wrath.

He went to the shower and let the warm water give him the energy he didn't get from sleep.

Emalynn, he mused, had her own vision of respect that had nothing to do with bowing. She behaved as though everyone around her were of the same rank. She gave respect where she expected to get respect and withheld it where she didn't get it.

No wonder she and Mother didn't get along.

"Tristan?" Davy's voice pulled him back to the shower. "Your wall is beeping."

Stars, he'd overslept and wouldn't get to eat before his first appointment. "Tell it to show schedule."

He rinsed one last time and let the hot air vents dry him. There were some luxuries he had missed. Not having to step out of the shower wet was at the top of the list. Living by the schedule that popped up every morning wasn't.

"Tutors, tutors, self-defense, and more tutors." He growled at the list of appointments. "All except the self-defense right here in his room. Oh, joy."

"Who makes your schedule?" Davy handed him a roll, still warm and filled with a nut paste he didn't recognize.

Tristan took it and shrugged. "What is it?"

Davy shrugged back. "It's good, and I haven't gotten sick yet. I think the guy said it was Hemnut or something like that."

Tristan took a small bite and let the flavor linger. Let the tutors wait. He couldn't learn about lords and trade agreements if he didn't eat. Oh holes, his first tutor really would teach him about lords and trade routes.

"So not fair," Tristan complained at the wall.

Davy looked up from the drop of nut paste that had fallen on his pajamas. "What?"

"I'm still scheduled with Miss Gingham. I'm not even the heir anymore." Tristan's roll flew from his hand and hit the wall right over Miss Gingham's name. That was a waste of a good roll.

"Seriously, who makes your schedule?" Davy handed him another roll.

"Why?"

"So you know who to complain to when you don't like it." Davy wandered over to the seating area and sat down. "I mean, when I didn't like my school schedule, I just slid on over to the scheduling office and said so."

Tristan dropped into a chair beside him. "That worked?"

"No." Davy laughed. "Mostly they told me it was a required class, but if I wanted to change teachers for that one, I'd have to completely redo my schedule."

"So did you?" Tristan tried to get them to talk about high school, but no one wanted to.

"Sometimes, if it would give me the chance to meet more of the students." Davy smiled but leaned forward. "The point is you have to know who to ask."

The door chimed, interrupting the conversation. "Sire, your tutor is here."

184

"She's early and I'm not ready." So much for breakfast. He might be able to eat during the lesson, but he wasn't going to sit through it in his towel.

"You'll want to get dressed, too."

He headed for the bedroom. "Do I have to?"

"Master Gingham isn't above making lewd remarks, and she's not likely to show you much respect anyway."

"Your classes suck." Davy joined Tristan in the closet. "What do I get to wear?"

"Anything that fits." They could match until Tristan figured out how to gain control over his wardrobe. He looked better in the rough woolens of Farthing Moon than these designer suits. Davy fit the clothes better than Tristan ever would.

"Sire," the guard called again. "Master Gingham says to open the door whether you are ready or not."

"She's still two minutes early. She can be patient." Tristan pulled a simple shirt and black pants from the racks and put them on.

"I think you just earned yourself a test." The guard laughed.

"Good. Then I won't have to listen to her lecture."

Tristan cut off the com with a gesture to the media wall. He waved away the schedule and pulled up the security report from last night. There were forty-two alerts, most of them mistyped access codes or unexpected movement. Then there was a series of alerts coded high priority. Tristan called up the report associated with that one.

"What's that?" Davy asked in a hushed tone.

Karen and Dom were mentioned in the first line of the written report.

"The stars have it in for that girl." Davy caught the back of a chair to keep from falling over. Tristan sank into a chair.

Tristan opened the video log.

"It's time. Turn that off and come sit properly." Master Gingham interrupted.

Tristan ignored her. The scene made his stomach churn. They weren't out of danger.

"This is not an appropriate activity." Master Gingham loomed over Tristan.

Tristan held up his hand to pause the playback.

"Master Gingham." He didn't turn to look at her. "Those are my friends. Do not tell me it's inappropriate to see what happened to them last night."

"You have a lesson to learn." She loomed darker over him.

Tristan stood to face her head on. "Tell me. Is this the kind of lesson I need now that I'm no longer the heir?"

For the first time since he'd met her, Master Gingham backed down.

Tristan nodded, then turned back to the screen and started the playback again. His heart nearly stopped when Karen disappeared from the cameras. The written report gave an estimated track through the sector, finally picking up with the heat sensors in an office that had cooled after the workday had finished. He held his breath through Thia's negotiations and gasped for air when Karen reemerged with Dom clinging to her side.

"Is she all right?" Davy asked.

"Says she made it back to Emalynn's rooms." Tristan pointed to that part of the written report. "I'm not sure that's the same thing."

Davy sighed. "It's not like she signed up for this."

Tristan nodded. They needed to do something to root out all the traitors now. Master Gingham would have to wait. Trade routes had nothing on the safety of his friends right here in the palace.

Karen

From the middle of the giant bed, Karen watched the ceiling shift from darkness to light. If she closed her eyes again, would it dim again and let them sleep in peace? Probably not. She could hear Ly and Dare moving about the other rooms, talking too quietly for her to hear the words. She didn't have to. Ly was complaining about the new requirements she still had to face. Only Ly would think becoming the heir apparent was the worst possible fate. Maybe not the only one; Tristan had a low opinion of the position as well.

Dom twitched in her sleep. She never did let go of Karen, not all the way, which made getting ready for bed interesting. It was a game they used to play. It wasn't a game anymore. How were they ever going to get back to normal? For now, while she still slept, most of the tension had left her body, and Karen could see the old Dom still there. She clung to that shred of hope as tightly as Dom clung to her.

"Karen? It's Dare. May I come in?" His voice should have been muffled by the door, but it sounded like he was already in the room.

"Yeah, but Dom's still asleep." Karen barely raised her voice. He shouldn't have been able to hear her through the door.

The door opened anyway, and Dare came in with a pile of folded fabric. "Clothes and towels for you when you're ready." He ducked into the bathroom and came out empty-handed. "Um... you know you could use all of the bed."

Karen just glared at him. The bed could have held her entire family comfortably, while she and Dom could sleep comfortably in her little bed at home under normal circumstances.

He came around to the side of the bed close to her. "How is she?"

"Sleeping quietly."

"That's a blessing." He kept his eyes on Dom. "How are you holding up?"

Falling to pieces, she thought. She couldn't say it out loud or she really would break.

He nodded in sympathy. "I'll get you some breakfast."

"That isn't your job."

He turned with a smile. "My job is to keep you safe and feeling safe."

Karen almost laughed. "How does breakfast keep us safe?"

"Safe from hunger." He slipped out the door every bit as sly and graceful as Ly.

Karen sighed and leaned back into the pillows. This was the luxury everyone at home thought they were enjoying. Giant fluffy beds with someone to bring you breakfast in the morning. Thia told her to enjoy the luxury as much as she could. She'd done exactly what she said she would do: walk with them back to Ly's rooms and leave her in Darius's care. They'd seen no one else the whole way back, not even a servant. The few words exchanged between him and Thia must have been code, because Dare didn't ask her anything about what happened. Either that or he already knew.

Dare came back with a whole tray of food. "Ly says good morning."

"Why doesn't she come in herself?" Karen stared at the door. Even open, she couldn't see the main room from here.

Dare set the tray on the little table in the corner. "She's busy getting ready to face the public relations liaison who will be here in about five minutes, according to the schedule."

Karen stiffened. "Public relations?" The last thing she wanted right now was a "conversation" with a reporter, even if they were from the palace.

"Don't worry." Dare came over to stand within reaching distance. "They won't get a chance to bother you."

"But they'll want to," Karen protested.

"They always do, but that's why I'm here." He smiled softly. "I told you my job is to keep you safe and feeling safe. If I'm not enough, there's Trevor. He'll be here to interfere, too."

Karen let herself smile a little, too. "What about Emalynn? I thought you were her guard."

Dare blushed but didn't look away. "Her orders were to keep you safe. She wants to know you aren't going to be used against her again. It's not like she needs me to do more than watch her back."

Guilt filled Karen for that. "It's not like I want to be used."

"Of course not." He put a hand on her shoulder. "You get used because she cares about you. That's just the way things are."

To say "palace culture is different" would be the understatement of the era. Karen hated it. The whole place felt like the worst of the cafeteria sniping. At least in school you didn't have to worry about being a pawn in someone else's assassination attempts. Reputation killing was the worst that happened there.

"So what are we supposed to do?"

The blush drained from Dare's face, but his posture rose to his pride. "This morning, stay here. I'll lock the door when I leave and turn off the com system." He paused to look around. "That wall is keyed to your voice and has full access to both the royal and standard nets, including central security, except for the highest level."

"No." Karen stopped him from going into more detail about the security. "I mean, how do we get our lives back?"

He struggled to keep his relaxed posture. Dare was the only one she'd ever seen who could turn stress and tension into loose muscles that were ready for anything other than Ly. Seeing him give in to the same tension she felt made her stomach tighten more.

"You don't." He spoke to the floor. "You lost your normal life as soon as you helped Ly with that image campaign. You became connected to the royals. All you can do is pick up the pieces and make a new life."

"I don't even know where to begin." Karen looked down at Dom but saw her own hand covering her lover's hair. "I used to think the worst thing that could happen would be for us to break up. I never once thought we would just break."

"I don't think anyone considers that possibility."

"Do you consider the possibility they aren't done yet?"

He sighed, but his posture returned to his usual relaxed look. "We never stop thinking they are out to get us."

"So they're still trying to... I don't even know what they're trying to do."

This conversation wasn't making her feel any better. Ly hinted about a life in dangerous places when she was growing up. That Dare called the palace worse said something.

"They are trying to take over the government." Dare laughed. "It's what everyone wants."

"Not everyone." Karen didn't think any of her friends would want to take over the government, least of all Ly.

"Everyone who tries anything." Dare laughed. "This time they've decided manipulating the princess will get them the power they want."

Karen snorted a single laugh. No one could manipulate Ly. That never stopped them from trying, and it never ended well for the manipulator.

They both looked up at the sound of voices from the other room.

"Go," Karen said. "She needs you."

He moved toward the door but stopped right in the threshold. "You start by learning to defend yourselves. We'll begin after lunch."

He left and the door closed behind him. A soft chime and a shift in the lights told her they were locked in. This room became as secure as a prison cell. It just felt a bit more comfortable.

"I didn't do anything," Dom murmured into her stomach.

"He's gone." Karen pushed Dom's hair aside.

Dom sat up without losing contact between them. She looked at the door with a smile. "I"—she waved at the door—"didn't do anything."

Dom's eyes were filled with hope and fear when she turned back to Karen.

"He's a good one." Karen agreed, and the level of fear dropped.

Dom threw herself onto Karen in a big hug. "I didn't do anything."

"I love you, too."

Tristan

Tristan and Davy arrived in the gym five minutes early for the afternoon's "self-defense" lesson and found it already crowded with women in civilian workout clothes. He recognized enough of them as guards to assume they all were. The schedule had him here for three hours, which seemed a bit much, but he wasn't going to complain about not meeting with tutors who still thought he needed to know the inner workings of government. Someone needed to explain that he wasn't the heir anymore.

"I saw you started your preferred file again." Grouse stood beside him with a grin on her face. "And you still need to learn how not to let people sneak up on you."

"'Because an assassin isn't going to put herself on my schedule.'" He managed the quote without a quiver in his voice, but his stomach threatened to give back his lunch if tried that again.

Grouse's expression turned grim. "Yes." She looked out over the gathered guards.

"Who makes my schedule?" Tristan asked before she could say anything else.

"Why? Are you going to slide into the office and request a new one?" Her grin was back in place.

"So you were listening." Tristan made a show of watching the guards warm up.

"Your schedule is set by the secretary's office." Grouse flipped back to serious mode. "And I would suggest before you start bugging them about your schedule that you ask for a private secretary to manage it for you." She nodded to someone across the room. Then in another complete change of mood, she chirped, "Good afternoon, Davy. Have you chosen your major yet?"

"Not yet," Davy responded.

"I've got some ideas for you if you're interested."

Davy shook his head. "Your ideas would probably have me staying in the palace. Sorry, but as soon as I can figure a way, I'm out of here."

"Take me with you." Tristan clasped his hands and dropped to his knees in the overly dramatic pose popular in old vids. "I beg you. I can't live like this."

Davy turned away. "What would you do out there? Why would you leave all this?" He waved at the women stretching and showing off their muscular bodies.

"Enough, you two." Grouse laughed. "Go get warmed up."

"Wait." Tristan jumped up to catch her. "What's with all the civilian clothes and so many guards?"

She wasn't smiling when she turned back to him. Then her eyes slid past him.

Tristan turned to see Emalynn, Dare, Karen, and Dom enter through the main door of the gym. Dom clung to Karen's arm while she scanned the room with wild eyes. Emalynn and Dare flanked them.

"That's why."

Tristan gauged the reaction of the guards, all of them relatively young. Protocol said Emalynn should have been on the interior of the group with Dare as her bodyguard just to her left. In this position, they were giving Karen and Dom the honored position. Tristan didn't have to guess why. Dom would have become a quivering pile of jelly seeing this many people. It was a wonder she was out and about at all after last night.

The women studiously went on about their warm-ups with only side-glances at the princess. Not one of them paused to bow or otherwise show respect to his sister. For that matter, they hadn't bowed to him when he entered either, though they were more direct in their looks. He was used to it.

"Hey." Emalynn walked up and hugged him. "Anything funny last night in your room?" she whispered barely loud enough for him to hear.

"A couple bugs," he whispered back.

She moved on to hug Davy, and Dare bowed to Tristan.

"Uh-uh." Tristan stepped in to hug Dare. "How many did you find?" he asked the same way Emalynn had asked him.

"Four, chairs and knobs in the bedrooms," came the reply.

Davy was already hugging Karen by then. Tristan waited his turn and found Dom clinging to him, too.

There were several women among the guard who weren't going to have much contact with them in the future. Tristan made note of the ones who looked scandalized by the greeting between friends. He could see Grouse doing the same.

"Come on." Dare ushered the four of them to the side while Emalynn stepped to the center of the gym with Grouse. "I'm supposed to work with you today."

"That was a test." Davy laughed. "I think some of them failed."

"Yeah." Dare glanced over his shoulder. "I don't think they're ready for this next bit either."

"Listen up." Grouse was in full military mode. "You think you want to protect Princess Emalynn."

Dom whimpered about not doing anything, and Karen hushed her, but Dare was watching the guards.

"She's not auditioning guards for herself, is she?" Tristan whispered.

Dare shook his head just slightly.

"That's a challenge none of us are up for." Grouse continued. "For one thing, the princess is a better fighter than you. She was trained in smuggling routes where they don't fight fair. She has more self-awareness than you. She pulled two inexperienced boys out of the middle of a gang war and kept all three of them intact."

Tristan closed his eyes to banish that memory. Her description was accurate and rather complimentary coming from her.

"She's smarter than you." Grouse continued. "She learned how to talk to the Others and use them to get past an entire armada. And scariest of all, she doesn't think like a royal. She puts others' well-being ahead of her own safety or duty. She's better than Prince Tristan at getting into trouble, and I promise you her trouble will be far more dangerous than tracking her through the old tunnels. Are you sure you want this challenge?"

A couple guards shifted uneasily, but no one opted out. They wouldn't. They thought this was too much of an honor. Tristan thought about objecting to the part about him getting in trouble, but he knew it was true. She'd be better at getting into worse kinds of trouble than he'd even imagined.

Grouse looked over the gathered guards a couple times, then stepped back. Emalynn stepped up. Tristan could see the leader in her from that simple move. Grouse didn't give her the floor. She took it.

"All right, ladies, the challenge is simple." Emalynn smiled. Well, it looked like a smile with the corners of her lips turned up and her teeth showing beautifully, but it felt like the gaze of a predator. "All you have to do is impress me."

The guards shifted uneasily. Some of them glanced toward the door. They'd had their chance to leave. Now they weren't so sure they'd made the right decision.

"The rules are simple." Emalynn turned around to catch everyone in her gaze. "If I point to you, it's your turn. We'll spar until one of us is on the floor. Then I'll point to someone else."

A young blond woman with military short hair and a red shirt raised her hand.

"Oh good, a volunteer."

Everyone backed up to leave the woman in the center with Emalynn. Tristan saw the subtle shift of attention that told him she was ready to fight.

It was equally clear the young guard wasn't ready. She got ready quick, choosing a wide-footed stance. The princess and the guard stared at each other for several long breaths. Then the woman lunged forward, flipped over Emalynn's arm, and crashed to the floor on her back. Emalynn waited only long enough to be sure the woman was still alive before pointing to the next guard.

"And you know how the rest of that is going to go." Dare turned his back on the auditions. "And if you ask, it took her fifteen seconds to put me on my back, if you don't count the staring time."

Tristan was impressed.

"What about Grouse?" Davy asked.

Dare looked back at the security chief. "She hasn't tried yet, and I think neither of them want to know."

Tristan agreed with that wisdom.

"How about some self-defense training?" Dare smiled with the glee only a sadistic tutor could really master. "Help me teach these three how to stand?"

Tristan snorted. He remembered when T— He remembered learning how to stand. It had felt so silly at the time. Then he saw how Emalynn used that to keep her opponents off guard. The feel of standing properly gave him power. He'd never be able to do what Emalynn did, but he'd settle for the ability to stand toe to toe with most of the guards and not have them laughing over him when they knocked him down.

Together, Dare and Tristan tweaked the balance and posture of Davy, Karen, and Dom. Tristan found Dom to be the most eager. She even allowed him to touch her so he could correct the minor flaws in her posture. They were an hour in when they finally managed to convince Dom to release Karen's arm and stand on her own.

As a break for the others, because learning to stand was far more taxing than anyone thought, Dare suggested they demonstrate the forms. Dare insisted Tristan should lead. Of course, it was a chance for Dare to watch and help Tristan improve. They started moving and were in sync by the end of the third move. Tristan could feel the influence of Dare's grace on his own movements. He'd always thought, when he practiced with Ly, it was their connection as twins that allowed that influence. Shift and turn, raise a hand to block, follow through and ready for the next. A flash in the corner of his eye became a knife. His body already knew what to do. Shift and block, catch the wrist and pull the opponent into his other elbow. She dropped to the floor, and Tristan continued the form, now with a knife in his hands.

"Tristan!" Dare stood in front of him. "Good work, but may I have the knife please?"

Emalynn

Emalynn offered her hand to her latest opponent and turned to select her next when she noticed everyone was staring at the far corner. Karen and Davy were standing like guardians in front of Dom, who cowered in a corner. Dare had hold of a knife by the dangerous end, but was wrapping it in a towel. Tristan stood over a woman who was being held down by three other women.

"What happened?" Emalynn asked the nearest of the recruits.

The woman shrugged.

"Your brother just defeated another assassination attempt." Grouse took Emalynn by the shoulder and turned her away. "This time he did it for himself."

Emalynn broke out of Grouse's grip. "What?" She turned to go help.

"Leave it." Grouse had hold of her elbow now. "He needs to step up to this, and Dare will bring him in."

Emalynn watched as Dare did just that, leading Tristan away from the woman who was being hauled to her feet. Her brother looked a bit like a zombie as he followed Dare. The knife disappeared so Dare could put his arm around Tristan's shoulder.

"How did this happen?" Emalynn turned to face Grouse directly.

"You were the one who predicted it." Grouse kept her tone even. "Why do you think I set up this little exercise?"

"I predicted they'd keep going after me."

"They did."

Emalynn tried to object but knew Grouse was right. "I'm too hard to hit, so they'll hit those I love."

Grouse nodded. "Now put that out of your mind. You still have evaluations to get through, and I haven't told Tristan his part in all of this."

Emalynn sighed. She couldn't call the chief a liar here, not when she wasn't sure if Tristan understood what they were doing. It doesn't matter, she told herself. So long as they were able to find enough trainable guards.

So far, the matches hadn't lasted more than a few seconds from the first attack to the candidate landing on the floor. The last three weren't any better on that front. And she'd thought Grouse was exaggerating during the introduction. It was clear none of these women had ever been in a real fight, one where the other person was determined to kill you.

Maybe, she thought as she stretched out and thought about what to do with the women still gathered here, they should send the royal guard recruits to police the smuggling routes. The two biggest drawbacks to that would be the reduction in smuggling income for those who relied on it and the reduction in recruits who survived training. Maybe that wouldn't be such a good idea after all. There had to be some way to give these women the experience of putting their life on the line to up their skills.

"Attention!" Emalynn took on Grouse's military posture and waited for most of the women to show their attention. The last conversation died slowly. The three women involved hadn't impressed her. "You three can leave."

Everyone turned to look at the offenders. They were struck dumb as well and stood paralyzed as though she would change her mind if they stood still enough.

"Go." Emalynn kept her voice under tight control. She watched them until the door closed. She turned back to the rest of the gathered guards. "This is a winnowing process. It is also a chance for you to learn, whether you meet my requirements today or not. For one thing, one-to-one rarely happens in real life."

There were nods throughout the group, but no one dared to take her eyes off Emalynn or even open her mouth. Good, she had their attention.

"You won't always get to choose who you go into battle with, so you'd better be able to fight beside any one of these women or anyone fighting for the same goal." Emalynn moved back into the center of the sparring area. "You, you, and you." She pointed to three of the most clever she'd seen in the individual evaluations.

The three came forward and spread out without talking to each other. This would be a good fight, then. A quick nod between them and they attacked from three sides at once. Emalynn dodged under the arm of the first and redirected the second into the third, but none of them went down. The second recovered first and relaunched her attack with a high feint that turned quickly into a leg sweep. Emalynn barely managed to jump the sweep but had to face the first in a bad position. She blocked the attack and used it to regain her footing. Now with all three in one direction, she begin her own attacks. With every move, she shifted between fighting styles and even tossed in a couple of cheer moves to throw them off. She needed several deep breaths to recover once they were all on the ground.

"Good." She sent all three to see Tristan.

She'd expected bruises from this part of the evaluation. She hoped she could hold up better in the rest of the matches. She picked her next three opponents from the bottom of her list. They performed as expected. One she sent to the corner opposite Tristan and let the other two go. She worked her way through all the women until Grouse stepped in to stop her last bout.

"You need a break."

"I'm fine." Emalynn gasped.

"Your friends are exhausted."

Davy, Karen, and Dom were seated with their backs against the wall, watching her. Dom smiled shyly when Emalynn glanced at her. She sat in the middle of the other two, a little closer to Karen, but not touching her. Emalynn smiled back, genuinely happy to see her friend showing signs of recovery.

"There's one more I would like you to consider." Grouse guided Emalynn toward the corner where Tristan and Dare were surrounded by her picks.

"Thia?"

Grouse gave her that look again. "Smart. Yes, Thia, though not specifically for you."

Emalynn followed Grouse's eyes back to Dom.

"She managed to get those two in without sleeping gas, though they probably needed it."

Emalynn laughed. "They just needed to feel safe, warm, and loved. Dare put them to bed, and they didn't last long enough for me to get out of the shower."

"Then you don't know anything more?"

Emalynn nodded. "Nothing concrete." Not that she'd had much time to observe anything. "Though Karen seems to be able to understand her."

"And you're sure about the ketalin?" Grouse's voice went dark again.

"Mix that drug with torture and..." Emalynn sighed.

"I think I don't want to know everything about your past." Grouse shuddered.

Emalynn stopped before they were within hearing. "Baba brought a boy home from one of her jobs. She called him a 'complication.' The poor kid quivered like gelatin every time he heard any sort of click, but all he could say was, 'It's in the bubbles.'" Emalynn hated to think how this boy had come to Baba's hand. "Baba told me it was ketalin, but this kid didn't act like any of the other addicts I'd known."

Grouse lifted her eyebrows and glanced sideways at Emalynn.

"I wish I could tell you it wears off, but Baba found the boy's family and returned him for them to deal with." Emalynn glanced at Dom. "It's probably a good sign she's trying to find a way around the limits of her mind."

Grouse nodded. "What does it mean? That phrase?"

Emalynn shook her head. "Anything or nothing." All this just because they knew her before she became the princess. "They aren't the only ones who could be used against me."

"Of course not." Grouse was all business again. All these rapid switches were going to give Emalynn a headache. "We've got your whole school under surveillance. No one else has gone missing."

Emalynn smiled.

"Hey." Karen tried to get up. "That was really impressive. Baba taught you to do that?"

"She wanted me to be safe."

Grouse left as stealthily as she came. Emalynn let her think she went unnoticed.

"I didn't do anything," Dom said in the same voice she would have used to say that she hadn't done her homework. "I didn't do *anything*."

"I know." Emalynn smiled at Dom as she squeezed in to sit beside her opposite Karen. If she shut her mind off, she could almost believe this was just like hanging out after cheer practice.

Dom leaned back against the wall. "I didn't do anything," she whispered with relief.

Tristan

Tristan walked alone to the small guest dining room. Not really alone. That couldn't be allowed with the current threat level. He had a set of uniformed guards with him. Davy had gone ahead to help set up the "picnic" with Karen and Dom, while Tristan was stuck with his tutor who didn't accept his excuse that he wasn't heir to the throne anymore.

"You can leave me here." Tristan attempted to get around the guards to open the door.

"Sorry, sire, we're supposed to stay with you," replied the lead of this group.

"No, you aren't." Emalynn poked her head out the door. "Go or be accused of sedition."

The guards scowled but left as ordered.

"Was that really necessary?" Tristan asked.

Emalynn shrugged. "It's what got my guards to leave me here. Besides, it's true." She stepped out of the way to let Tristan into the room.

"I thought you had Dare."

"He came with Dom." Emalynn sighed. "She freaked at the sight of the uniforms. We need her as calm as possible this afternoon."

Tristan agreed with that but didn't say anything. He was shocked by the way the room was set up. The table was folded into its smallest configuration and pushed against the wall and covered with more food than they should need for this exercise. The chairs had been removed and replaced with old blankets scattered about the floor.

"What is...?" He waved at the room.

Emalynn laughed like she had when they were accepted into the community on Farthing Moon. It was a sound made only of joy. "This is a picnic. Sure it would be better in the gardens, but we aren't ready for that yet."

"Oh, don't laugh too much, Ly." Karen came over with a glass of some yellow liquid. "It's called lemonade." She pushed the glass into Tristan's hand. "You have to have lemonade at a picnic."

Tristan took the glass, but his attention slipped past Karen to where Dom knelt in the middle of a blanket, doing something with one of the guards he'd chosen for this test. They were very focused on something Dom had just scattered between them.

"You really eat like this?" Tristan looked around. Two of the other guards were sitting with Davy, looking rather skeptical at the food on their plates. The fourth was with Dare, picking food from the table.

"Usually only for celebrations, though sometimes just to do something fun." Emalynn pulled Tristan farther into the room. "It depends, but since Dom was able to tell us she wanted this, it's a good enough reason for a celebration."

Tristan wasn't so sure about this, but it couldn't be any worse than the commons on Farthing Moon, a great hall filled with wooden tables lined with wood benches where they ate their stew from wood bowls with wood spoons. He'd learned to eat fast at those tables. There wasn't time for a leisurely meal when the cows needed milking and the sheep were hungry. This was supposed to be a leisurely lunch. They'd scheduled three hours for it, not including the setup time. No one was rushing here.

Tristan grabbed a plate from one end of the table and started picking his way down the table. There were grilled meats that looked safe and bowls of cold pasta with vegetables mixed in. He took a little of each just in case he didn't like them. The chips he recognized from his brief stint as a normal teenager. How had Emalynn managed to convince the kitchen to come up with all of this on such short notice? Right on the end he found the corn, just the way they'd eaten it on Farthing Moon the day of the harvest. There they hadn't even removed the husks. Here they'd been shucked and cut into manageable pieces. He would have grabbed two if there'd been room on his plate.

He went to join Davy.

"I'm serious." Davy laughed at the two women who were poking at their own cobs of corn. "You just bite it off."

"But how do they get it to stick like that?" Nari, the darker of the two, picked it up to look at it more closely.

"It grows that way." Tristan picked up his corn.

The guards started to bow but stopped before they got too far. Tristan could forgive them this gaff.

"How would you know that, sire?" Raul asked.

"Call me Tristan." He took a bite of his corn to give him time to decide how to answer her. Could he reveal the months they spent on Farthing Moon without putting the colony there in danger? Officially, there were still two months of their travels unaccounted for. The current prevailing rumor was they had gone to an Others world.

The door, which should have been locked, opened, and two uniformed guards entered. Tristan recognized the slight differences in their uniforms to know his father would be the next through the door. That didn't matter to Dom, who scrambled to get to Karen. The four trial guards moved just as fast but with more grace to get between her and the guards without looking too much like guards themselves. The two sets of guards were facing off by the time King Levon stepped into the room.

"Hello, Father." Emalynn rose slowly, brushing crumbs off her legs. "Could you please ask your guards to step outside?"

Tristan shook his head. She still hadn't learned the proper etiquette of dealing with the most powerful man in the galaxy. Or, more likely, she still hadn't realized it was important.

"What is going on here?" Levon looked around at the plates and cups scattered about the blankets.

"It's called a picnic." Emalynn tilted her head to one side while twisting her lips into a smile that was anything but friendly. "And please send your guards out."

Dom and Karen were muttering behind the wall of guards.

"Father." Tristan rose and bowed in one movement. "The uniforms are scaring our friend."

The king drew himself up as tall as he could with his chest puffed out. "I—"

"I didn't do anything," Dom screamed over the king's voice. "I didn't do anything. I didn't do anything."

Karen hushed her, but that only lowered the volume a little. The king glared at Tristan but waved for the guards to leave. They hesitated only long enough to bow to a king who wasn't looking.

They stood there awkwardly looking at each other until Dom's cries faded.

"Thank you." Emalynn bowed.

So she did know the etiquette and chose not to follow it. Tristan winced at the thought of what that would do to their family dynamics. Father might be willing to forgive some of her insolence, but not all. Then he had to think of what Mother would do if she learned of this lapse.

"You two are being rather difficult." Father started right in.

Tristan lowered his eyes. Father only skipped the pleasantries when he was upset.

"If this is about our little trip to orbit, Chief Grouse already lectured me, and I get it."

"It's about you not responding to my requests for a meeting." Father's jaw was set and his voice tightly controlled.

Emalynn looked at Tristan. He could feel her confusion mixing with his.

"We've been following the schedule that pops up every morning." She locked her gaze with his but talked to Father. "I haven't seen any communication from you."

"I will not tolerate lying from the heir to this throne."

"She's not lying." Tristan couldn't break the look between them. "All I get is the schedule, too. I thought you were mad at us."

The sense of feeling he received from Emalynn threatened to overwhelm him. She was cycling between confusion, anger, and fear so fast he couldn't keep up. It didn't help that he felt the same way.

"Look at me, both of you."

Emalynn broke the gaze first. The look on his father's face wasn't the anger his voice suggested. His eyes were filled with fear Tristan had never seen before. Tristan fought against the paralysis that threatened to take him with all this fear swirling around the room.

"Then it would seem we have more rebels to flush from the system." Emalynn looked as relaxed as always, which meant she was anything but. "Davy?"

Davy jumped up. Tristan envied their ability to act as though everything were normal.

"Sire." Davy bowed. He too understood his place. "I can try to trace the problem. Can you tell me when you sent the messages?"

"You can trust him, sire." Dare stood beside Emalynn, also without bowing. "He's the most skilled hacker we've found."

"I'll send it." Levon turned to leave.

Emalynn stepped forward. "That's not going to work. We aren't getting the messages. Besides, that's not why you wanted to see us."

Tristan wanted to kick her. She just didn't know when to let things be.

"You're right." Father turned back with a smile on his face. "I'll send a messenger."

Tristan felt the world spinning. When had he learned to switch personalities so fast?

"You still haven't said what you wanted." Tristan sucked in a breath after saying something like that.

Father and Emalynn shared a look and laughed. "I was wondering if you were ready to try a family dinner again? I think not." He waved at the mess all around. "It would seem your manners have regressed further."

"The schedule does say we are having a picnic," Emalynn said.

"Actually, my version said you were doing some sort of security testing."

"I didn't do anything," Dom screamed again.

This time Emalynn ran to help calm her. Tristan sighed. So much for Father's good mood.

"We are." Tristan took his father's attention off Emalynn's breach. "We're trying to avoid certain words and sights."

He waited for things to calm down a bit more before continuing. Father's eyes were on Emalynn. His posture softened as he saw how his daughter reacted to her friend's need.

"It may be a while before we can try again." Tristan stepped around to stand next to Father. "She won't do anything that isn't in some way helping get Dom back."

"Where did she learn to do that?"

Tristan smiled to himself. "She didn't."

The look his father shot him was priceless. He'd have to see if he could capture a still of it later.

"She just loves her friend. They all love each other and would give up just about anything to spare the other's pain." Tristan swallowed the jealousy that welled up at that thought. "They are all like that. Out there."

The king stood as a father watching his daughter deal with a problem. Tristan stood beside him, aware he should be helping with Dom as well and that he was a prince who had to be aloof from everyone. He sighed.

"You've changed." Father spoke just as quietly.

"Thank you."

Father bowed to Emalynn, who didn't notice. The guard candidates did and barely managed to hide their shock. Then he turned to Tristan and bowed as well. "Keep us informed."

Tristan returned the bow.

Emalynn

Emalynn dropped into the big chair that no one else liked with a huff of breath. "It was just a picnic. Why are we so exhausted?"

Everyone else flopped around the suite with similar huffs. Everyone except Dom, who had been given a sleeping pill and was sleeping already. The apartment felt cramped with so many people lounging flopped out on the furniture in the main room. She didn't know what Tristan had told the elite candidates, but they were acting as though they weren't guards enough that she could almost forget. They had the same ever-vigilant gaze Davy used when they were hanging around. At the picnic, they were social and relaxed enough to keep Dom calm until a threat presented itself.

"Picnics are exhausting." Davy lay up against the wall with his tablet in his lap. He wouldn't sleep tonight if he didn't find something in the net about why the king's messages weren't making it to Emalynn and Tristan.

"Remember the annual picnic?" Karen laughed. "We were just supposed to show up, and it was still exhausting. Imagine being on student council."

Emalynn laughed with her. "We never just showed up." The cheer team became the unofficial publicity arm of the council. "The council was great for planning, but they couldn't convince a clown to be funny."

"Hey." Karen mocked, "Don't mock the council. They are our future politicians."

"Oh, well then, I'm glad I never got elected." Emalynn tossed an arm in the air.

"You did get elected." Karen laughed even harder. "Last year. You were a write-in and took the class seat in a landslide."

The horror of that announcement came flooding back. It took a week of pleading with the principle for the teachers to come up with a reason she wasn't eligible. "Well crud and double crud, that explains a lot."

"What?" Tristan lifted his head.

Karen crumbled with laughter and brought Davy down with her. Emalynn couldn't help but join them. Dare, Tristan, and the guards passed confused looks between them.

"It's a joke about student council." Davy gasped at them.

Emalynn pulled her breath under control when Davy started laughing again. "Everyone knows the highest political position a civilian can reach is mayor, and mayors don't have a lot of power." She shook her head. "So the kids in student council are the ones who think they could somehow breach that limit. It never happens."

"The closest anyone gets is to rise to power in a corporation." Karen took up the explanation. "That's not elected either."

"So the joke is Emalynn never wanted to be on council but got elected anyway?" Tristan raised his eyebrows at her.

"And she became the heir apparent," Karen confirmed.

The door chimed. All laughter stopped and they were all on their feet. Emile got to the door first, but waited to be sure the other three were between the door and Emalynn. The illusion that they were all just friends burst. She closed her eyes against all the memories of guards who weren't mixed with the ones before.

"Stop." She sat up in time to keep them from opening the door. "I can't do it this way." She turned to Tristan. He might understand. "I can't live like this."

"Like what?" He held her eyes.

"Depending on people we barely know to keep us safe against threats that may or may not be there." Emalynn turned to Dare. "We are in the palace and we can't open the door without putting someone at risk?"

She pushed her way past the four to the door, checked the vid feed to see a girl in a messenger uniform. Baba insisted she never stand in front of an open door. At school, they teased her about that habit until the gelatin incident. As the only student who made it through that day without changing her clothes, she'd kept the habit.

The girl on the other side jumped when the door opened. Surprise became confusion, which shifted to mortification as her eyes roamed from the empty space where a servant should have been to the princess standing just inside the door.

"Oh, um…" She bowed in a hurry and came up with a small data stick in her hand. "His Royal Majesty King Levon sends this to Davy Carlise." She thrust the stick at Emalynn.

Emalynn took it. "Thank you." She gave the girl a small bow in return.

The girl looked about to explode from blushing as Emalynn stepped back and let the door close. She gave the four guards who'd jumped for the door a nod and walked back to where Davy was nose deep in his tablet.

"Remember that bit from Chief Grouse?" Dare grinned at the other four. "She really is better at protecting herself than we are." He'd remained in his seat, but she could see the lie in the way he forced himself to relax.

"No need to worry about me," Emalynn dropped back into her chair, "I've lived in more dangerous places. It's just a door. It takes a little caution, and I don't have to put any of you at risk."

They stared at her as though she'd done something amazing or horrible. She didn't want to live with that either.

"The risk is just there." Tristan looked around at all the guards. "It's odd to try and hide it."

"You mean you've lived with this kind of threat your whole life?" Emalynn sat up again. "You're telling me there's always a threat?"

Tristan nodded.

"Haven't you?" Dare asked. "You were a smuggler. That would seem like a threat-filled life."

"That's different." How could she explain? Karen wasn't any help. She didn't know about that part either. "We know the people we work with aren't trustworthy, but as long as you're on the job, you're all working for the same pay. You can trust a thief to do what will get her paid."

"It's not so different." Dare stood and faced her in a casual challenge. "We are all working toward the same goal and have to trust each other even when we know there are untrustworthy people among us."

"But when does it end?" Emalynn rose to the challenge. "When's the payout? When do we all change our IDs and head off to enjoy our winnings and live like normal people for a while?"

He held her gaze for three breaths, then turned away. "We don't. This job never ends." He allowed her to hear defeat in his voice.

It was unfair, and she knew it. He didn't control this system any more than she did, nor did he ask to be a part of it. It was just as bad that she was stuck as the cargo in this job. She was also the mark in someone else's game. Tristan had unwittingly used their one gambit to walk away. If they disappeared from the palace again, if either one of them walked away, everyone who looked even remotely like them would be in danger.

Dare held his defeat only as long as required by tradition, then faced her again, this time with his right shoulder and hip a little forward. He knew this game too well. "I ask you to trust me."

She shifted to the same stance. The game was offered and accepted. "Can I trust you?"

"Emalynn!" Tristan protested.

Dare didn't flinch from his stance, but waited while one of the other guards closed on Tristan to keep the prince from interfering.

One step to the right. "I've been with you now for five days. Have I done anything suspicious?"

"You let us out of the palace when you were supposed to be guarding us." They circled slowly, right hands palm in still by their hips.

He smiled. "I could have kept you in, but would you have regained Dom?"

"Were you under orders to let us go?"

"My orders were to stay with you."

"Who gave the orders?"

"Security Chief Grouse, in her office, with the door closed."

Step by question and step by answer they walked around each other until their hands had risen to shoulder height. He turned the questions on her about her devotion to Dom. She couldn't lie, not during the game, or prove she couldn't be trusted. She couldn't care about what Karen would think of her answers. Dom was a friend, a close friend, who was in danger. Emalynn would have done the same for any of their classmates.

He challenged her, so she had to end it. She closed the distance between their hands in one swift move and asked the one question she didn't already know the answer to.

"Your favorite color?"

"Green, specifically holly green." His hand didn't move within hers.

Emalynn smiled. "So did I pass?"

Tristan gasped.

"Yes. Did I?" Dare asked.

"One last question." She kept hold of his hand. "Where did you learn to play?"

Dare leaned away, letting his shoulders rise as he prepared to reveal something he'd kept up to now.

"I was abandoned when I was ten. After Mom left, Papa couldn't hold a job. The company took everything of value to cover Papa's expenses. I got out before they finished the inventory, but that only meant I was an unregistered orphan."

"Then how'd you end up here?" Tristan pushed past the guard.

Dare dropped his eyes. "Techani Kenchi. I got caught and he claimed me before they finished filling in all the forms. He had proof I was his nephew or something like that. All he told me was I was ready to prove myself to the royals."

Emalynn's chest tightened around his story. Baba had told her the same thing about her teacher. She'd said her mentor did more than teach women to fight; he taught the universe to care. His was the one name that never changed in all their moves. "If anything happens to me, you find the man named Techani Kenchi and tell him I raised you." Emalynn would have done that had she not watched his transport ex—

Emile stood before her in the right-facing position. A short nod from Dare told her to play the game again. Emalynn matched the position but waited for Emile to issue the challenge. The questions she pushed with focused on the public aspects of Emalynn's and Tristan's "travels." She didn't turn to their time in the palace until their hands were close to touching. Emile projected her choice to end the game with the final question with more than enough time for Emalynn to avoid it.

"Will you become queen?"

Emalynn swallowed all her emotions to keep her hand from revealing any of them.

"If I must."

Emile smiled and squeezed her hand. She nodded to the rest, who released tension Emalynn hadn't noticed.

"This is just wrong." Davy pushed through to show Emalynn his tablet, but it didn't make any sense to her. "None of the king's messages are getting anywhere. Most of them, the ones that would be noticed, are rewritten and sent from a dummy account."

"What?" Tristan grabbed the tablet. His expression darkened as he saw what Davy was talking about. "Are you sure?"

"As sure as anything in a computer is." Davy took the tablet back, ran his fingers over the display, and thrust it in front of Emalynn again. Now it showed a map of the palace communication system using navigation symbols.

She took the tablet gently so she could orient herself to the map. She found her suite and Tristan's just down the hall, where most of the lines of communication were severed. The king's chamber had only one line still intact, but that wasn't one that should have been there.

"This can't be your everyday plot." She handed the tablet to Dare. "We have a job to do."

He nodded. "Flush them out."

"Let them think they're succeeding."

"How do we do that?" Karen inched toward the door to the room she shared with Dom.

"By acting as though we haven't seen this."

Emalynn

Emalynn paced around her room, still in her pajamas. Three days and they were no closer to flushing out the conspirators. Davy made some progress on finding the source of the breach in communications, but only to the council wing of the palace. The schedule said she should be meeting with her Lords Master, the tutor who was supposed to teach her about the rest of the royal family. Master Therin stood just outside her room with arms crossed and one foot tapping a bit faster than twice per second. The only thing that kept the master, glorified tutor, out of the room was Darius standing in the doorway. This also kept the door from closing. The media wall chimed again to tell her she was late for her lesson. She threw a pillow at it. The wall shut down. A programmer had a sense of humor. It was probably just a snooze function.

"Isn't she ready yet?" Master Therin demanded, shifting the foot she tapped with and the timing of the tap.

Dare shifted to face the master. "Not since the last time you asked."

"Can she teach me something practical?" Emalynn growled.

"Knowing the lords is important," Therin shot back.

Dare gave her the signal to keep quiet. "Master, just pretend she's run off like Prince Tristan used to do. We'll call you when we get her back where she belongs."

"She's in there. I can see her." Therin stepped forward into Dare's suddenly threatening posture. "She just needs to—"

"Not hear the next words you were planning to say." Emalynn heard the frustration in Dare's voice.

"Well, I never. This is unacceptable."

Dare sighed. "And yet it's how it's going to be. Now, if you have any questions, may I suggest you watch the vid from the challenge King Levon offered her in the library? If that doesn't convince you, you could check the feed from her selection process."

Emalynn snorted. She wouldn't attack the master the way he was suggesting. Although, the thought of taking off for a few hours was tempting. Completely irresponsible and likely to get her into bigger trouble than she could get out of on her own. Besides, she'd promised Grouse she wouldn't do that kind of thing anymore.

"Are you threatening me? Young man, I don't think you know who you are dealing with."

"No threats from me." Emalynn heard the insincere smile that pulled at his lips. "I'm just warning you that you've said enough for one day."

"She needs to learn—"

Emalynn didn't see what Dare did, but the tutor huffed her way out of sight. A moment later, the main door cycled open and closed. Emalynn sighed a small breath of relief. That was one frustration out of her way.

"That's going to have consequences." Dare returned to his post just inside the door.

Emalynn turned away to keep from glaring at him. It wasn't his fault.

"Have you considered running forms?"

"I don't want to calm down." Being calm hadn't gotten her mind working in the right direction for the last three days. Maybe being worked up would shake a useful thought loose.

"How about a bout?"

She always loved a good bout, and he'd give her a good one. For all their jokes about her taking him down in fifteen seconds, he was good enough that it wouldn't happen again.

"That would calm me down, too."

He laughed. "That's the point. You need to calm down. I'm not going to be able to get you out of all your meetings today just because you're in a bad mood."

"I'm not in a bad mood," she snapped. "Okay, I'm in a mood. I just need to be." She kicked the pillow she'd previously thrown at the wall. It still didn't break, so she ran up and kicked it again.

"Differential mind?"

She stopped in surprise. Of course, he'd been raised by the master Baba learned everything from.

"How about a public challenge?" He rescued the pillow and put it back on the bed.

"How long will it take to get the public here?" She started stretching.

He shook his head. "Not that kind of public." He started pulling the blankets up on the bed. Emalynn couldn't let him make the bed on his own.

"What kind of public are you thinking?"

"Palace guards in one of the courtyards. I've heard rumors of a pool to see how many of them it would take to get you off your feet."

214

They finished making the bed, and he pushed her toward the shower. "But what's the public?"

"Invite public relations." He toggled the bathroom door closed between them.

She toggled it back open. "That's cruel."

"It's the only way I'll be able to get it on your schedule for today."

She smacked the switch to close the door again. She kicked the door for good measure and winced at the stupid pain. Fine, let public relations be there. The warm water helped her calm enough to see the real brilliance of his plan. Everyone would come out for something like that. They might catch a glimpse of the conspiracy. It would also be a public reminder that she wasn't the usual kind of royalty.

A simple sweat suit with a blue top and purple pants lay on the bed when she got out of the shower. They had embroidery on them in the opposing color to prove they were a set. They were also the perfect advertising for some designer.

"Feeling better?" Dare sat in the main room with two of her elite squad.

Emalynn nodded. "How long?"

"You have time to eat something small and log in to prove you're studying the lords." He looked up at the media wall where the official complaint from Master Thorin glared down at her.

"You've got to be kidding me." Emalynn read it again and burst out laughing. "She's really full of herself."

"Yeah, so you have to prove you don't need her before your father reads that," Emile said. "Tristan uses that trick all the time when he's skipped out on tutors."

Emalynn hated they were right but grabbed her tablet and muffin from the breakfast bar. She started by setting up a chart for herself. County, main export, primary industry, personality, rank in the family, and connection to LeBlanc. There, no chance they would think she cheated on this part. She managed to research and enter three lords by the time Dare told her it was time to head down to the challenge.

She walked obediently, followed Emile, and let Yali follow. Dare walked by her side, explaining the rules of the challenge. First, it would be one-one until all the guards had been thrown. Then they would come in groups no larger than three. The third round would allow groups up to six. If she was still standing after that, it would be a free-for-all. "At anytime, you can stop it by dropping to one knee." Dare glanced at her as though expecting her to object.

"Sounds like you've thought this out." She glanced at the crew from public relations setting up the cameras. "Can you convince them to let Dom edit the video?"

"I'm not that kind of magic." Dare laughed. "Now, don't get hurt out there."

She leaned over and kissed him on the cheek. "Yes, Daddy."

The courtyard was filled with guards. Some in full uniform around the edges and corralling the civilian spectators. Most in practice uniforms, forming one large circle in the middle of the courtyard. Raised stands behind the guards were filled. She entered the ring to find it was filled with sand. Good for a soft landing, but it would make it hard for some moves.

Chief Grouse was in the center of the ring, explaining the challenge rules to the gathered guards. "Remember, the point is only to knock the princess down, not kill, maim, or otherwise hurt her. Good luck to all of you. Medics are standing by to treat your bruises."

The gathered guards laughed.

"Emalynn." Grouse spoke much quieter. "Are you sure about this? They will eventually put you on your ass."

"Of course they will." Emalynn smiled. "The point will be how many it took to get there."

"You've thought this through?"

"As promised. If I need to, I'll put myself out."

Grouse nodded, then turned to the far side of the circle where a special riser with sun guard had been erected. King Levon and Queen Treylyn were seated there with Tristan and Davy. What a set of targets they made, and the little wave Tristan gave said he at least knew it.

"Your Majesties." Grouse bowed to them. "With your permission…"

King Levon rose as though he were going to make a speech. "Begin."

The first guard attacked before Grouse was out of the circle. Emalynn blocked to the right and let the sand trip her. The second came from behind, going low. Emalynn jumped aside with enough of a twist to come down facing the right direction. The guard redirected her attack right into Emalynn's twist and landed several feet away. The third guard jumped the second and came with good form. Emalynn had to block three strikes before she was able to push this one off balance. By then the fighting trance had set in. Her conscious mind faded into the background and her body reacted to the incoming threats.

Did Grouse know about the fighting trance? Would she have allowed Emalynn to fight like this if she knew? Emalynn's awareness expanded past the circle of guards. She picked out little details, like the four women gathered away from the stands and the new woman on the shelter. Little details that she could barely put in context as her body moved to control the fight.

216

They were coming in multiples now.

Her body moved with its usual grace through the first few attacks. They were supposed to all step forward at once when called as part of a group. That woman shouldn't be there, hanging back with a knife sliding down her sleeve. Another glint caught her attention behind Tristan.

Emalynn changed styles to grab the knife from the woman attacking her. She would remember the screams later as she flipped the knife to get its feel, then threw it. The screams continued as she returned to the challenge. They couldn't have made it to the final round yet.

The trance faded, and her conscious mind took in everything at once. Men screaming, women issuing orders, Dare beside her.

"You need get out of here."

"What happened?"

"You just frustrated another assassin." He pulled her through the crowd to the elite guards who surrounded her even as they matched her pace. Tristan and Davy joined them at the first checkpoint. Thia caught up to them at the lift with Dom and Karen. Dom had a death grip on Karen's arm again, but she wasn't muttering.

In the lift, Dom hit the emergency stop and grabbed Emalynn's arm.

"I…" She shook her head and tried again. "He… He…"

Emalynn reached out to stop Thia from restarting the lift. "The man?" She kept her focus on Dom. They could celebrate the fact that she had broken the phrase later.

"He… I…" She took a deep breath and put her hand out like she was touching a wall. "I didn't do anything."

"Thank you." Emalynn restarted the lift but changed their destination.

"What are you doing?" Emile asked.

"Being unpredictable. They won't expect us in Security Central with this much chaos." She winked at Karen, who would get the reference to their wild days on the cheer squad.

Dare smiled to himself and faded back into a corner of the lift. Tristan took the other back corner.

"We shouldn't be in Security Central." Thia reached for the lift controls. "We'll be in the way."

"We'll be dead if we head back to the suite now." Emalynn blocked Thia and stood in front of the control panel.

Emile took a position in front of the other one with a nod to Emalynn.

"Now you distrust me." Thia looked for support from the others in the lift. None of them took sides other than to leave Thia to face Emalynn alone.

Emalynn shook her head. "I don't think you're trying to kill us. You wouldn't be standing there if I did."

"Then what is it?"

"Dom recognized the assassin on the dais."

Emalynn waited for that to sink in. Thia flushed but didn't look away. "How is being in Security Central going to help?"

"I don't know yet." Emalynn shrugged. "It's just the safest place I can think of where we'll be able to look through the vids of the crowd and maybe figure out who's trying to kill us this time."

Tristan

The guards in Security Central ran about the office like wild turkeys while the techs had every screen available tuned to the chaos of the assassination attempt. That wasn't right. Tristan knew they shouldn't be watching the assassination. They should be looking everywhere else in case the chaos was a diversion. Worse than that, no one noticed they were standing there.

Dare looked just as uncomfortable with the situation as Tristan felt. They caught each other's eyes and Tristan glanced at Grouse's office. Grouse should have beaten them back to her command central where she could coordinate the response from a position of knowledge.

Emalynn didn't bother to wait for acknowledgment; she just picked a tech and started giving her orders about what to look for. Dare signaled the elite guards to scatter, except Thia, who stayed with Karen and Dom. Tristan moved away from Emalynn to keep attention off her.

"Ahem." He stood like a good prince is supposed to when he wants the attention of people who are working. Someday, this would make a funny story about how the tutors might know a little about what they were talking about. No one paid any attention to him. So much for being a good prince. "Hey! Where's Chief Grouse?"

A guard with a poorly fitted uniform and insignia out of place looked up. She turned to Dare. "Get him back to his suite."

"No," Tristan said. He didn't have to yell or growl to be shocking. Everyone stopped what they were doing to see why the prince was being stubborn today.

"Sire, you need to return to your rooms." This time the "commander" looked directly at him. She didn't bow or show her respect in any other way.

"No," he said again with the same mild expression.

Dare moved closer with a show that he was protecting the prince.

"There is an assassin loose in the palace, sire. You will be safer in your suite."

Tristan shook his head. "I don't think so." He stepped up to one of the techs and leaned in to see what the tech was doing. She stiffened to have the prince looking over her shoulder.

The woman stepped around the desk with an open hand, attempting to guide Tristan away. It would have worked before his adventure. Rather than let her turn him aside, he backed away.

"I would think Security Central should be the safest place in the palace." He kept his smile in place as though this were all a game. That's what they expected of him. He never took security seriously and only followed orders when they came directly from Grouse. He hadn't been home long enough to change his reputation. "Can you show me the feed from my suite?" he asked the tech he stood behind now.

The tech looked to the woman for confirmation, which she didn't get. That was enough to convince Tristan they were on their own and facing the conspiracy. Dare shifted again, this time closer to the woman. Tristan could see this woman wasn't aware of her surroundings like a true fighter. He would be willing to bet she was part of the conspiracy they were fighting.

Tristan turned back to woman. "Where is Chief Grouse? I'd like to talk to her."

"She's not here." The woman tried again to turn Tristan away. That's what she wanted him to believe, with that open hand aimed at his shoulder. "I'll be sure to tell her you were looking for her."

Tristan stayed out of range of her hand, though he was getting close to where Emalynn and Dom were looking through the vids of the challenge.

"You didn't answer his question." Dare spoke louder than he needed to, considering how close to her ear he was standing. "Where is Chief Grouse?"

Tristan wished he could laugh at the woman's expression. It was the classic frustrated-at-dealing-with-kids look too many adults had perfected.

"She's up dealing with the crisis, where she should be." The woman turned on Dare. "Aren't you supposed to be guarding the princess?"

"I am." Dare cocked his head in a mimicry of Tristan's move. "Oh, you mean that's not Emalynn? Who can tell them apart? You did know that they were identical twins. Right?"

Tristan stepped in a little closer, though still out of effective fighting range. "I'm not sure she knows what she's talking about."

She drew her weapon, but Dare took it from her before she could bring it to firing position. "You should know these aren't permitted in Security Central." He tossed the weapon to Emile, who appeared from behind one of the dividers. He still had the woman under control by twisting her wrist.

Tristan ran to the supply cabinet by Grouse's office and brought back plastic restraints. "Do we tell her how long we've known she isn't who she claims to be? Or just start the interrogation?"

"Brat," the woman spat at Tristan.

"I think someone didn't do her homework." Dare tightened the restraints with enthusiasm.

Tristan took that as a yes. "You should probably know I spend enough time in these offices to know the procedures for a crisis, and Chief Grouse never takes point anywhere but here. The techs know they should be looking anywhere but at the crisis itself unless Grouse tells them to, because any crisis could be a diversion. And no one would order me back to my suite if I showed up here during a crisis." Tristan looked at the woman. "And that doesn't cover anything about your appearance or fighting skill."

"He!" Dom yelled, making just about everyone jump. She pointed to a screen over the shoulder of the tech.

"Get away from there," the fake commander yelled. "Stop them."

Several guards moved in to follow the woman's orders. Tristan could have kicked himself. Of course this woman wasn't the only traitor in the ranks of the security force.

"Run," Emalynn said as she rose to face the guards coming at her.

Dom and Karen fled deeper into the security offices. Thia engaged the two guards who tried to follow them.

Emalynn attacked the nearest of the guards coming toward her. It was just like during the challenge. She moved like water over and under her opponents. Somehow she was never where they tried to strike. The emotional connection between them went dead. Unlike the challenge, these women were trying to kill her. Simply dropping them to the floor didn't prevent them from getting up again. The only thing that prevented them from using their weapons was that Emalynn took them before they could use them. The strain of all that fighting started to show, and the two best fighters of the guards were able to knock Emalynn to the floor, but that didn't stop her from marching on.

The fight ended with a sickening crunch. Emalynn crawled away from the fight and gagged.

"Look away," Dare whispered.

Tristan didn't need Dare to tell him that was Emalynn's first real kill. The roiled emotions that returned now that the fight was over told him that. He closed her off and turned his attention to the one who was still able to answer questions.

"Who do you work for?" He didn't growl like Emalynn did, but he lowered his voice and eliminated all aspects of play. The flighty prince wasn't the one who came back, and it was time to let someone know that.

She stiffened at the change in his manner but didn't answer.

He reached for the collar of her uniform and twisted it tight around her neck. "I said who do you work for?" He released her collar just enough for her to speak.

"Lord Degrase."

Tristan dropped her. Of all the possible names she could have said, that wasn't one he expected.

"Degrase?" Emalynn limped up to him.

"Aunt Elise Degrase, one of Mother's sisters."

"So not royal by birth." Emalynn shook her head. "How did she take the county seat?"

He shouldn't be surprised that Emalynn learned so much about the family so quickly. "By marriage. Her husband abdicated to her just after their wedding, before he even took the seat."

"I remember now. It was all over the net." Emalynn limped to a chair and dropped into it. "He had two sisters who died within weeks of each other, leaving him as the only heir." She huffed a small laugh. "Rumor had it he'd had them killed so he could inherit, but then he abdicated to his bride almost as soon as the vows were said. That got him off the tail of that comet. Some conspiracy nuts shifted their blame to the bride, but it didn't stick. Guess it should have stuck."

Tristan sighed. "It should have, because of all the sisters in that family, the only one without a title of her own is Mother."

"How many aunts do we have?"

"Four."

Emalynn groaned as she sat up in the chair and pointed to the screen she'd been looking at. "Those four?"

As expected, his aunts were framed on the screen with two serving boys attending them. "From left to right, Lords Philia Henning, Elise Degrase, Regia Warren, and Hestia Lerring. The sisters born to a corporate executive all managed to snag titles of royalty."

"Let's not invite them to any family gatherings." Emalynn limped her way back to the screen and started the playback.

The sisters stood, chatting among themselves during the challenge. They weren't watching Emalynn, but the rest of the crowd. The serving boys entered. One approached Hestia; the other served Philia. The blades were evident as the boys walked away. The one from Philia was wrapped in a white cloth. The serving boys split and entered the crowd. Tristan would bet the cloth covered blade was the one intended for him.

"Find that cloth and you'll find legarum—and probably a fair number of unresponsive people."

"Legarum?" Dare asked.

"An illegal neurotoxin." Emalynn flinched. "It won't kill you directly, but if the dose is strong enough, you'll die of thirst before you start to move again."

Tristan flinched at that thought.

"Guys," Davy called from the terminal where he was seated. "We have to get out of here."

The screens had turned to a countdown with only forty-two seconds… forty-one.

Karen

When Emalynn told them to run, Dom took off without hesitation. Karen didn't react fast enough and nearly lost Dom as she ran deeper into the offices of the security operation. Karen zigged and zagged around the desks, terminals, and offices, putting all her effort into closing the distance between them. She was only steps behind her when Dom slipped between two large computer towers. Karen nearly missed the turn, then lost sight of Dom in the darkness. Why were these here? Shouldn't all the computer storage be in the communications wing? The towers went deep, with little light to show just how far. Karen followed the shadow of movement she assumed was Dom still running.

Dom stopped dead in the intersection between towers. Karen's reflexes weren't fast enough to prevent crashing into her and taking them both to the floor.

"I'm sorry, sweetie. I'm sorry." Karen tried to comfort Dom while checking to see if she was injured.

Dom shook and reached out for a deeper shadow just around the corner. "I didn't."

"You're safe now." Karen pulled Dom closer to her. "I'll keep you safe."

"No." Dom pulled away. "I didn't." She pointed to the deep shadow. "No. I didn't."

Karen looked closer. It wasn't a shadow, but a woman lying at the base of the computer tower. They crawled closer to the woman.

"Are you okay?" Karen asked as they approached.

She reviewed all the first aid and first responder training she'd received as a captain of the cheer team. Don't move a body without a medic present. You never know what kind of injury there might be. She didn't have access to a med kit either, so there wouldn't be much she could do. Still, she couldn't just leave her there.

"Karen, back away," Thia called from behind her.

The woman didn't even twitch, though Karen jumped at least a foot.

Karen ignored the guard's warning. Something wasn't right about this woman. She lay in an unnatural position and didn't move. She didn't show signs of breathing. Karen moved closer and touched her shoulder. The woman was still warm.

"Hey, are you hurt?" Karen moved her hand to the woman's neck. She thought she felt a pulse, but it didn't happen again right away. "She's alive I think."

"Live." Dom crawled past Karen to a second body.

"Girls." Thia grabbed Karen's arms. "We have to get—"

An explosion ripped through the towers and pushed Karen back down with Thia on top of her. What little light there had been was gone now. Karen could feel dust floating in the air and something warm dripping on her.

"Thia." Karen pushed against the weight holding her down. "Thia, are you hurt? Thia?"

"Mmm." Thia shifted above her.

Karen reached up to feel the woman who was supposed to be protecting them and found her covered in something sticky. A quick sniff told her it was blood. She'd dealt with blood before. It was part of being in a dangerous sport. Broken bones and head wounds were nasty side effects of learning spectacular builds and unorthodox dance moves. This is just like any practice injury, Karen told herself, except for the complete lack of light and the bomb and the people trying to kill them. All the politics and maneuvering were just like the school hall intrigues that had consumed her life until Ly disappeared. If she thought like that, she just might get through this.

A light flared to her right. Dom had her tablet turned to a bright-white screen. Of course, they didn't have to be in the dark or all alone.

"Thank you." Karen reached out for Dom to come closer. "You were always better at that kind of thinking."

"Good," Dom breathed. "Meds?" She scooted closer to Karen and looked up at Thia.

With light to see, Karen had to look away from the blood covering Thia's head. Head wounds were the worst for blood. Mix in hair and dust, and it was hard to tell if any of it was something more than just blood.

"Thia?" Karen put her hand on the woman's cheek. "Thia, I need you to wake up." She started wriggling out of the little jacket that came with the outfit she was wearing that didn't do anything for warmth. It was going to have to take up duty as a bandage. This space they were in was too tight and she had to struggle to pull her arms out of the sleeves until Dom wriggled in close enough to help.

"Down." Dom waved for Thia to lie on the ground.

"Mmmm." Thia groaned, but her eyes flickered open.

Karen managed to get the little jacked around Thia's head in this awkward position and tie it tight enough to stop the blood from dripping. Then Dom was right. They needed to get her down to lie on the ground. She would be more comfortable there and she would have a better chance of recovering, assuming there weren't any neck or back injuries to be aggravated.

Together they were able to get Thia down.

"What are you girls doing?" Thia asked just as they were laying her next to the other woman.

"What we can to keep you alive," Karen said.

"No, you need to get out of here." Thia gasped. "You are in danger."

Karen looked around as far as the light would reach. "We're stuck." Karen hated to admit it, but they were probably safest in this little hole that was still open from where the towers crashed into each other. Karen could see the design that would allow these gaps if anything should happen.

"What are all these towers for?" She wanted to keep Thia awake so she wouldn't die.

"Security keeps our own backups." Thia gasped. "The entire history of the monarchy is here."

Karen looked up in awe. She wondered how far in the past the vids on the machine above her were. What about the tower behind her?

"What do you do with them?"

Thia didn't answer immediately, but her eyes were still open and moving. Karen tried to imagine what kind of security threat records from over five hundred years ago could help.

"We learn what plots have happened before and how they were stopped." Thia's voice was getting weak. "We learn how to handle a prince who likes to run away." She paused to smile. "Tristan isn't as original as he thinks."

Karen laughed. "But he gets away with it."

"Lordy, lordy, lordy, lord," Dom sang out. She turned the tablet for Karen to see. The four sisters were walking through the palace as though nothing had happened. Only the dust and other dirt that covered their clothes proved this was a live feed.

"Where are they?" Karen asked.

"One." Dom gaped and gasped, trying to find more words she could use. "One and one. Sire." She bowed to an imaginary person as much as the space would allow. "One and one."

Karen closed her eyes and tried to just understand what she was saying. It worked best when she listened the tone, not the words. That wasn't saying much, but it was better than ignoring Dom. "Are they going to King Levon?"

Dom shook her head. She thought a bit, then changed the view on the tablet. "Lie, lie, lie. All a lie." The screen showed the rubble after a bomb. It was hard to see where this part of the bomb had been until Karen saw a half round of wood that could only have been Emalynn's precious wood plate.

"We have to warn them," Karen said.

Dom smiled and held up the tablet in record mode.

Karen turned to the tablet as best she could. This would be the worst recording of her life, but she braced herself for it. "Princess Emalynn, don't return to your rooms." Karen chose the blunt approach. "If you stay out of the way, the other bombs won't be able to find you. Don't worry about us. We are safer here than anywhere else for a day or so."

Dom smiled as she took the little vid into the editor. Karen knew she would add enough to make the video confusing to anyone who wasn't Ly. She lay back with a sigh. She'd just ensured people would come looking for them. She could only hope it would be Ly or her followers who found them first. If not... well, that wouldn't be so bad in about a day when they were tired, thirsty, and faint from hunger.

Tristan

Tristan became aware of himself from the ringing in his ears and the pain that covered his body. Dark and dust with the smell of fire and blood filled his senses. No, this was just a dream. He'd survived the blast. That was in the past. He just had to wake up. Wake up, like Emalynn taught him when the nightmares were worse. Only this wasn't a nightmare and he wasn't asleep. It took all his wits to remember he'd been running for the safe room in Security Central.

"Sire, are you hurt?" A face he didn't know coalesced from the haze in front of him.

He opened his lips to a mouthful of dust. Coughing made all the pain flare.

"Sire?"

He succeeded in making a grunt his rescuer could hear. He tried to sit up and sparked another round of coughing. A weight lifted from his chest and something pushed up under his shoulders so he could sit. All of which caused more coughs and the attendant pain until he could only whimper.

"Tristan, thank the stars." Davy appeared beside him. There was a thin line of dried blood down the side of his head. "You look a mess. Are you fine?"

"Ow." Tristan managed to say.

Davy pressed a bottle to his lips. Tristan could smell the tang of citrus before the liquid hit his lips. It tasted horrible but cleared his throat enough to stop the coughing and give him a chance to catch his breath.

"What happened?" Tristan pulled himself to his knees to look around.

As the dust settled and his eyes adjusted to the dark, he realized all the light they had was coming from the independent status lights. Nothing that was connected to the main power showed any signs of operation.

"A bomb happened." Davy offered a hand to Tristan. "No clue of all the damage and no way from here to find out." He held up his tablet. It didn't look damaged, but the screen was blank.

Tristan took a long breath, testing the limits of his lungs. It hurt, but he would live. Good, they didn't get what they wanted.

"No!" Emalynn's voice came from somewhere to his left. "No. It's not fair. Her voice faded away.

He and Davy limped in the direction of her voice. A woman in a guard's uniform joined them. Tristan was tempted to order her away until he recognized her as Emile. She held her left arm tight against her body. She didn't say anything, just nodded to him and turned her attention back to navigating the rubble in the dark.

"I'm sorry." Emalynn's voice filled him with dread. "I tried. I'm sorry." She was hunched in the rubble.

Tristan sank to his knees beside her, and in the light of a flash, he saw Dare with a lump on the side of his head caked in dried blood. He wanted to cry out too, but Ly needed him to be strong. She would never be able to forgive herself if this were what it looked like. Tristan reached out for her hand, but she pushed him away.

"Ly." He tried again.

"No," she growled at him. "Get away from me."

Tristan's hand fell on Dare's chest. It was still warm and moving. Tristan held his hand steady on Dare's chest until he was sure the movement was from breathing, not from Emalynn's rocking.

"He's not dead."

Emalynn continued rocking and muttering how sorry she was.

"Ly, look at me." He put a hand between her and Dare, then pulled her attention toward him. Her eyes were dead, the way they were when she had to talk about Murphy. "Dare's going to survive." He held those dead eyes with his.

He hated to see her like this. This pain she endured just for loving all the people around her. Tristan felt the pang of jealousy that he couldn't make that kind of connection. What a horrible thing, to be jealous of the pain she felt. No, it wasn't the pain he wanted, but the joy she got from those deep connections. For now, he had to get in the way of that connection so the medic coming to help would be able to do her job.

"I couldn't stop it," Emalynn whispered.

"No one could have."

"I should have protected him."

Tristan had to stifle a laugh. Dare didn't need protection. He was the only one on staff who could stand up to Emalynn.

"I was mad and scared him. I scared him and he died." She wasn't talking about Dare.

Tristan pulled her into an embrace. He wanted to tell her it wasn't her fault. He wanted to comfort her. It was Darius's job to protect her. Neither of these things would calm her. They didn't make him feel any better either. In her current state, he wasn't sure she would see the medic as a positive either.

"Ly," he whispered in her ear. "We are in Security Central at the palace on Prime."

She stiffened as he spoke. He tried not to flinch from the strength of her embrace. She managed to find all his bruises and press them.

Davy came close and waved for him to come away. Tristan shook his head a little. He needed to get Emalynn back to the present before he could let her see what had happened. The medic working on Dare kept glancing up at them with the fear that Emalynn would catch her molesting Dare.

Tristan shifted to pull Emalynn a little farther from them. He tried to fill himself with compassion and empathy for her pain. She didn't feel the connection the way he did. That didn't mean it couldn't be useful.

"We have to get out of here." Emalynn's voice was quiet and devoid of emotion. "We can't let them catch us here."

Tristan couldn't tell if she was talking about now or then. Either way, it would fit. Either case would lend to getting her up and away from this event horizon before they were both torn to bits. "Where should we go?"

Emalynn glanced around with those dead eyes. "We need to assess our injuries and defend ourselves."

"There's a secure room at the other end of the office," Emile suggested.

"No." Tristan shook his head. "Too close and easy to lock us in."

"The library?" Davy suggested.

"That's on the other side of the main hall." Emile shook her head. "We'd be too exposed on the way there."

Emalynn looked at Emile and Davy with a hint of confusion. He needed to get them moving before she broke from either her illusion or reality.

"The staff classrooms are close. Just a couple halls away." Tristan pulled Emalynn up and kept her hand in his. "They should be empty now."

"The lounge." Dare groaned more than spoke.

Emalynn turned so fast she pulled Tristan off balance. She was on her knees beside Dare again but holding back from touching him.

Dare struggled to sit with the medic's aid. His head was covered in a bandage that looked more like a strange skull-clinging hat than a medical device. Tristan moved to take the medic's place, telling her to move on to the next patient. Emalynn's eyes had their shine back when she watched him drape Dare's arm over his shoulder. He didn't need to tell her to get his other arm.

Between them they were able to support Dare enough for him to lead them to the lounge he spoke of. A room with a food service machine, two tables, and sixteen of the most uncomfortable chairs Tristan had ever encountered. The clock over the door was blank and the walls were the dingiest shade of white possible. Holding cells were more comfortable than this room. They lay Dare on the one couch, though it might have been more comfortable on the floor.

Emalynn pushed the tables and chairs aside to give herself room to practice her forms. Tristan wanted to join her, but his legs wouldn't put up with the stances, so he joined Davy on one of the tables instead.

"The internal net is down," Davy told him.

"Then what are you doing?"

"I'm getting just enough signal from the standard net, but it's slow." Davy showed him a vid that was running at one frame every two seconds.

He stopped the vid and shifted to a different feed. "No one outside the palace has figured out the government is in danger yet."

Good, Tristan thought, *unless that's what they wanted.*

"Are you getting enough signal to send?" Tristan asked.

Davy shook his head.

"What would you send?" Emalynn asked without breaking her moves.

"I don't know." Tristan sighed. "A distress signal."

Emalynn shifted gracefully through the moves, showing him all her injuries and the places where her clothes were torn. He'd fared better, a little. She finished the set and bowed to the wall. She went to kneel beside Dare, who'd slipped into unconsciousness. Her hand brushed lightly across his hand. In the emergency lights that still worked here, Dare's wounds were laid bare. It was hard to find a place to look that wasn't scorched or covered in blood or both.

"Did you lie to calm me down?" Emalynn asked him without looking away from Dare.

Tristan knelt beside her. "I didn't lie."

She sighed. "I don't like this. How can they care so little about the people around me? Around us? How many people have to die?"

He didn't know how to answer that.

"We don't even know how many people died this time." Emalynn continued, still in that flat voice that sounded like she wasn't really there. "Where are Karen and Dom? What about Thia and the others?"

Tristan's heart sank. Last he'd seen them, they were running off into the back offices. The other elites had been sneaking about the offices, looking for traitors. He couldn't know where they were.

"They're alive," Davy said, "but stuck in the servers." He turned the tablet around to act as a little screen to show them the vid Karen sent out.

"In the servers?" Tristan could see the stacks leaning around each other. "That's a relief."

"What?" Emalynn looked over her shoulder at him.

"The towers are designed to fall safe, and there are emergency supplies hidden among them." Emile stood by the door, doing her best to be a guard despite her injuries. "This isn't the first time the palace or Security Central has been bombed. Then there have been natural disasters; the engineers have had plenty of lessons to learn from."

The vid was short, so they had to play it several times before they understood all Karen had put in there. The obvious warning about other bombs covered a much deeper and more worrisome hint. Emalynn saw it first. There were three bodies visible in the dim background. One of them was Thia, but the other two were women Tristan couldn't identify. Emalynn found more meaning in Karen's words, though how she knew all the depth she claimed...

"We don't have much time," Emalynn declared after the tenth time through the vid. "But we are going to have to wait for the rescue mission to get them out. In the meantime, tell me as much as you can about our aunts."

Tristan sighed. He'd never really trusted his aunts. They were always too focused on their media image. Davy added bits and pieces from the net to fill in a picture of his family that showed too many skeletons. They weren't just in the closets, but stuffed under all the furniture.

Emalynn

Emalynn felt the strain of living in a drama-filled world taking its toll. No one they knew had been confirmed dead, yet. Karen and Dom were trapped but apparently stable. A blessing of sorts. Darius drifted in and out of consciousness on the little cot in the first aid office.

"I'm sorry," she whispered again. "I have to leave you here."

"Go." He moaned. "I'll be fine."

She couldn't argue with him. They had to move on, disguise themselves, and fight back. Her aunts were going to be sorry they'd tried to mess with her. She'd faced people like this before, mostly in the form of Baba's clients. Women who had the privilege to not know where the kitchens were or that a large enough kitchen would have a first aid office. They wouldn't know kitchens were a playground for a criminal seeking a new appearance.

"Emalynn, we need to keep moving." Emile spoke softly from the doorway. She looked dashing in the casual clothes they were able to borrow from the kitchen staff. Flour dusted into her hair changed the color enough to transform her whole appearance. They'd even found a way to hide the worst of the scratches from the bomb.

The cooks found ways to lighten Davy's complexion and darken his hair. The younger staff quivered to be in her presence the way boys at school did when there was a rumor of a vid star coming anywhere close. Emalynn couldn't bear to tell them she wasn't that special. Instead, she spent a few moments personalizing their tablets before following the others back into the servants' halls.

"Where are we going?" Emalynn asked.

"I've found a clear path to the secondary media offices." Davy handed her the tablet showing the route. "We'll be able to get a better view of what's happening from there."

Emalynn nodded. "And equipment?"

Davy smiled. Of course they'd be going for the kind of equipment Karen and Dom would need to produce the kind of vids that went nova as soon as they were released on the net. Karen's network of followers was the reason Emalynn's plan to confuse the galaxy about Tristan had worked at all. It wasn't the kind of network her aunts would know about or be able to control. Unpredictable, that was the key. Never mind they'd done it in the past; she only need to do things her aunts wouldn't anticipate in the same way they'd managed to get away with their plots so far, because no one thought them capable of doing that kind of thing.

Emalynn kept her breathing steady through tight control of every move she made. If she let her thoughts wander too far, she would drive herself mad for the sake of these women who'd been so manipulative. What kind of woman was her grandmother to send her daughters off to take over the royal families like this? She was still a corporate leader, so unable to come to her homecoming.

"You really think they won't think of this?" Tristan caught up to her. "I mean, they have public relations people to keep track of the net."

"Exactly." Emalynn thought of all the advice Baba had given her about keeping out of trouble. "Everyone thinks their plan is unique and their tactics are theirs alone," she quoted. "They have manipulated the media to their advantage to keep people from figuring out what they did to their husbands' families. They aren't going to think we would dare try to use the media against them. They have it all locked up."

Tristan nodded. "Is that how you win so many fights?"

Emalynn felt the heat rising to her cheeks. "I win so many fights because I fight like a bilge rat."

"You fight dirty?"

"I fight to win, however that needs to happen." Emalynn remembered the first time she'd had to fight her way out of trouble. She hadn't reached four feet tall yet, and the dock guard wasn't one of the honorable ones. She would have sold Emalynn to the first slaver or corporation to come along once she was done with her fun. The desperation gave her strength she couldn't have summoned otherwise. Baba taught her to control that reaction after that. The next time she'd had to fight her way out of trouble, the fighting trance kicked in.

The secondary media offices were empty and dark when they arrived. Tristan tricked the lock into admitting them. Emalynn found it amusing that this office looked so similar to the studios at school where Karen spent most of her time when she wasn't required to be somewhere else. They were so similar Emalynn was able to find the handheld cameras that made for better vids than the tablets.

"Oh stars and dust." Davy had the main media wall running as many windows as possible, all showing different parts of the palace.

"How many bombs were there?" Emalynn looked over the images. Security Central had emergency lighting and teams of rescue workers crawling over the destruction. The throne room looked pristine and abandoned, but the courtyard where the challenge had been sported a crater and piles of twisted metal that might have been the spectator stands. That gave her a chill. The main hall and library were little more than charred rubble. So were the main media offices. "And why aren't the media using this office?"

"They've opened the office in the business wing." Emile pointed to another view, an office similar to this room. That room was crowded with women and men tripping over each other with tablets cradled in their arms.

"Can we see what kind of images they're putting out?" Emalynn was sure at least one of those women was in league with the aunts.

Davy's hands glided over the controls. "No, I can't get a good feed on it." He pushed that image to a closer screen. "You're worried they're working for your aunts."

"They are." Tristan took over the main screen with a selection of the top gossip and news feeds. All of them reported the apparent death of both Emalynn and Tristan.

The reports contained just enough contradictory information that any one report could be discredited with little effort, but together they could bring the whole system into chaos. Emalynn hated to admit it, but they were good at this.

"Can we cut them off?" She leaned over Davy's side of the control panel. "I mean, most of these are saying the crisis is over except for the cleanup and investigation. So we can prove that a lie if the palace suddenly goes dark."

Davy turned to look at her with his mouth open, but it was Tristan who answered her.

"Only by taking down the whole royal network."

"Do that, then."

The boys looked at each other with an expression she didn't want to understand. They had reservations about going dark. Tristan she could understand. Despite all he'd been through, he still believed in the system.

"Princess." Emile stepped away from her position at the door. "Taking down the royal network would be extremely risky. We would be cut off from all our resources."

"Resources we can't trust." Emalynn stood to confront the guard. She'd only been with them for a couple days, but she'd proven herself a useful person. Still, she, like Tristan, believed in a system that had been rotted from the inside. "Assume this conspiracy predates Queen Treylyn. Who can we trust?"

Emile's lips tightened as she tried to stare down Emalynn. "What do you intend to do?"

"Break their strategy." Emalynn smiled. They were going to go around all the systems her aunts knew and understood. "Guys? When we take down the royal net, we'll have access to the standard net, won't we?"

The look on Tristan's face said it all. The wide-eyed, open-mouthed look that froze for a moment while he put his thoughts back together. "We'll have to adjust the tablets, but yeah."

Emalynn grabbed the nearest tablet and flicked to the settings.

Karen

Karen sat in the makeshift infirmary next to Dom, watching Thia sleep. No one would tell them where Emalynn was or anything about what had happened. They gave different excuses about needing to help other people or it being nothing to worry about. She worried because this wasn't the first time since arriving in the palace that she'd narrowly avoided death. She worried because Dom had gone completely silent since the rescue workers had found them. Dom didn't want to leave with them until they took Thia. She didn't want them to do that either, but couldn't stop them. Karen felt the same. These women couldn't be trusted, but her best bet was to stay with Thia, even if the guard was unconscious.

Now they were all worried about something they still wouldn't tell her about. It wasn't hard to figure out they were out of communication with anyone else. So the network went down or was taken down. Karen would lay even odds for the stars that Emalynn had something to do with that.

Another pair of rescue workers came in with someone on a litter. They deposited the body on the far side of the curtained-off area.

"Hey, how are you two doing?" One of the workers came over. She looked as if she'd been close to the blast, with cuts all over her face and hands.

"Fine, I guess." Karen gripped Dom's hand. "I wish someone would talk to us."

The woman laughed. "Yeah, I doubt that's going to happen." She came closer, keeping her face turned down. "You see, they want to be free to blame you."

"Free and then go." Dom pulled her hand free of Karen's grip and reached out to the woman who let Dom push her face to the light.

Nari held the position for a few seconds, then brushed Dom's hands aside to lower her face again.

"It won't be long. Are you two ready to go?"

Karen nodded. Nari gave a short bow and left.

Thia still lay as still as death on the table they'd made into a bed for her. It didn't look comfortable, but the one person who acted like a doctor declared she would live and could be left to sleep for now. Someday, all of this would make it into one of her stories. She had to hold on to that to keep from screaming.

"This way." A whisper called her attention to the curtain wall behind Thia's bed. "Come quick."

Dom grabbed her hand and pulled her to the curtain. They ducked under the curtain into the dark war zone outside.

"Karen." Ly wrapped her arms around her. "I'm so happy you're safe. Thanks for the message."

"If you got our message, what are you doing down here?" Karen held Ly tight. "And what did you do to the network?"

Ly laughed. "What do you think I'm doing? I'm going to take down four lords this time, and I need your help."

Karen hugged her friend tighter. "Of course you are. What's the plan?"

"Not here." Emalynn pulled away and hugged Dom just as tightly before leading them through the rubble to a hole in the wall that led to a back hallway where Davy, Tristan, Emile, and Nari were waiting.

"Where's Dare?"

"In the same state as Thia." Emalynn's voice went strangely flat. "Oh, here, I got you these. Have fun, but you'll probably have to give them back."

Emalynn handed her a large tablet and handheld independent camera. She gave a similar set to Dom. The camera was the best of the best, the kind Karen had only ever drooled over in the catalogs when she dreamed about becoming a professional vid maker. The tablet was even better. The screen resolution would allow for vid editing on the fly and maintain the quality without having to check for flaws on a media wall at its highest setting. It had all the programs she was used to using and a strong connection to the net.

"I thought the net was down." Karen looked over at Davy. "I heard the rescue workers complaining about it."

"Check which network you're on." He grinned.

The standard net. Then the royal network really was down. They weren't playing around.

"How long do we have?" Karen directed that one at Tristan, then to Emalynn. "What do you want us to do?"

"Make one of your nova videos and get it out before the aunts have time to rein it in," Emalynn said. "And you'll have about three hours now, maybe more, maybe less depending on how quickly they figure out what we did."

"So no pressure." Karen sighed. Being Ly's friend had never been easy or lazy. As a student, she laid on the homework worse than any teacher and worried so much about graduation no one around her could do anything less. Now that she was princess, she found new ways to make things interesting.

"Well, how do you feel about interviewing the king of the galaxy?" Emalynn grinned the way she did when she'd come up with a new move for cheer and wasn't sure if the team would be able to do it.

Karen looked at the dusty, bloody, and cut-up clothes she was wearing. "Could I at least get changed before we meet the king?"

Emile showed her the clothes they had and promised there was a shower where they were going. Emalynn outlined the plan to create a short documentary outlining the way her aunts had manipulated their way into the royal family. The key would be getting King Levon to provide the damning quotes. They'd already loaded the relevant historic vids.

"It would be best if we could get at least one of the sisters to confess," Karen said as she started digging through the vids they'd given her to work with. Emile took her shoulders to keep her from running into the walls as they continued toward the king's chambers.

"Not Mother," Tristan said with a firm look at Emalynn.

"You'd better have the vid mostly ready before we confront any of them," Emalynn said. "Something you can just drop in place and get out there."

Karen laughed, just like working on a group project with all the over-achievers in communications class. She could already see some of the structure of this project. She fought when Nari took the tablet so she could take her shower. Her hair was still wet when they arrived at the king's private chamber.

The king's guards expected them and opened the chamber doors before Tristan could ask. King Levon sat in his main room in a chair that looked like a comfortable throne. He wore a suit as always and smiled in the way that had become his signature in any press releases.

"Father." Tristan bowed.

"Tristan, Emalynn." The king held out his hands.

Emalynn took his hand and let him pull her close. Tristan hesitated before doing the same.

"Can I assume you are getting in trouble again?"

"Yes," Tristan answered.

"And out." Emalynn shot a look at Tristan. "We've come to ask you a few questions." She smiled at the king.

King Levon laughed. "And brought an amateur camera crew with you." The king raised a hand to Karen. "Is it because the net is down and you're going to be loud and embarrassing? Or is it because you're going to be loud and embarrassing that you took the net down?"

Karen blushed and wished she could hide somewhere else. How did the king know that much about what they were up to before they even started? Tristan wouldn't look his father in the eyes. Emalynn only stepped back a bit.

"It worked against Lord Leblanc." Emalynn took her father's hand in both of hers. "It will work against your wife's family, if you help us."

Dom had her camera on and trained on the royals. Karen didn't know if they would be able to use this intimate family moment in the vid they were about to create, but she would find a way to use it sometime.

The king blinked first with a short laugh. "You really are his sister, without all the propriety training."

The look of shock and love on Tristan's face was priceless. Emalynn's confusion was equally rare.

"Leave your mother out of this one. She's suffered enough since your return. I can assume you've already retrieved the records they didn't succeed in destroying."

"You can." Emalynn left to get a chair she could sit in so it would look like a normal family evening. Normal for a regular family living in the colonies. Their plan was to pretend Karen had pulled all the files from the archives, including this interview. Emalynn knew her part here, and she started the conversation as though she were just trying to get to know the family. Then the questions about how her aunts had managed to become royal.

"What about Mother? Was she part of the plan?" Emalynn looked so concerned Karen wasn't sure if she was still acting or if this conversation had become something real.

The king wasn't acting when he shifted his gaze to the floor. "She did as her mother ordered and found her way into court." He described a tangled web of courting and intrigue, with several prominent families all vying for his hand in marriage. An unwed prince is a prize worthy of battle to those seeking power, and they were all tricked onto the princess' transport for some sort of contest. "Treylyn warned me about the sabotage, but I couldn't convince anyone to take it seriously. By the time the dust settled, she was the only suitor."

"But you love her."

"I came to love her before we needed an heir." Levon reached out to Emalynn and Tristan. "You were born of the love that comes from trust in the face of adversity."

Karen felt her own stomach tighten around that thought.

"Did she ever ask you to abdicate?" Tristan stood beside Emalynn now. He wasn't supposed to be in the shot. He wasn't much of an actor, but that line came out perfectly.

King Levon paused a long time, looking mostly at his lap before he looked up at his son. "She told me she was supposed to, but she never did."

That was perfect. Karen had never had a shoot go so smoothly. Nothing to retake or trying to rough cut pieces that didn't really fit together. She would be able to put this vid together quick and easy. She could get the first part out before they planned to confront the aunts. It would be out on the net before those media hacks had a chance to slow it down. It would be better if she could get part two out, with their confessions or at least threats, before things went sour.

"Thank you, Father." Emalynn rose and bowed deeply to the king.

The look on King Levon's face told a whole story of hope and love. Karen wondered how long he'd been waiting for her to do that. Something about this not-so-staged conversation had broken the wall between them. Ly would become his heir without reservation now. He stood and bowed back to her.

Karen was late to bow with the rest of them as they got ready to leave.

"Miss Toya," the king said as she rose. "Make this work. My daughter has faith in you."

"Thank you, sire. I will."

"And if you make me look too human, you'll have to watch out for my publicist." He smiled.

Emalynn

Karen's vid was perfect. Emalynn loved how it showed just enough of the evidence against the aunts to catch the attention of the conspiracy freaks while not being something that would scream fiction. Since her clips weren't verifiable yet, that would have to do. Karen even added a bit about how the sisters of the queen were masters of manipulation, so be sure to keep your copy of the vid safe and put It back out if you ever find it's gone from the net. That should keep it circulating long enough to cause problems. The title itself would be an issue if they failed in the next phase. *The Royal Succession: Part I.*

They waited only long enough to see someone had seen it. Then they pushed the vid to all the screens in Aunt Philia's room. Hers was the closest, and they had to tap directly into the feed. The added advantage was access to the media eye so they could watch her reaction. One thing people in power never seemed to notice was just how much they depended on the invisible systems working properly. Philia wasted time yelling for a connection to Hestia before realizing she was going to have to walk next door. Time Emile and Nari used to clear the hallway of bodyguards and others who might get in the way.

Emalynn timed her next actions carefully. They were in a small room meant for favored servants, but it was unused. Timed right, she would catch Philia before she noticed the lack of staff in the outer halls.

She stepped out as soon as she heard the cycle of Philia's door, but that was just a moment earlier than she wanted.

"Oh, Aunt Philia," Emalynn called when the lord finally came into view. "Do you know what's going on?"

Philia jumped. "What are you doing here? I thought everyone was supposed to be in their rooms."

Emalynn shrugged. "My guards brought me here, then took off to go deal with the crisis. I guess it's safe enough."

Philia continued to stare at Emalynn as though not quite sure she was really there. Emalynn just stood there, letting her look as though it were nothing. Eventually, Philia shook it off.

"The safest place is always your own rooms. We should get you back there."

Emalynn shrugged again. She let Philia back her into the room. Let her aunt assume she was the spoiled brat she expected. As long as Emalynn played that part here and now, Philia wouldn't question it. She might wonder how this brat managed to escape the bombs. That presented her with a bigger problem—getting Emalynn back to where their plot could work.

"I don't want to go to my rooms." Emalynn added just a hint of whine to her voice. "Why do we have to be locked down anyway? All the commotion's over by now."

Philia sneered at Emalynn. "Child, we have to be careful. Let those who know what they are doing handle that kind of thing."

"What more are they looking for. I hit both assassins." Emalynn threw her fist toward the ground. It had been a long time since she'd played a temper tantrum. It felt just as fake now as it did when she was little and needed to distract some dockworkers.

Philia fell for it. She didn't notice she'd been cut off from her guards. She fell into the adult role so easily. "Honey." Her voice dripped with false sweetness. "We never know what they're looking for."

"Because an assassin isn't going to put herself on your schedule." Emalynn pulled the quote Tristan told her to use. It was false. Baba often made appointments with her intended victims.

"Exactly." Philia smiled with the same saccharine emotion she'd spoken with. She pulled something from her pocket that Emalynn couldn't see. "You just need to relax and let the professionals handle things."

Emalynn dodged Philia's attempt to pat her on the shoulder. There was a small needle in her hand, poisoned without a doubt. Things just got a lot more interesting.

"Professionals like you?" Emalynn turned to face her aunt directly. "Is that what you told your husband?"

Philia took a step back. "What do you know about that?"

"Only that you and your sisters were really lucky to find five royal men in need of wives to take over their holdings." Emalynn braced herself for the rage that was about to erupt. "Oh, only four of you were that lucky."

"You little..." Philia closed the distance between them with surprising speed.

Emalynn caught her outstretched hand and pushed it aside. Philia lost her balance with the change in her own force and landed in a heap. She twitched a couple times before slumping as though asleep.

246

"Crud." Emalynn rolled her over to find the small needle mark on Philia's thigh. "You just couldn't leave well enough alone, could you?"

"What happened?" Tristan came out of the back room.

Emalynn shook her head and carefully removed the needle from her hand. "Have they pushed the vid to Regia yet?"

"They just started." Tristan came to help pull Philia into the next room. "We didn't get any good quotes off her."

"Can't we use any of her ranting in front of the screen?"

Tristan shrugged. "You'd better get going, and be careful."

Emalynn left Tristan to deal with Philia and went to ready that little scene again. They were running out of time to neutralize the aunts. Emalynn hated this game of intrigue and counter intrigue. Why couldn't the lords just play it straight, have their fights, and go home to lick their wounds like everyone else?

She heard the door cycle farther down the hall. Three deep breaths and she stepped out.

Regia kept her guards around her more tightly than Philia had but still fell for the opportunity to put her upstart niece in her place. This time the scene played out with the guards in the room doing most of the intimidating until Emalynn brought up the succession. Regia's anger burned slower than Philia's.

"You think you know anything?" Regia stepped in front of her guards at Emalynn's taunt that one of her sisters hadn't followed the plan. "Men aren't fit to rule."

"Oh?" Emalynn feigned shock. "So you just happened to marry a man who would be forced into a position of power. I suppose you're going to tell me you don't really want the power. You're just stepping up to fill the void."

"What are you saying?" Regia narrowed her eyes.

"I'm saying it's amazing that all three of your sisters-in-law died in such horrible accidents." Emalynn gave her aunt a sly grin. "I mean, my tutor told me how awful it was to have so many fine young women lost in just over a year. If they weren't nobles, we'd say it was just bad luck. I mean, it happens in the colonies."

Regia had a very sour look on her face.

"The funny thing is I don't remember hearing about it. Something like that would get talked about all the time. I mean, we keep track of the royals." No, they didn't. Most people lived just fine without talking about the nobles for years at a time. "So it's odd that no one would have said anything about three noble heirs dying to leave only a boy to take their place." She almost gagged on that line. "Something like that almost feels like it had to be planned."

"Watch what you say." Regia spoke through gritted teeth.

"Why? 'Cause I might stumble on the truth?"

Regia jumped back as though Emalynn had slapped her. Karen would be able to use that, if the camera angle worked out.

"All I'm saying is you and your family got really lucky to snag five royal titles. I mean four titles."

"Luck had nothing to do with it." Regia drew herself up to look intimidating. It might have worked on someone else. "It wasn't luck. It took years of planning to get us where we are, and we won't let a little brat like you destroy it."

"Planning?" Emalynn lifted her shoulders as though weighing that word. "How do you plan for so many fateful accidents? It sounds more like luck to me."

"You may rely on luck, but we plan. That's the main difference between those in power and those without." Regia loomed over Emalynn with a finger pointed at her, ready to jab at any moment. "You'll get nowhere in this universe if you don't figure that out."

Close enough.

"By planning, you mean sabotage?" Emalynn let her stay this close but changed her attitude from cowering to power. "All those accidents, poisonings, random killings were planned. That sounds like the definition of conspiracy to me."

Regia grabbed for Emalynn's neck with more speed than Emalynn would have guessed. Emalynn allowed the move with a slight twist of her neck to keep it safe. Three, two, one—Emalynn broke the hold and twisted so she had Regia's arms pinned behind her and her body between Emalynn and the guards.

"Disarm." Emalynn ordered the guards. A small twist got Regia to squeak. That was all the guards needed to comply.

"I'm a lord. You can't do this to me." Regia again spoke through gritted teeth.

"I'm a princess." Emalynn pushed her toward the inner door. "I outrank you."

Emile and Nari came to deal with the guards while Tristan helped bind Regia to a chair in the back room.

"Let's get Hestia started." Emalynn headed for the main room.

"That's not going to work," Davy called through the media wall. "Royal net has been restored and Hestia's already looking for you."

Crud and double crud. Emalynn took a couple of deep breaths while Tristan stared at her. "Lock us in." She told him. With the net back in place, she wouldn't have to face her aunts directly. "Davy, get Dom and Karen somewhere safe and try to contact Grouse. Directly if you can figure a way."

Davy nodded and the wall went dead. Emalynn braced herself before reopening to the wall with a direct connect to Philia's rooms. The connection completed through automated response just in time for Emalynn to see Hestia and her guards, all six of them, enter the room. It didn't take long for Hestia to notice Emalynn on connection.

"What have you done?" Hestia rushed the wall as though that would intimidate Emalynn.

"Lots of things." Emalynn smiled with her lips only. "Which things did you want to know about?"

"That vid that's already gone nova."

"Oh, that." Emalynn shook her head. "I'm not much of a vid editor. That wasn't me."

"You upstart little brat." Hestia's face reddened under her dark complexion. "I'll discredit everything in that vid."

Emalynn shrugged. "You can try, but there's a reason it didn't run through the reputable channels. Oh, you didn't notice that part, did you?"

Hestia turned to verify that with one of the guards.

"So." Emalynn interrupted. "I just wondered what you did to get your husband to cede his power to you?"

Hestia glared at the screen, her cheeks twitching.

"Did you steel his puppy? Or maybe his favorite servant." Emalynn dropped her smile. "Actually, I know what you did. You promised to hide the scandal of his birth. The fourth son with no daughters? What could his mother have been doing?"

"Shut up." Hestia yelled. "Just shut up. What do you know of anything?"

"I know your youngest sister got the best prize and chose not to follow the plan."

Tristan huffed his disapproval of this line of the game. He would have preferred to leave Mother out of it, but it was the best way to push this otherwise cold and calculating woman over the edge.

"I also know how many people have died in your family's bid to become royal. At the latest count, not including today, you've racked up five hundred thirty-one bodies. That we know of. There may be more we haven't traced to you yet." Emalynn shifted about, allowing herself to gesture as if this were just a casual conversation. "I also know your sister Philia has an unfortunate fascination with illegal poisons such as legarum. That got the better of her today."

Hestia's eyes got big when Emalynn moved out of the way to show Philia lying stiff on the bed. Regia struggled in her bindings beside the bed.

"You stupid bilge rat." Hestia gestured to her guards. Then the connection went dead.

Emalynn turned to Tristan. "Sorry about that."

"Let's just get out of here." He shook his head.

The door slid open. Emile and Nari fell through, bound and gagged. Emalynn prepared for a fight until she saw the laser pistols in the hands of Elise's guards.

Tristan

Tristan watched his aunts argue about what to do now that Elise had done the unthinkable and kidnapped the princess. He sat against the wall between Emile and Davy with his hands bound behind his back. Davy shouldn't have been here, but he couldn't find a way to ask without revealing Karen and Dom. Nari, on Davy's far side, and Emile were gagged and had their ankles bound as well. Emalynn lay in the far corner, bound hand, foot, elbow, and ankle. She was gagged and blindfolded as well. Elise insisted on that much for her citing her upbringing. Tristan had to agree it was probably best to keep Emalynn that tightly bound if you wanted to keep her at all. He wasn't sure whether to be honored or insulted they didn't give him the same respect.

He'd seen Emalynn moving in small ways that were probably attempts to loosen her bonds, so he copied them. Pulling against the ropes they used hurt his wrists and didn't get him anywhere. He couldn't imagine how Emalynn put up with all of that without so much as a whimper. His aunts kept looking over at her and never seemed to notice the strain she put on their knots. He feared the thought that she'd been through something like this before. For all that she complained about the intrigues in the palace, she'd lived a much more danger-filled life than he.

Davy wasn't so subtle about straining at his bonds. Not that it made any difference. Like Tristan, his feet weren't bound. No one took notice of his struggles, even when he fell over onto Tristan.

"Part II made it out," Davy whispered while his head rested on Tristan's shoulder. "I wonder how long until they notice."

Tristan wondered the same thing. Karen's network of fans was extensive, as seen by the response to her call for the Tristan images. Since these involved references to the royal family and images of Emalynn, they would circulate widely. Of course, that width would be mostly among the underage crowd until it was too late to pull them back, which was the whole point. He wondered how many times they would be able to count on that before the adults learned how to block them.

Tristan toppled onto Davy's shoulder. "Where are they?"

"Don't know. Safe I hope." Davy helped him sit back up.

When Tristan looked at his aunts, only Regia looked back with a sneer. Tristan grinned at her with the practiced sweetness he'd learned as a child. He wasn't supposed to use that one anymore, but it was so effective. Just as Regia turned away, he stuck out his tongue.

"Really?" Emile slid a hand behind his back and put something in his hand.

It took every ounce of willpower not to look at her while he turned it over in his hand. It was a small knife sharp enough to cut the ropes with little force. The hard part was not cutting himself.

"We can't kill them," Hestia declared loudly over the building argument between Regia and Elise.

"We can't just release them either." Elise glared at him. "As soon as they get the chance, they'll blab about all this."

"They've already done it." Regia pushed past Hestia to get at Elise. "They have a vid with archives in it. I thought those were destroyed."

"Where did you see this vid?" Elise shot back.

"On my media wall."

Elise looked at Hestia and the two of them started laughing.

Tristan freed his hands and leaned over to pass the knife to Davy. "Should we tell them?"

"Not yet." Davy took the knife.

Tristan sat back up with his hands still behind his back. He glanced at Emalynn and saw she'd managed to adjust her blindfold enough to see him.

"You are an idiot." Elise pushed Regia against the wall. "The net was down. They couldn't put it out, and we are in control of the publicity office now. Nothing leaves the royal net without publicity approval."

True, Tristan thought. But technically that vid was never on royal net. So the fact that it went out without publicity office approval didn't break the rules. Technically. Maybe the archives they used would be considered broken rules. They did break the rules about putting out unapproved images of the king, except Father approved them himself.

"What are you looking all smug about?" Elise grabbed Tristan's chin and pulled his face around to face her.

"I don't think I broke any rules this time." He twisted his chin out of her grip.

"What?"

"Well, I didn't ditch my security team." Tristan pulled his knees up to his chest preemptively. "In fact, I'm still with them. And I didn't leave the palace. I'm trying to remember if there's a rule against royals using the servants' halls. I know it's discouraged, but I don't think it's actually against the rules. Besides, that's what Emile told me to do." Tristan pretended to think for a moment. "Nope, I didn't break any rules this time, so it's not my fault I'm in trouble. It's yours."

"Does that logic work for me, too?" Davy asked. "It'd be nice to not be at fault for once."

"I would think so." Tristan looked up at Aunt Elise. "What do you think?"

Elise pulled her hand back to slap Tristan across the face. Tristan flinched away, but the slap never came.

Emile had Elise by the wrist. "I arrest you in the name of Princess Emalynn for attempted assault on Prince Tristan."

"You can't arrest me." Elise tried to pull away.

Emile twisted Elise's arm around to pin it behind her back. Nari had dropped three of the guards already and had the rest pressed against the wall with their own laser pistols aimed at them. Davy rushed to Emalynn and had already released her legs. Tristan quit pretending his hands were tied and used them to lever himself up without touching Emile or his aunt.

"Security breach. Code Tristan other two." Tristan spoke to the systems that had ruled his life since birth. The failsafe, if somehow the guards failed to protect him. No one, not even him, would be able to leave this room until Chief Grouse or one of her generals came to extract him. He'd never used one of these codes for anything other than a drill before.

He heard the locks on all the maintenance vents and access panels slide into place. The palace techs would complain about that until all of them were manually reset. Tristan would apologize later, if he wasn't able to get them all reset before they were needed.

Emalynn exploded from her place in the corner only to find that no one resisted her. She stopped in the middle of the room and turned to him. "What did you do?"

"Set the automatic security system. Nothing gets out except the beacon until security comes to release us." Tristan smiled at his aunts. "Oh, and they will have the video and audio feed."

Emalynn stared at him for a beat, then started laughing. "This could take a while." She gasped. "I mean, they blew up Security Central."

Tristan took his turn to look at her dumbfounded. He didn't see the humor that had her almost doubled over with laughter. A glimpse of the horror on his aunts' faces gave him a clue. They'd really dug themselves in deep this time.

"Oh, I hope you ladies had a good lunch." Emalynn continued to laugh.

Davy joined her. "Oh, but they don't know the best part." He came over to lean on Tristan's shoulder.

The laughter was contagious now. He had to force himself to breathe. "You're talking about the vids Karen released."

Emile and Nari were shaking as they held the aunts and guards under control.

Looking at his aunts' faces made Tristan laugh even harder. He couldn't get the rest of the thought out, not in one breath.

Emalynn sucked in air. "Last we had a chance to check…"

Davy picked up from there. "Fourteen thousand views, on the original site."

"Her best yet." Emalynn clapped Davy on the shoulder.

Regia turned ghostly pale and crumpled to the floor. Elise and Hestia glared at them.

"What are you talking about?" they said in unison.

Tristan had to close his eyes to regain enough control to explain how they got around the restrictions. Hestia joined Regia on the floor, just as pale. Elise squared off with Emalynn, though her jaw quivered.

"It won't have the effect you're looking for." Elise promised.

Emalynn sobered as though it had all been an act. "Can you be sure of that?" Emalynn closed the distance between them. "It's out there in a way you can't clean up. It will only take one legitimate question and you'll have to face what you've done."

"And who's going to ask that question?" Elise stiffened but didn't back away.

"I will." Tristan spoke before Emalynn had the chance to. "It would be unseemly for the heir to attack her blood relatives."

Elise twitched, and Emalynn put her on the ground with a hand around her neck.

"Stand down." Dare ordered from just inside the door.

When had they opened the locks? Dare had two dozen guards with him who took control of the room.

"Emalynn, that means you." Dare came closer. He moved with a care that revealed his injuries.

Emalynn released Elise to the guards and stood facing Dare. "Did we get it all?"

"Enough," he said.

"Are you…?"

"I'll fight. I'll live."

Tristan found somewhere else to look.

Karen

The guards outside the queen's chambers waited patiently for Karen to approach. The two who had found them in the servants' halls of the guest levels were waiting at the closest corner, after announcing her and Dom to the two who were standing beside the door. None of them had moved. They didn't sigh or shift their weight. None of them said anything about hurrying up or even that they were welcome. Best of all, they kept their eyes off Dom, who clung to Karen's hand and shook. Dom stared at the queen's guards standing beside the door.

Karen agreed with Dom about one thing; this was the scariest door they could have been brought to. Queen Treylyn was scary enough in her own right, being the most powerful woman in the galaxy with a reputation for being strict about etiquette and propriety. She was also the sister of those four lords who had kidnapped Dom and ordered Davy beaten in order to control Ly and Tristan. Most likely, they were also the ones who set off bombs around the palace that had nearly killed them. That's why she would be scary for anyone.

Karen and Dom had released the vids that detailed the horrible things her sisters had done to win their place in the royal family. Karen didn't think the guards were the scary part here.

On the contrary, the guards were in the process of convincing her it couldn't be all bad simply by not rushing them into the queen's suite. The sisters never gave Karen or Dom an option. When they wanted to talk to them, they simply kidnapped them right out of the school cafeteria in what looked like a ceremony to award them their prize for the contest they'd made up. These women, despite their uniforms and the family of their employer, used patience and logic to get Karen where they wanted her.

"We should go," Karen muttered as much to herself as to Dom. The logic that brought them this far was still true. They needed to be someplace safe and unexpected, and what could be more unexpected than Queen Treylyn's private suite?

Dom gave one small nod in response.

Step by step, inch by inch, they moved closer to the queen's door. The guards showed no sign that they noticed the two girls heading toward them. No sign at all when the door slid open for them. They didn't so much as blink when she and Dom inched past them into the queen's private rooms.

Inside, the main room, while a little bigger than Emalynn's, was laid out the same. A small dining area just to the right was dominated by a gorgeous wood table with elaborately carved legs and three chairs to match. Display shelves over the buffet counter displayed decorative sets of dishes in a wide variety of styles. Beyond that were two seating areas. One with individual chairs clustered around a low steel and glass table and a second area with double chairs arranged for viewing the media wall.

Queen Treylyn sat in one of the double chairs with her back to the main room, watching the scene on the wall. Emalynn and Tristan stood larger than life on that wall, surrounded by guards. A faint bruise was forming around Emalynn's left eye, and Tristan kept rubbing his wrists. Other than that, they looked happy.

"Welcome, Miss Toya and Miss Quell" The queen rose from her seat to face them. She looked much older than any of her media images Karen had seen. Instead of her usual tailored suit, she wore a simple shirt with relaxed pants. Even her hair was down from its usual styled look. "Please come sit with me."

Karen bowed deep before moving farther into the room. She would never have imagined she'd be alone in a room with the queen. That struck her when she was about halfway across the floor. There were no guards or attendants here. There were just the three of them. She had to assume the cameras were as prevalent here as they were everywhere in the palace, but who would be watching? Most of the palace staff were dealing with the aftermath of the bombing.

"Thank you for inviting us, Your Majesty." Karen bowed again when they were closer.

"Don't thank me yet." The queen spoke in a low, sad voice. "I haven't told you what I want." She waved at the chair across from her. "As my daughter would say, enough of the bowing and majesty talk. I'm just a person."

Karen couldn't keep the grin from her face to hear the queen quoting Emalynn. Although, Emalynn usually sounded more angry than sad when she said it.

"Please, turn your cameras on." The queen returned to her seat. She gestured at her wall, and the image changed from the little room where Emalynn and Tristan had been to Karen's netsite. The queen called up the royal succession video so fast it was clear she had practiced.

She set the video to play with the volume low, then turned to Karen. "You are either very brave or very foolish, possibly both. In any case, I want you to make at least one more of these vids."

Karen lowered her camera, though Dom kept hers trained on the queen.

"You... you want me to continue?" Karen bit her tongue to keep the "Your Majesty" from leaking out.

"It's about time, don't you think?" The casual words sounded odd coming from the queen's mouth. "I've been living under my mother's dictates all my life, and they haven't made me happy. Now I see my son smile even as he faces the worst problems of his young life, and my daughter has more personality than all my sisters combined."

Dom laughed. It was a low, soft sound filled with sadness.

The queen smiled, a real joy-filled smile that looked as odd on her face as the casual clothes on her body.

"They like to pretend they're in control, but not one of them would dare break the plan." Queen Treylyn looked up at the vid still playing in the background. King Levon was speaking about how he met Treylyn. "Not one of them would dare to love her husband. The men were convenient stepping stones to power."

"Forgive me, but I thought your mother was dead." Karen winced at the question herself.

Treylyn shook her head and turned back to the camera with a sad smile on her face. "I thought, when I heard about the accident, that I would be free of that stars-blighted plan." The queen continued to describe the plan where they would seat a daughter, properly trained in the family's values, on the throne just as soon as they could manipulate the succession properly. Treylyn wasn't supposed to get pregnant when she did, and then the rebel's successful plan to kidnap one of her children threw even more of a wrench in the works.

"They tried to kill me, but that just made it easier for those hooligans to secret my daughter away."

"Everyone says Emalynn was a surprise." Karen had her tablet out for notes. She would have to get back into the archives for supporting vids for all of this.

"A mother knows how many babies she delivers, even when she almost dies." Queen Treylyn remained calm, but her eyes were staring through time. "I had enough time to think it out before anyone started asking questions. But I lost track of her the same way the rebels did."

Karen shuddered. As though Emalynn needed any more complications in her history. She listened as the queen, Emalynn's mother, described the real moment when she lost her daughter and struggled to keep the tears from her eyes. This would make a great vid, but not in the same one as the troubles between the sisters of that otherwise ordinary family. No, the queen's family wasn't ordinary. That was the problem. They were rich and thought that entitled them to more.

"Have you spoken to Emalynn about any of this?" Karen asked when the queen paused for more than a breath.

"It's impossible to talk to her." Treylyn looked away. "She sees me as some sort of horror."

Dom laughed again.

"She doesn't hate you." Karen pulled Dom's arm to get her to lower the camera. "You know Baba gave Emalynn as much as she could, even though she hadn't signed on to be a mother."

"What relevance does that have?"

Karen took a deep breath and steeled herself to look at the queen directly. "Baba died in the most gruesome way you could imagine, just before Emalynn met Tristan. Emalynn loved her as a mother because she never knew who she really belonged to. I can't begin to imagine what it was like to loose her foster mother, and with her all connection to her birth mother, yet somehow she still managed to find her way home."

Dom put her hand on Karen's shoulder, forcing her to pause. Dom took Karen's tablet and ran her fingers over it. The media wall jumped to her command, bringing up Emalynn's use record. Dom highlighted the searches on proper etiquette. Karen couldn't hide her shock at how much time Emalynn had managed to put into her attempts to learn what her mother expected of her.

"When did she have that kind of time?" Karen let her breath cover the words a bit. The question wasn't needed. All the records were time stamped in the middle of the night.

Queen Treylyn rose slowly and walked to the wall. Her hands traced the lines on the report about etiquette. "What is this?"

Karen would have joined the queen if Dom didn't hold her back. "It's Emalynn trying to live up to your expectations."

Emalynn

The grand hall recovered from the bombings remarkably fast. Emalynn remembered how it had been decorated and arranged for her homecoming. That first time meeting her parents had been a strange and public event. Now, however, the room was transformed into a courtroom, complete with a judges' bench, jury box, and tables for the prosecution and defense. All at Emalynn's insistence. Typically, anything involving the royals would have been handled by the council, in private and away from scrutiny. Emalynn would have nothing of it, and siting the release of Karen's vids making it already public, she argued anything less than open court would be seen as a cover-up.

The council might not have cared what she said if she hadn't received support from an unexpected source. Queen Treylyn publicly agreed with Emalynn, which was only slightly more surprising than Karen's *The Succession: Part III* that had somehow made it out without approval of the public relations department.

Now they were ready to begin the first ever trial by jury of a royal. Four royals. The aunts had found a team of lawyers willing to defend their actions. No doubt they would run through most of the family fortunes doing so. They'd already forced several changes to the way courts are supposed to run. The jury was the council of lords, not a randomly selected group of citizens. The prosecutors were judges pulled from the outer colonies. The judge herself was the same. Emalynn and Tristan were required to attend even though they were also witnesses. In fact, they were required to sit on the dais above the judges' bench with their father. Mother was sitting with the rest of the witnesses in isolation since, as she pointed out, she wasn't royal.

"Are you feeling well?" Father whispered while looking out over the gathering crowd.

"Not really." Emalynn clenched her face in a similar pose and held it by sheer will. "It would be bad form to show how many backflips my stomach is doing."

Father broke his pose to give her a small grin. "Is that what I'm feeling?"

"I shouldn't be here," Emalynn complained again. "I'm a witness."

"You are a princess first." The king returned to his frozen expression. "You'll leave before anyone else gives testimony. We want to be fair, but we also have to be proper."

Funny that he was the one pushing that line now. Mother had decided her lack of title meant she could ease up on the propriety since the bombings. That did make family dinners more bearable. Now to have Father the one making these calls chafed a bit. Granted, he only did it when they were in the public eye. She could learn to live with that.

"This is the hardest part of the job." He raised his hand to someone who'd just entered. "I suspect your performance experience will help."

"This isn't anything like a cheer competition."

"No? Do you get to show the judges how painful that build is?" He'd done some research. "Do you have to look as though everything were effortless despite all the work you had to put in?"

Stars and dust, he was right. "So it's all an act?"

"It's all showing what the people expect to see." He acknowledged another member of the crowd.

"Who are you waving at?"

"It doesn't matter. They all think I'm waving to them. It makes them happy."

Emalynn looked out to the gathering crowd. Most of them were recognizable members of the media. Yet another reason for her stomach to twist. They all watched the dais carefully without seeming to. She copied her father's movement and six people waved back, all with smiles on their faces. She wished Dare were by her side, but he was shut out until he testified, as were all the elites, Karen, Dom, and Davy. Grouse selected a few guards who would look impressive to stand behind her and otherwise stay out of the way.

The council entered as one and made their way to their seats in the jury box. They lined up in front of the bench and bowed as one to the three royals on the dais. Emalynn knew most of them found this role tedious and would have preferred to quietly strip the sisters of their titles, but the threat of the vids kept them in their roles.

Following the jury, the prosecutors entered with as much ceremony. Emalynn could feel the influence of the media office in the scripted way they moved through the crowd to their table and bowed to them. The sisters and their lawyers came next. They didn't follow the script so well. Emalynn let her smile become a little more real. The lack of respect they showed didn't play well for them.

"All rise," a guard at the back of the room yelled.

Emalynn stood beside her father and Tristan before most of the rest of the court participants moved. According to the etiquette sites she'd researched, there was no mandate for the sitting monarch or heirs to stand for any person. Emalynn argued they should anyway, to lend their authority to the judge. Who would be able to argue with her if the king himself stood when she entered? That had been the argument with the king's advisors who never wanted him to cede any of his power for any reason. Tristan won the day with the argument that if Levon wasn't willing to delegate to the judge, then he should sit as judge himself. No one liked the idea of King Levon sitting in judgment of his sisters-in-law, least of all Father.

The judge, a white-haired, spry woman who didn't jump at the idea of judging the royals, bowed to each of them in order before turning her back without waiting for permission and sat.

"You may be seated." She spoke quietly but clearly enough to be understood throughout the room.

Emalynn counted to three before King Levon moved to sit. He was as good an actor in manipulating the impression he gave through subtle movement. He waited just long enough to show the people were still waiting for him to signal the move, but not long enough to take back any of the authority he'd given her by rising in the first place.

"This is usually the time when the court clerk reads out the docket number and names the prosecuting and defending parties, but this isn't a usual court." The judge began with quiet dignity. "To pretend otherwise would be folly and turn this whole exercise into a farce. We won't do that. During this case, in this courtroom, by order of King Levon, my word is law and my rules of conduct are in effect. If any of you are unable to comply, I ask you to leave now. If I have to remind you of these rules, you will be removed by the court guard."

The judge was just as skilled as the king in using the subtleties and well-placed words to manipulate the power dynamic in the room. If she had been one of the examples in Presentations, more of the students would have passed the test. That gave her an idea for some of the changes she would make when she became the crown princess.

"What are you smirking about?" The king's voice caught her attention.

"Just thinking." She pitched her voice the way she used to when having a side conversation in class. What a scandal it would be if the judge had her and the king removed for talking out of turn.

"Not about getting into trouble again?"

"I don't have to think about that."

The judge had finished reading the charges brought against the four sisters and called for the prosecution to make their opening statements. Two women and a man stood behind the prosecution table. They had been chosen to represent the crown because of their deep well of experience in their professional lives. The man stepped forward to speak, but before he could say a single word, Regia yelled that she wouldn't stand for someone like him accusing her of anything.

"The defense will keep their clients under control or the accused will be removed from the court," the judge said.

The lawyers dragged Regia back to her seat with a heated conversation in tones too low to be heard. That gave most of the people in the room permission to chat with their neighbors or comment into their tablets.

"You aren't planning anything, truly?" The look in her father's eyes when he looked at her showed just how much he worried she was planning something.

"Just tell him already." Tristan leaned forward to grin at her.

At first, she couldn't imagine what Tristan thought he knew. When he winked, she caught on to the joke.

"We agreed to keep it secret." Emalynn waited for their father to shift his gaze to Tristan before winking back.

Order was restored before the king could respond, and he was left to worry over their declarations during the first opening statement, which revealed more than Karen had about the activities of her aunts. Emalynn took many deep breaths to keep herself under control. What they had found of her aunts' activities was bad enough. In just this first opening statement, their body count doubled, and he was only talking about the actions against the Degrase and Henning families.

The second prosecutor stood immediately to lay out the case for the Warren and Larring families, and the argument that these women had taken once thriving families and winnowed them down to make the succession they wanted. Whole branches of the families were wiped out to make way for the men her aunts had targeted to take power. Emalynn couldn't help thinking they wouldn't have gone so far if it were easier for a man to inherit a title.

In the colonies, men inherited frequently when their wives left them a business or their parents divided their assets in their wills. Why wouldn't the royals have the same kind of system? They should. Men weren't weak and sickly like they once were. There was no reason they shouldn't be given the same rights and opportunities.

The third and final prosecutor spoke about the crimes leveled against the monarchy itself. These weren't as much of a shock to Emalynn, not after she saw Karen's latest vid. It went nova before anyone at the palace knew she'd filmed it or dug through the remaining archives to add support. Emalynn found it the way everyone else did, when someone sent her a link. A lot of someones, most of them she didn't know.

"Tell me now." King Levon turned to Emalynn as soon as the judge announced a short recess. "What are you keeping secret?"

"Um…" Emalynn smirked. "I learned the Other code because that's how smugglers get around checkpoints."

The king fixed his gaze on her, ignoring the image he was presenting to the cameras.

"Not that secret." Tristan leaned back this time to wink at her around their father's head. "The other one."

"Oh, that one." Emalynn enjoyed this game. She'd seen other kids play their parents like this, and being able to tease the king just made it better. "I have a son."

The words came out faster and smoother than she expected. She stood quickly to cover her surprise and the casual tone of the bomb she'd just dropped in his lap. Almost everyone else in the room stood and stretched as well. It was hard to believe they'd all been sitting for close to two hours.

Levon stood and followed her around the side of her chair. "You have a son?"

Emalynn gave him a little nod. "Hey, Tristan, are you ready to become an ambassador?"

"I can't wait." Tristan met her behind the monarch's throne. "It's like they knew it was my lifelong dream job."

"They might have." Emalynn bounced a little on her feet. "I've always thought they knew more about us than we'd figured out about them."

"You think so?"

"If they're asking for an ambassador, that means they've figured out how to provide you with a safe place to live in one of their worlds."

"In?"

"They live in gas giants."

"Oh, right."

Levon put a hand on their shoulders. "Enough, you two. Tell me about your son."

Emalynn suppressed a laugh.

"Really, Father." Tristan pushed Levon's hand off his shoulder. "What is your publicist going to say about you acting like this during court? I mean, everyone is watching us right now."

Every camera she could see was pointing in their direction.

"I don't envy you when he gets you alone tonight." Emalynn grinned at Tristan.

"Your mother had something to do with this." Now Levon's gaze was leveled at Tristan, who met it with a smile to match her own.

"And her publicist." Tristan grinned. "They wanted to be sure our aunts didn't completely control the message coming out of these proceedings."

Emalynn let out her laugh. "And a little scene of the royals playing during a recess will take the net like a black hole."

"Be prepared for another round of the gossip sites," Tristan added.

Now the king let out a strong laugh of his own. "I will, and so will you as soon as you explain about this son I've just heard about. Who's the father?"

Emalynn shot Tristan a quick look of warning. "Tristan."

They had to bite their tongues to keep the laughter to a respectable level as their father tried to decide which of them to glare at. Then it hit him. "That's impossible. You two were only together for three months."

"We adopted," Emalynn admitted.

"How were you able to legally adopt?" Levon asked.

Tristan shrugged and started sneaking back to his seat.

"Well, according to the laws of the colony we were on at the time, he is legally our son."

"And what colony is that?"

Emalynn sucked her lips between her teeth and shook her head. She wouldn't say anything more where there was any possibility that someone who had reason to hate her might hear. So far, no one knew about their stop at Farthing Moon. How that had been lost in the net traffic about their wild adventures, she would never know. No matter how she searched the coverage and gossip about her, she saw only the great mystery of the six weeks they were completely out of range of any known net-enabled camera.

"Fine, we'll continue this later."

"Under strict security."

He drew himself up as if about to argue but deflated without saying anything. "Is there anything else you want to tell me while I can't yell at you?"

Emalynn thought for a moment while playing up the guilty teenager body language for the cameras. "Well, there were the three shuttles we... uh... borrowed and will have to replace." She gave him a big cheesy grin.

"That will come out of your allowance."

"I get an allowance?"

"Not anymore." He gave her a sly grin.

The call to order cut off Emalynn's response.